All on a Summer's Night

All on a Summer's Night

BY

MAURICE EDELMAN

THE BOOK CLUB
121 Charing Cross Road
London W.C.2

First published in Great Britain 1969
by Hamish Hamilton Ltd
90 Great Russell Street London W.C.1

Copyright © Maurice Edelman 1969

This edition by arrangement
with Hamish Hamilton Ltd 1970

Printed in Great Britain by
Western Printing Services Ltd Bristol

TO
DOMINIC

Chapter One

THE finger in the tendrils. He sat on her breasts with his palms pressed against her nostrils; and she was suffocating and groaned into the pillow and awoke. For a few seconds she lay with her eyes open, gulping relief and listening to the diminishing drumbeats of her heart.

Against the yellow-striped linen her forehead was wet, and she raised her hand slowly, following the line of her body beneath her house-coat, as if she were inspecting an alien surface, till she reached her throat and her brow and her outspread hair. At eye-level, the miniature electric clock was a blur that came into focus as she pushed it away. Though the curtains were drawn, the afternoon sunlight burst into the room in violent patches, enclosing the clock in an aureole where the second hand jerked in an unrelenting pause and thrust.

For a short while she watched the serene minute hand that marked twenty-three minutes past six. Twenty-three minutes past six. The time seemed mysterious, majestic, as if every clock ought to strike twenty-three minutes past six endlessly. Twenty-three minutes past six. She wanted to cocoon herself, fixed in the torpid hour, with the curtains and the door closed while the second hand twitched inside her.

For the last three days she had stayed at Marfield, away from Grosvenor Square and the constant mutter of traffic that rose to their flat. Here the sounds were different. All the sounds except for Harry's anxious voice, the service call from London asking for assurance that she was still there at half-past eleven at night, at half-past eight in the morning. 'Hello, Isobel. Baby! How're things? Any news? Yes—I can't wait. ... Going up to the works in Manchester . . . Macclesfield . . . Halifax. See you Friday. Ring you tomorrow. 'Bye now, baby. Love!'

She lay on her back, listening to the sounds of summer in the woods around the house and the grumble of doves below her window. From the swimming pool came scrambled voices, laughter, a cry, a silence, then the slap of a diving body. A silence again. Through the open bedroom door she could see her bathing suit folded carefully over a rail, a violet shadow against the pale silk of the walls. Should she swim again before they had to dress for dinner and the twenty-minute drive to the Orme-Campbells'?

Unwilling to stir in the sullen heat, she raised her foot, kicked away the covering, and looked along her body where the house-coat had opened, and frowned. On her right leg about six inches above her knee was a tiny network of veins, almost invisible in the immaculate expanse of her thigh. She put a finger on it, watched the skin go pale and then redden as she took her hand away. Then she turned and pressed her clenched eyes into the pillow. At a quarter to seven she would begin to make up her face. She would hear the Mercedes swivelling around the gravel in the drive, and she'd pour a whisky and soda for Harry, part of the rituals of his daily life which were a secular transference from those he had given up in his youth. But now for a quarter of an hour she wanted to blot out thought.

Crouching by the wall, so that her tall body couldn't be seen through the windows that reached to the floor, Isobel went to the curtains and pulled them till the room was filled with a blaze of light, falling over the chintz of the four-poster bed and the vast bowl of yellow roses sent by Harry for her birthday two days earlier. Not yet fully awake, she returned to the bed, heavy and inert while the first stir of evening touched her body. Lying on her face again, she struggled out of her house-coat and tugged the cold sheet over her, leaving only her naked back with the faint rivulet between the shoulder blades exposed. A finger in the tendrils. Drift and remembrance.

She chose her memories like books from a shelf. In the spring of that year, the hills had been flushed with anemone and narcissus and broom and oleander, with herons flying over the Sea of Galilee. She and Edward had walked through the ruins of the synagogue at Capernaum, and then at night they had driven to the hotel, high above the lake, where they had watched the fishermen's boats dragging their nets by the shores of Tiberias, the lights of 'Ein Gev to the east and behind them the darkness of the Golan Heights. The next day he was to have lectured at the Institute, but he didn't want to sleep. *Herod, son of Bonimos and Justus his son, together with his children, erected this column.* Enlaced in the silence above the miraculous waters, they had recited the inscription, and death happened to everyone but themselves.

The next day, while she waited in the hotel, Edward and his chauffeur Avram, driving to Rehovoth, hit a tank-carrier on a downhill curve. She and Edward had been married for eleven years. At the memorial service in London, Lord Pinner said that Edward was the most promising endocrinologist of his generation. And the Rabbi had said that what mattered wasn't how long you lived but what your life contained. And her father, Henry Canley-Mills, O.B.E., an Anglican looking ill-at-ease in his hat during prayers, had borrowed another fifteen pounds from her because he didn't want to go straight back to Rottingdean. Jonathan, their ten-year old son, had cried when the Rabbi told him to remember what a fine man his father had been, and syllable by syllable, following the Hebrew words spoken by an uncle, had recited the Kaddish.

It was over, all gone except for the pang, the longing that sometimes rose, urgent and hopeless, for an impossible ghost.

So now, after the pillow-clinging, the poignant ascent and the

3

convulsion, there was emptiness and desolation. She turned slowly face upwards, and looked at the manoeuvres of two flies under the canopy. 'Get up,' she said aloud to herself after a few minutes. With an idle hand she took her house-coat, and let it trail on the floor.

Her son had entered the room, and stood silently waiting for her to speak.

'I see you don't knock,' she said.

'No,' he answered.

She sat up, pulling the sheet under her armpits, and he leaned forward and kissed her forehead.

She said, 'You've grown in the last term. What are you now, Jonathan? Six foot?'

She knew that he wasn't. He preened himself, and stood next to the window, his amber-coloured eyes lightened by the sunburn beneath his fair eyebrows.

'Five foot eleven and a half,' he said. 'Why should I knock? I'm not Luigi. He's hanging up the lights.'

'What about the barbecue?'

'Don't fuss,' said Jonathan, sitting in a chair and stretching his legs. 'I've put it by the yew trees—you know, near the river.'

'Well, I hope you won't burn the place down. Your father wouldn't like it.'

She saw his face redden, and his throat swallow where his check shirt was open.

'I'll be very careful,' he said slowly, 'not to damage Harry's property.'

'Don't be silly,' Isobel said. 'I just—' and the sentence faded.

*

After Edward's death, she had lived alone with Jonathan in a service flat in Wimpole Mews, not understanding the complexity of debt that Edward had left behind, the relics of his

4

arrangement to buy a house in Devonshire Place for a research project, her days of grief spent in a counterpoint with bank managers and accountants and income-tax men, till the final recognition that she had only enough to live on for about a year. That, and the letters from her father in Rottingdean, explaining that he had his own troubles and couldn't help her.

She had worked at the B.B.C., at the British Council, for a short time in a boutique, fearing each time she left home that something terrible would happen to Jonathan. When she returned and found him already back from Marylebone High School, relaxed on the divan in the large room which was both their sitting-room and their bedroom, she felt gratitude and wonder, as if Edward himself had returned from death.

'I see you don't knock.'

The words echoed in her mind. Until six years ago, there had been nowhere to knock except the front door. She had lived with her son in a frantic intimacy, each day's separation a torment, each return a hysteria, their conversation a calling-back of Edward.

'I've been thinking,' said Jonathan. 'Something special.'

It was a childhood formula that meant he wanted her advice.

'Come and sit down,' she said, and watched with pleasure his taut body and brooding face as he walked from the window and sat on the bed. She took his brown hand in her long fingers, and said,

'You must scrub your nails.'

'I wish you'd—', he began in exasperation, and then he stopped.

'I've been helping Luigi.'

'I was teasing,' Isobel said. 'What d'you want to ask me?'

'Well,' said Jonathan, frowning, 'do I have to go on calling myself Levenson?'

'Why not?' asked Isobel. 'Isn't it rather a nice name?'

'No—it's an ugly name.'

'Why?'

5

'It's got nothing to do with me. It's *his* name.'

'Would you rather be called Canley-Mills?'

'I don't think so. That's just a boring name. Dad's name was Ross. That's what I'd like to be called.'

'I suppose,' she said, 'you can call yourself anything you like. . . . Shall I tell you something? Your father's name was short for Roscofsky.'

'Roscofsky,' said Jonathan thoughtfully. 'That's a new one. Why didn't you tell me before? Roscofsky—' he sipped the name as if he were tasting a wine—'Roscofsky—I like it. There's something more to it than Levenson—it's got more body—it's more *challenging*.'

'How would it have gone down at school?'

'I'm glad to say I'll never know. But you're quite right—it's not much of a school name. It's a good university name. "A New Theory of Nabatean Aqueducts," by Jonathan Roscofsky. How d'you like that?'

'I don't,' said Isobel. 'Anyhow, they're dropping the *-ofskys*, even in Israel.'

'Yes,' said Jonathan, releasing her hand and examining an ivory paper knife by the bedside. 'It's all very puzzling.'

'What is?'

'It's puzzling to be the sort of half-Jew that I am. At school —to choose not to go into prayers, and yet wondering what they're all about. Not liking the name Levenson. Meeting people and when they ask you if you're a Jew, not knowing the answer.'

Isobel said, 'Run my bath, darling.'

Jonathan turned the taps in her bathroom, and went on talking through the open door.

'Take yourself. Why are you always marrying Jews?'

She laughed and lit a cigarette.

'I've only been married twice.'

'No, seriously,' Jonathan went on, 'I'd have thought you'd have wanted a change after Dad was killed.'

6

'Well,' said Isobel, 'I married Edward because we met on a plane going to Paris, and I loved him, and that was that.'

'What about Harry?' said Jonathan. 'I've made it lukish warm.'

'That's fine. You'll have to go in a minute—he'll be back by a quarter to seven, expecting me to be ready. . . . Harry? Well, that was slightly different. Your father was the consultant when his mother was in hospital. Harry liked and admired him. They became—not exactly friends—acquaintances at any rate, and I met him by accident after your father died. And that's how I came to marry two Jews.'

'What about grandfather—your father?'

'He didn't like it when I told him I was going to marry Edward. But by the time I married Harry, he was resigned to the idea.'

She watched him as he walked around the bedroom, picking up the ivory-backed brushes on her dressing-table and reading the inscription on an unopened bottle of scent, his face withdrawn and thoughtful.

'I can't understand,' he said, 'why he doesn't stop. It's become a disgusting habit. Just look at him! He's got all the money he could possibly want—you both have.'

'It's got nothing to do with money,' said Isobel. 'After a bit it becomes a pure intellectual exercise.'

'Pure?'

'Yes—pure. Your father—Harry—likes efficiency—and don't move his brushes. You know how tidy he is. He can't stand loose ends.'

'Your hair's all loose.'

Jonathan stroked her hair on the pillow.

'I haven't done it yet.'

'I suppose he plays take-overs and mergers instead of snakes and ladders. It's revolting,' said Jonathan.

'Why?' said Isobel. 'You take his money.'

'Not if I can help it.'

7

'But he pays for everything—your school, your university, your party tonight.'

'I hate it all the same.'

She smiled at his stern expression, and said, 'Let's not quarrel. I see you rarely enough. Nothing is absolutely right in life. We all have to do a deal with it.'

'You're even using his language.'

'Yes,' said Isobel. 'It does grow on one. Come and sit next to me, darling.'

'I suppose it was very convenient,' said Jonathan, sitting on the bed again. 'I mean, when you became rich.'

Isobel looked at him, hoping he was being frivolous, but his face was unsmiling.

'My father was never very well off,' she said. 'He was an exceptionally incompetent business man. His problem was that he never realized it.'

'Do you like being rich?' Jonathan asked, looking at the Vuillard over the fireplace.

'I didn't like being poor,' said Isobel. 'You'd better go. What's the matter?'

His face had darkened, and she looked at him anxiously.

'Is anything wrong, Jonathan?'

'No, nothing. I just hope the party goes all right, and no one falls in the river. We've got the Upminstrels playing at eleven, and I've worked out a few places for snogging—the Roman temple, the summer-house, the cottage, the ruins near the main road.'

'And what about Henrietta?'

'She's coming with Mark.'

'Do you like her?'

'She's all right.'

'She's very pretty.'

'So are you.'

Their conversation paused, and she held his hands at arm's length, inspecting a stranger who had been away at school or

8

out of sight during her travels with her husband for over half the years of her second marriage, a sudden and unfamiliar young man.

'You're not so bad yourself,' she said teasingly. 'I suppose all the girls—'

'I prefer archaeology,' he said.

'I don't believe you.'

'Well,' he said, 'I've done more archaeology than girls.'

'You're disgusting,' she laughed.

'You too,' Jonathan answered.

In the marquee, by the river, someone at the discothèque had put on a record, and the music jolted the window.

'I wish they'd turn it down,' said Isobel.

'Next dance?'

Jonathan stretched himself at her side, lying on top of the sheet, and put his face against hers.

'I thought young people danced apart nowadays,' she said after a few seconds.

'You're not young,' said Jonathan.

'I'm forty-two,' said Isobel.

'That's what I mean.'

'I'm going to shake you,' she said, raising herself and gripping his arm. 'I'm going to shake you.'

Laughing, they wrestled till he lay beneath and Isobel, with the sheet wrapped around her, kissed his face as her fingers pressed his shoulders. Jonathan drew away, and then stood awkwardly by the bedside while she reached for her house-coat.

'All right, Jonathan,' Isobel said, and their eyes didn't meet, 'I'll see you before we go to dinner.'

They turned to the door, which had opened quietly and surreptitiously.

'Hello, darling,' said Isobel. 'You're early.'

With a quick glance at Jonathan, Levenson walked over to the window and opened it wider.

'It's nearly seven,' he said crisply. Then to Jonathan, 'I thought you were having a party.'

'I was just leaving,' he mumbled, and walked out.

'What's all the girlish laughter?' Levenson said.

When he spoke he scarcely moved his lips, like a prisoner talking at exercise.

Isobel drew on her house-coat.

'Whisky—or would you like something cooler tonight?'

'Whisky.'

He sat in the armchair by the striped-silk curtains and shut his eyes. His thick brown hair, youthfully barbered, was a contrast with the greyness of his cheeks. He was ten years older than she was, but the face she was examining looked older by at least twenty.

'I don't like him hanging around the bedroom.'

She poured the whisky and didn't answer. A quiet rage bubbled inside her, and she handed the glass to her husband slowly, unwilling to speak.

After Edward's death, Levenson had asked her to dinner a few times, but she had always declined. She knew that he was wealthy, an industrialist who was chairman and managing director of a famous engineering firm and other businesses besides and whose name and photograph regularly appeared in the newspapers, and sometimes on TV. Always the same image—off-guard and disadvantageous, a melancholy portrait taken at a company meeting, that made him look shorter than his medium height, his broad nose more squat, his cheekbones more Tartar.

One evening after a reception at Lancaster House where Levenson had been invited because he had endowed a Commonwealth University chair, and she because she had remained on an old social list, he drove her back to Wimpole Mews. Jonathan was away at a summer school in Dorset.

She offered Levenson a drink, and they sat and talked about her childhood and her school and her marriage. And since nothing seemed remote from his power, though he said nothing about himself, he created in her a despair that looked for rescue. Then, without pleasure or regret, as it had been with Armitage and the man from the U.S. Embassy, she lay naked in the darkness. And Levenson's head was heavy against her neck, and between them there was an intimacy and a nothing.

Afterwards he stirred and said,

'Cheltenham Ladies' College.'

'You sound,' she said as he rolled away and lit a cigarette, 'as if you've just made love to the whole school.'

'I have,' he said.

Miss Bell, Miss Cheadle, Miss Fretts, Miss Bolton.

Isobel switched on the light, glimpsed his satisfied expression and turned the light off. It didn't matter. Four months later, after she had twice refused, she married him in a Registry Office, and for their honeymoon they went to Japan where he had to visit a machine-tool exhibition.

*

'What sort of day did you have?'

She asked the stock question, a request for the agenda of their evening's conversation.

'Oh, fair,' he said. 'It's a race, but they're coming along nicely. It all depends on the institutions. We only need another twenty per cent and we're home and dry.'

The bath was running and he had to speak above the hiss of the water, exaggerating each vowel.

'He is a very good husband,' she said to herself, smiling to him, 'and I hate his voice. When he says "nicely" and "home and dry", my toes curl up and something runs down my back.'

'That's very good,' she said. 'Will you get them?'

'We'll know tonight. They're fighting back. Budd's going to be there.'

'What's he got to do with it?'

'Everything. He's the Minister responsible. The Monopoly

Commission's divided, but they do as he says. If he says "No" to a merger, it's off.'

'He's very unpredictable.'

'Yes—the insurance companies and the trade unions won't commit themselves till Budd approves. Ever since he took over from the Board of Trade, as Minister of Industrial Reconstruction, Budd's the big boy.'

He rose, and began to take off his tie, turning away to the window so that she knew he didn't want to talk any more about the bid.

She stood next to him and he put his arm around her waist.

'Jonathan's got a very good evening for his party,' he said.

The sun was still high, and they could see Jonathan and a dark-haired youth with a red towel around his shoulders sitting on the edge of the pool. As they watched, he threw off the towel and dived neatly beneath a girl who was swimming on her back.

'Who's that?' Levenson asked.

'Adrian something-or-other,' said Isobel. 'He's at Trinity with Jonathan. We've met him a few times. You've forgotten.'

'Looks much older than Jonathan,' said Levenson.

'They're making them bigger nowadays,' said Isobel.

He took his arm away from her, and straightened himself. 'I hope they don't make too much mess,' he said.

'Oh, come on, darling,' she said. 'They're not savages. It's all going to be very civilized. Luigi and Carmella have organized a buffet at the top of the Cypress Walk, and they're only going to drink hock and fruit-cup and beer—and there's a barbecue later on and strawberries and champagne for breakfast. It's looking very pretty.'

The gardeners were hanging the last of the Chinese lanterns leading from the pool to the river.

'It's going to be even prettier when it gets dark,' Isobel said.

'And very noisy,' said Levenson. 'I hope that dance floor and the marquee won't damage the lawn.'

'It won't,' said Isobel, putting her arms around him. 'At the Trinity May Ball—'

'I never had anything to do with May Balls,' he said. 'You're mixing me up with your old friends.'

'Don't be silly,' she said. 'Everyone's going to have a lovely night, and I hope we get back in time to see some of it.'

'Come and lie down,' said Levenson, putting his hands on her shoulders. The spatulate fingers of his left hand, each nail carefully manicured with the half-moons exposed, gathered the petals at the neck of her garment. It was the day of his weekly visit to Bond Street for a hair-cut, shampoo and manicure. She could mark the calendar by looking at his hands. Hands were important. Edward's lean hands had been phantasy and fulfilment all at once. And there were Harry's hands.

She hesitated, listened for a moment to the young voices rising from the pool, and said,

'No—not now. We'll never get to that dinner. It's a long drive.'

He shrugged and picked up his glass.

'You're quite right. Let's get dressed, Isobel.'

Finishing his whisky, he telephoned Lattner, his personal assistant and legal adviser.

'Lew? This is Harry.'

From the other end came the familiar voice, whose undertone of intimacy had steadily grown as their fortunes had progressed.

'Can't quite hear you, Harry.'

'Well, listen harder, old chap,' said Levenson. 'Budd's going to be there. Orme-Campbell asked him personally.'

'Yes—I told you.'

'What if he can't get away from the House?'

'He'll get away all right. I saw him this morning.'

'Why didn't you offer to drive him up?'

'Listen, Harry, I know Budd. If you start rushing him—'

Levenson grunted.

'What about Kenton?'

'He'll do what the Rt. Hon. Alf Budd says. The unions won't sell unless they're sure the Monopolies Commission will keep out, and that Budd will let the deal go through. There's nothing you can do, Harry, unless Budd backs it . . . Budd! That's the man. See you later. I'm just leaving.'

Levenson put the telephone down without saying good-bye, and as he took off his jacket he began to read the catalogue of a Sotheby sale.

'A pair of salvers on foot by Joseph Walker, Dublin, 1702-3. Diameter 10 inches. Weight 36 ounces.'

He liked the description of the salvers, and intended to bid for them. He studied the room—the *guéridon* with its marquetry of tulip and violet woods, the Aubusson carpet with pinks and blues and yellows picked out by the sun, and the Vuillard reflecting the colours in the carpet, and he decided that objects of art had a tranquillizing effect.

*

Isobel wore a long white dress with a flowered pattern. He took her hand and examined her.

'You'll do,' he said.

'Is that all?'

He smiled a slow, sad smile. 'They'll all be jealous of me.'

She liked the prospect of flattery, and took his arm as they walked down the steps to the hall where Jonathan's guests were already assembling.

The theme of the party was '1820', and the tapestry that covered one wall made a dark green background to the group, all dressed in black and white. Jonathan in velvet trousers and a white ruffled shirt ran halfway up the steps to greet them.

'And who are you?' Isobel said.

'Byron,' he replied.

'You seem to have an awful lot of Byrons,' she said.

14

'Yes,' he answered. 'Four Byrons, so far, three Caroline Lambs, a couple of Teresa Guicciolis, one Lady Blessington, various Maids of Athens, and a few Augustas.'

'That's a lot of concentrated vice.'

'Not bad,' said Jonathan. 'I'd better introduce you—Henrietta Martin you know. Annabel Saunders, Charlotte Rogers, George Mayne-Erskine, Venetia Cohen, Sylvia Stanhope and Adrian Sinclair—you've met before—I told you we're going to share rooms in Cambridge next term.'

Levenson nodded, and Isobel said to Henrietta Martin,

'You look absolutely lovely—such beautiful shoulders. Who are you supposed to be?'

'Teresa Guiccioli,' she said. She stroked her long black curls, and said, 'I had them specially set.'

'I like the roses.'

Henrietta put her hand over the roses at her bodice, and said,

'Yes—they all used to wear them—so demure, when you think how they really lived.'

'And you?' Isobel asked Adrian.

'I'm just a corsair,' he answered modestly.

'Yes,' said Isobel. 'I saw you walking the plank. What are you reading?'

'English,' he said.

'You're a bit younger than Jonathan, aren't you?'

His expression changed from meekness into a private self-confidence.

'A year older. ". . . grown aged in a world of woe".'

'That's very Byronic,' said Isobel.

He smiled into her face.

'I'm not surprised,' he said. 'Byron wrote it.'

'I know,' she said stiffly.

'Come on,' said Harry, pressing her elbow. 'We're going to be late.'

Isobel waved, and they hurried to the drive where Wardle the chauffeur was waiting with the Mercedes.

15

'The young are very self-satisfied,' she said.

'Not all of them,' said Levenson.

'I really meant those friends of Jonathan's. That bumptious dark-haired boy with the blue eyes. They always seem to be mocking one.'

'You know,' Levenson went on as he helped her into the back of the car, 'you hardly ever call me by my first name.'

'How very strange!' said Isobel. 'I'd never really thought of it.'

16

Chapter Two

'YOU'VE got a numismatic head,' Elaine Orme-Campbell said to her husband. She had a faint stutter, and pronounced the 'n' three times. He turned to the looking-glass decorated with golden *putti* on a see-saw facing the bookshelves of his study, and examined himself with satisfaction. His hair, once flaxen, was receding from a marmoreal forehead that seemed only to lack a laurel wreath to give it a Roman gravity. His straight nose, his firm mouth, the port of his thick neck in a massive frame added an Imperial grandeur. But his eyes, he thought, as he had thought at his prep school and at Eton and King's and in the boardroom of the Orme-Campbell Engineering Corporation, were too small. Too small. Too small in relationship to the glabrous jowls. Too small except to twinkle. He changed his expression. His lips turned upwards, and his eyes puckered.

'Augustus or Tiberius?' he asked his wife in his resonant voice, watching her fingers as she ruffled the roses in the bowl on the desk and teased their heads into position. They had been married for thirty years, and when they were alone they often communicated with words which to a stranger would have seemed isolated irrelevancies.

'Augustus in the boardroom, Tiberius in the bedroom. You ought to be cast in bronze.'

'Yes,' he said, accepting her homage, and because he was the handsomer of the two, added graciously,

'You're looking extremely pretty tonight. She'll have to watch it.'

She touched her black-rinsed hair, pleased with his compliment.

'Isobel Levenson's beautiful,' she said. 'She can't be so young. But she always stands out wherever she goes. She looks like a butterfly among a lot of old moths. Did you tell him it's not black tie?'

'Oh, Lord—I forgot. Does it matter?'

'She'll be wearing a long dress, that's all. She might feel uncomfortable.'

'I'm sorry he's bringing her here. It's tiresome having a woman around when you want to talk shop.'

Elaine said, 'That's not very nice, even to me.'

He took her arm and walked to the window, from which they could see the beech woods on the hills and the terraces where their guests were gathering. In the afterglow of sunset, the lawns and gardens with the elevated entablature of the Orangery lay spread out before them like a tinted landscaper's drawing. Orme-Campbell's great-great-grandfather had bought the ruin of a Stuart manor and three hundred acres in the early nineteenth century, rebuilt the house entirely to a design by George Hattersley, and had added a Graeco-Roman pediment with Doric columns to the south front. He had also planted twenty thousand trees, including an avenue of limes; and as a distraction from their commercial affairs, Orme-Campbell's grandfather and father had occupied themselves in the restoration of the estate, studying its history in seventeenth-century memoirs and manorial records, and reconstituting from the old stonework the chapels and the Orangery, and decorating the approaches to the woodlands with shrubberies. Two enormous lead sphinxes, cast in Birmingham, looked down from the staircase over the lawns, a memorial to the second baronet and to the technical skill of the Industrial Revolution and, in Elaine's eyes, the only blemish in the physical harmony of Orme House.

'I'm glad to say you're always around,' her husband said, pursuing his thoughts.

'Am I?' said Elaine. 'I hope everything will be all right. I'll take her away when you begin your meeting.'

'They're a strange couple,' he said.

'Yes,' she answered. 'He's more like a manager than a husband. Are you worried?'

'There's nothing to worry about,' he said.

For a few seconds he watched his manservant handing out drinks to the five executive directors of O.C.E. who were attending the dinner arranged for them to meet Levenson and discuss his bid. 'Fortescue—Lord Hamblett of Gorsay—Henderson-Kerr—and Howell,' he counted them. 'There they are. The Praetorians—all set for battle with their martinis.'

'They won't let you down?' Elaine asked.

'Why should they?' Orme-Campbell asked simply. 'I invented them.'

'Isn't that a reason to be careful?' said Elaine, patting the hair at her temples.

'Oh, I am careful,' he said. 'Careful but relaxed. . . . First of all, we're not going to sell. Levenson needs at least another twenty per cent of the voting shares. And second—whatever the pressure, Budd will veto it.'

'Are you sure?' she asked. 'Is he reliable?'

'Well, he is the Minister responsible. Perhaps reliable is going too far.'

There was a knock at the door and Tom Howell, the financial director, came in. Howell had worked in the firm from the age of fifteen, moving upwards in a steady progress based on a tenacity and patience that enabled him to outsit his rivals. Respectful to his seniors, tough to his juniors and flexible to his contemporaries, he had climbed by acting as personal assistant to heads of departments till their removal by misfortune or failure had enabled him to consolidate a new advance. A director of Orme-Campbell Engineering at the age of forty-nine, he was remembered as a junior clerk only by Orme-Campbell himself and a few of the long-service men in the firm. Till three weeks before he died, old Orme-Campbell used to refer to Howell as the Tea Boy. Howell knew it, and had smiled complaisantly when the mourners at the funeral in Leicester had stood around telling anecdotes of the Chief's unfailing memory for the names of his staff and his nicknames for those he disliked. Nor did he mention how, when he saw him for the last time, the senile chairman of the firm, with a long-standing sense of guilt, had insisted on pressing a ten-shilling note into his hand.

But that was six years ago. When Geoffrey Orme-Campbell succeeded his father, Howell had moved up with him. Orme-Campbell and Howell. The two names were now always linked in the Business Section of the newspapers. The *Sunday Times* had called Tom Howell 'one of the most dynamic of the middle generation', and the name had stuck. With the new flotation, Orme-Campbell had given him a large allocation of shares. It had meant security, joining his interests irrevocably with O.C.E., and confirming that he was no longer just an executive director but also a substantial shareholder in his own right.

Over the years his Northern accent with its flat a's had passed imperceptibly into 'mid-Atlantic', expressed in the prefabricated phrases and homogenized tones of the executive world that he moved in—of advertising men and business conferences and TV interviewers and general managers and salesmen and Labour M.P.s and Tory public relations men and Alf Budd, Minister of Industrial Reconstruction, and all the others of the dun army advancing on 'the broad front of change', as the Prime Minister put it. Howell liked it that way. Once upon a time, he had tried to imitate the easy public-school voices of Orme-Campbell and his friends, and to adapt his accent to Lady Orme-Campbell's clipped Roedean voice; but it had never come off. All that was over now. He had a villa

20

in the South of France. He no longer minded. It was only his wife Marion who did.

'Hello, Tom,' said Orme-Campbell. 'Everyone here?'

'Budd's just turned up, Sir Geoffrey,' said Howell. His tone was resigned but apprehensive, like that of a patient in a doctor's waiting room.

'In good form?' asked Orme-Campbell.

'The usual,' said Howell. 'Never changes. Full of love for mankind, and ready to break into a hymn at the drop of a hat. Mind you, it's not always a good sign with Alf. When Alf's like that, you've got to keep your pockets buttoned.'

'I think,' Orme-Campbell said thoughtfully, 'that's going to be Levenson's problem—not ours.'

'Do I really have to have Budd next to me?' Elaine asked.

'You'll enjoy him,' her husband replied. 'When he puts his hand on your thigh to attract your attention, just smile.'

'Of course,' said Elaine. 'Pimp away!'

'I'm sorry,' he said. 'He's really quite harmless—he just likes touching people. Budd's our long-stop. In case anything goes wrong, his job is to say "No." What's the news from the institutions, Tom?'

'All set,' said Howell. 'I spoke to Hurstcombe today. The Manchester and General were a bit uncertain. But I've got their promise. They won't sell. Not for the time being. Neither will the Transport and General—or any of the other Union Trusts.'

'Sure?'

'Quite sure. . . . On the assumption, of course, that Budd's against it.'

'I'm very glad,' said Orme-Campbell serenely. 'Very glad.'

He looked at the folder in Howell's hands.

'I think it might be better if we limited the agenda tonight to Levenson's offer.'

Howell began to speak, but Orme-Campbell interrupted him.

'I don't want the accounts discussed tonight, Tom.'

'They might be raised,' Howell began to protest. 'How can we—'

'By ruling it out of order. You've got the agenda. It's pretty flexible and informal. There's no point in talking about losses when we're beating Levenson off. For God's sake, Tom, use a bit of sense.'

'Oh, Tom,' said Elaine, 'help me on with my jacket. I think I can hear the rumble of the Mercedes.'

'Funny,' said her husband, 'how chaps like Levenson always buy German cars nowadays.'

'Levenson is very sensitive,' said Elaine. 'He probably thinks a Rolls Bentley too Jewish. Don't forget to bring the cigarettes, Tom.'

'No,' said Howell. He could hear his dutiful tone, a hangover from the past, and regretted it as he opened the door and stood aside while Orme-Campbell and Elaine, arranging themselves into the role of amiable hosts, advanced towards the entrance, where Levenson was helping Isobel from the car.

*

An hour later, Elaine looked over the candles towards Orme-Campbell, waiting for his nod. Howell had worked out the time-table. At a quarter to ten, Orme-Campbell would have a final word with Budd for confirmation that he would veto the take-over if Levenson's bid seemed menacing. At a quarter past ten, when Gregory Stapleton would have arrived at Orme House after flying into Heathrow from Montreal, the Board would meet to record the situation—their own rejection of the offer, the Minister's statement, and perhaps even Levenson's hoped-for recognition that he had failed. The tactic, Orme-Campbell said, was a two-pronged instrument for Levenson to sit on. What with Stapleton's intervention, perhaps a three-pronged one. At midnight or thereabouts, Orme-Campbell would inform Levenson in person of the

22

result. To the press, who had been telephoning all day about the meeting, he had promised a statement at 12.30.

Though the windows and a door were open, there was no draught and the candles burned steadily. At the end of the table, Elaine could see the directors, a subdued and subfusc cluster, sweating gently over the Soufflé Grand Marnier. Perhaps it was a mistake, she thought. Too hot for a sultry night. Why weren't they talking? Lord Hamblett, with his bald freckled head bent over his plate, was preoccupied with his fork. Henderson-Kerr, the sales director, was wheezing; the pollen count was high. And Tom Howell had the remote look that often came over him when he was contemplating her husband. It was strange that she hardly ever noticed him. He was like a familiar house-dog, brooding by the table.

And then there was Isobel in her long dress next to Geoffrey, occasionally throwing a few words to Hamblett on her right to prevent him from being unhappy and un-talked to, her face thirtyish in the candle-light, attentive, her small teeth glistening, determined to back her husband up. And on her right Levenson, reticent but impatient for dinner to end, never looking at his wife, awkward in his well-tailored dinner jacket among all the casual lounge suits, mumbling an occasional message to Lattner, who also wore a black tie, two places away from him.

Orme-Campbell was in his teasing mood, exhilarated as he always was when he was host, dominating the table with his resounding voice and his emphatic and fluent conversation.

'Elaine,' he said, 'has got into a splendid racket. She's chairman of the Friends of Foreign Museums.'

'That's very exciting,' Isobel said. 'Does it involve a lot of travel?'

'Oh, yes,' he said loudly, so that Elaine could hear what he was saying at her end of the table. 'Elaine's always travelling—leading some chartered plane-load of eminent ladies to Acapulco or Bogota or Syracuse or Baalbec.'

23

He spoke each name like an insult.

Budd wagged a finger at Elaine. 'I'll have to report you to the Chancellor,' he said, 'for exceeding your travel allowance.'

She laughed, and said, 'His wife's coming with us to Brasilia next month.'

Budd shook his head in mock disapproval.

'Terrible decline in public standards,' he said, smiling. The candle-light brightened his thinning ginger hair and flashed on his glasses as he addressed her.

'What an unattractive man!' Elaine thought, smiling to him. Orme-Campbell had often spoken to her of Budd, the former fitter and shop steward in a Midland motor factory, who through his determined specialization in trade and industrial affairs had risen steadily through three Parliaments to his present position in the Cabinet. With his self-education reinforced by a year at Ruskin College, Oxford, he was at ease among the Party's dons and a social figure at Westminster, though he never drank. He added to his political energy what his supporters called 'a moral thrust'. On the other hand, a promising Junior Minister once said of him in the Smoking Room that 'he went grubbing for scandals as if they were truffles', and that his activities 'went well with his porcine snout'. Budd had laughed when a friend reported the story to him, and had added, 'The lad will grow up.' He had also taken the opportunity of telling the Prime Minister that his colleague would go far, if only he'd stop 'womanizing'. At the next Government reshuffle, the Junior Minister was dropped without explanation. But the report of Budd's part in the matter leaked out—some commentators thought that Budd himself 'leaked' it in order to emphasize his influence with the Prime Minister and the lesson that he never forgot an insult. It circulated both in Whitehall and the City, and Orme-Campbell told Elaine about it. Accepting that few politicians had Budd's talent for elevating a private grudge into a public cause, the

Orme-Campbells viewed him from that time onwards with a special caution.

*

'Never mind, darling,' Budd said, raising a glass of tonic water. 'For your sake I'll drink to the Friends of whatever-they-are.'

'Thank you,' said Elaine with a friendly nod in reply to his toast, and then, when her husband smiled to her, she stood, accompanied by an uprising of all her guests and a rattle of glasses as they pushed their chairs away from the table.

'Come on, Isobel,' she said. 'We'll leave them to their brandy.'

*

After they had left, Levenson sat without speaking, frowning at the detritus of the table and ignoring the guffaw that followed Budd's anecdote about a peasant woman who mistook a visiting bear for a man in a fur coat, and asked him to call again. The subdued atmosphere around the table had become boisterous, and the Minister was addressing all his neighbours by their Christian names.

'You see, Fred,' he said to Lord Hamblett, 'the trouble with Parliament today is that it doesn't represent anything. When I first got into the House, there were big men who stood for big interests—the law, business, trade unions, the universities. What've you got today? ' ('No,' he said in parenthesis to the butler, 'I want a Partago.')

He took a cigar, and the clatter around the table dwindled as he lit it.

'What've you got today? A bundle of dons and P.R. men. I'll tell you, Fred . . . since you were in the Commons, the whole quality of Parliament has changed.'

Hamblett protested, 'There are some very good young men, I'm told.'

25

'Political eunuchs,' said Budd simply. 'At their age I was fighting for causes. All they want to do is sit on their seats and hope for a job.'

Orme-Campbell was listening with a benevolent and detached smile. He goaded Budd a little.

'But, Alf, what you lack on the back benches you make up for in Government. Horsham, Mary Peters, Gronow, James, yourself, the Prime Minister.'

Budd raised his hand deprecatingly.

'I can't speak for myself. But when you talk about the P.M., I must agree. Trevor's the best thing that's happened in British politics this century. Just consider. . . . Here was a young man thirty years ago—the son of a senior Colonial Administrator—very well off on his mother's side—public school, Oxford, Middle Temple, the lot. But he chose to come into our Party because he wanted to serve. That's the point—he wanted to serve.'

'Yes,' said Hamblett reminiscently. 'I remember his maiden speech—very earnest and dedicated from the last back bench. Mind you, he didn't stay there long.'

'Well,' said Budd, 'Trevor has integrity. And there's a premium on that.'

'It isn't only integrity,' said Hamblett. 'He's got a brutal mind.'

'Brutal?' Orme-Campbell asked. 'It's not a word I would have used. I would have said tough rather than brutal.'

'No,' said Hamblett. 'When Trevor's mind is made up, it becomes brutal. I've seen him in action.'

'Not brutal,' said Budd, shaking his head. 'Logical—determined—not brutal. I'm pretty close to him, you know. He's basically a kind man. Too kind. It's some of those around him—'

He stopped, and then went on as the others waited.

'His trouble is that they get between him and the public. It's days since I've seen him myself.'

Levenson, who had been waiting restlessly for a lull, broke in. 'I think we ought to get on with it.'

'Yes,' said Hamblett. 'Political exegesis gets one nowhere nowadays.'

'It's political eschatology that counts,' said Budd.

'Too deep for me,' said Henderson-Kerr.

'Well, I'll explain,' Budd said sharply. 'It's the doctrine of death, judgment, heaven and hell—the doctrine of last things. That's what counts, lad.'

Orme-Campbell commented, 'Much too gloomy. Let's stick tonight to first things.'

'Can't we have some more light?' said Levenson. 'I'm not sure the romantic atmosphere is quite right to talk business in.'

'Put the lights on, Tom,' Orme-Campbell ordered.

Howell rose reluctantly and pressed a switch so that the great chandeliers bloomed in crystal, brightening the ormolu wall-lights and the gilt chairs.

'Thank you, Mr. Howell,' said Levenson with a friendly smile. 'Lattner, come and sit next to me.'

In a shuffling minuet the places were rearranged, so that Levenson with Lattner at his side faced Orme-Campbell flanked by his directors, while Budd and Howell sat at each end of the long table.

'Perhaps you'd better open,' said Orme-Campbell courteously. He had pushed back his chair, and was looking at those opposite with a relaxed, ironic expression which set a standard for the demeanour of the other directors.

'Thank you,' said Levenson. He waited like a conductor till his audience was comfortable. Then he began,

'Let me just recap, Sir Geoffrey. On May 3rd we put up our offer of £73 million for O.C.E. A week later you turned it down on the grounds that a merger between Levenson's and your company wouldn't be the best way of reorganizing the industry, even though at that time'—he paused and glanced at Budd, who was staring fixedly at a picture by Stubbs above

27

Levenson's head—'we had, or thought we had, the support of the Minister of Industrial Reconstruction. We were offering, in fact, fifty-seven shillings a share. We made at the same time a forecast of your pre-tax results that didn't look very cheerful. Right?'

There was no reply from Orme-Campbell.

'All right then. You came back at the end of the month with your own profit forecast. Marvellous! A record profit. Oh yes! You could do without us. Our friend Budd then decides that there is no need for the time being to refer our offer to the Monopolies Commission, or to give it a straight veto, because O.C.E. are in a position to hold it off without intervention.'

He drained his glass of Armagnac.

'Then the Minister has second thoughts, and refers our bid to the Monopolies Commission, who report they're divided. So the Minister of Industrial Reconstruction still has the last word.'

'I don't want to interrupt,' said Orme-Campbell, 'but, if I may say so, all this is past history. The important thing is your final offer, and that's something we've got the last word on. Our shares are up to sixty-five shillings in the market. You're now offering seventy-two shillings. It's a good price—and it'll find a lot of takers.' He paused and added, 'But we're turning it down. And the others will follow suit. I think that sums up the position.'

There was a mutter of assent from around the table. Unmoved, Levenson waited for it to subside.

'Perhaps we can come back to that. Let's look first at the structural position.'

*

For the next ten minutes, he engaged in a disparaging analysis of the company's assets, its managerial hierarchy, its distribution of functions, and its work in progress.

'What do you conclude from all this?' his host asked, leaning back in his chair with his eyes closed.

'I conclude,' said Levenson, '—and I'm going to be frank— I conclude that your whole organization needs to be reconstructed from top to bottom.'

He traversed some of the faces of those sitting around the table—Budd, Arliff, Sutton, Cranston and Howell. They were passive, apparently uninvolved. Orme-Campbell put a walnut carefully between the strong silver legs of a nut-cracker, and slowly pressed it till the fair hairs on the back of his large hands bristled.

'Very good of you, Levenson, to offer us this advice. Very useful indeed.' He looked around for approval. 'As a matter of fact, we've anticipated you. We've decided to do our own reconstruction. Fred—Lord Hamblett—is our new deputy chairman-designate, and I'm hoping that next year, Levenson, we're going to set a pretty hot pace.'

'Yes,' said Levenson patiently. 'Yes. But it's a long way to go till next year. What we've got at the moment is uncertainty. You see, Sir Geoffrey, it isn't just a matter of a bid. O.C.E. is a splendid company—your grandfather built it up in the Industrial Revolution—'

'My great-grandfather,' said the other. 'I'm not as old as all that.'

'It was a first-class family firm—your grandfather developed your lathe—and you lived on it for eighty years. Then ten years ago you moved on—but only ten years ago. You started pretty late on numerical control machines, transfer machines— all the stuff based on advanced technology.'

'We've got the finest research and development shops in the engineering industry,' said Orme-Campbell, still smiling but stung.

'Yes,' said Levenson sadly. His heavy eyes were commiserating. 'That's been the trouble with O.C.E.—a lot of research and not much applied. You developed your punch-control borer and grinder. Then you sat back and waited. . . I've just got back from Osaka. Franzoni and Schultz were everywhere. You, Sir Geoffrey, were nowhere. I'm sorry. It's a fact.'

He paused, and Orme-Campbell placed his cigar carefully on the edge of a tray before replying.

'I think, Levenson,' he said, 'you can leave us to look after our business.'

'That's just the point,' Levenson said, putting on a pair of horn-rimmed spectacles that accentuated his heavy features. 'I've got in front of me some advance figures of your accounts.'

'What do you mean?' Orme-Campbell asked, his lips tightening and a patch of red on his forehead. 'Our accounts are confidential, and haven't been published. How—'

'Don't get excited,' said Levenson. 'These are just intelligent guesses that my statisticians have worked out. Extrapolations, they call them. They show that your profits will be £4 to £5 million down—not up, as you forecast. That's quite a lot of money. Right?'

There was no reply.

'You may find, Mr. Levenson,' said Lord Hamblett, 'that publishing figures of this kind at this stage of play might be pretty near libel.'

'There's no stage of play,' said Levenson stiffly. 'We're not playing games. If there's any reason for me not to publish these figures, it's because I believe our forecast of your losses is too low. What I'm saying is that you need help in managing your business.'

'That's an impertinence.'

'I'm sorry. It's very relevant. But you mustn't take it too personally. Things have changed since your father went round the workshops chatting up the boys with fifty years' service. The Guv'nor figure is dead. And I'll tell you something else. There aren't any British companies any more either.'

30

'How d'you make that out?' said Budd, seeming to wake from a catalepsy.

Levenson paused and recomposed his stance.

'What I mean,' he said, 'is that the British engineering industry has to face international competition—American, German, Russian. Last year, I saw some of the industrial complexes in Eastern Siberia—fantastic engineering groupings based on hydro-electricity at a fraction of our costs. If we're going to compete with the Russians, we've got to face up to them on their own scale. Otherwise, we might as well pack up. It's the giants versus the pygmies.'

'That's not what you said,' Orme-Campbell insisted. 'You said there aren't any British companies any more.'

Levenson answered, 'That's right. There's no room for companies with only a domestic market.'

'No, you don't get off the hook all that easily, Levenson. You've just stated a principle that I find singularly objectionable—I think a lot of us do. I don't want to be offensive—but our families were here a long time before your crowd came on the scene. We built up our industries—or our fathers did— with hard work, skill, enterprise—everything. It wasn't a lot of paperwork that made our works in Leicester and Coventry and Manchester. It was work with machines and metal—'

'I think,' said Levenson, 'we can skip all that.'

'I don't think so,' said Orme-Campbell. 'We built it up. What have you done for our industry that makes you think you can walk in with your accountants and your bankers and imagine you can take over the work of a century?'

He turned to Howell and addressed him.

'I'm sometimes baffled by the sheer cheek of it all.'

'If you mean by cheek—', Levenson began, but his host interrupted.

'Listen, Levenson. You said there aren't any British companies any more. If you had your way, there wouldn't be. Your father came to Hackney from Roumania or somewhere.

Jolly good luck to him! He was a cap-maker, and I'm sure made very good caps. In 1909, my father was running the biggest lathe-manufacturing plants in the world. . . . Well, I claim no credit for that. Except that while I was reading blue-prints, you were selling neck-ties. When I was working in the machine-shop, you'd never as much as seen a lathe. When I was making machine tools in America, you were working for an East End estate agent, touting office space. . . . When I was a gunner in North Africa, you were a part-timer in the National Fire Service and a so-called manager of a tin-hut factory, sub-contracting Government contracts. And when the war ended, there you were—you'd made it—an engineer-cum-property man with a stake in our industry.'

'Why not?' Levenson asked quickly.

'Indeed, why not?' Orme-Campbell echoed. 'But you didn't just want a stake. You wanted a bit more—and a bit more—and then the lot. Company flotations, property companies—more and more. . . . Well, I can tell you, Levenson, that "more and more" stops here. There are still some British companies, and O.C.E. is one of them. And while I'm chairman, it will continue to be.'

A growl ran round the table, and Orme-Campbell pushed his chair still further back as if he intended to rise. Levenson didn't move. The faces, no longer neutral, had suddenly become angry, as if towards a gate-crasher at a private party.

'There's something you ought to know,' he said, ignoring the hostility. 'I had a report from our bankers half an hour before I left to come here. At this afternoon's count, we had over thirty-four per cent of acceptances—and all those despite your whispering campaign.'

'Paranoia too,' said Orme-Campbell, encouraging a burst of laughter.

'Paranoia?' said Levenson. 'You don't really think it paranoiac if I object to your friends writing "Go back to

32

Poland" on some of the application forms, or "Plotsk is calling you"—and all the other muck you dredged up?'

A second wave of smiles passed over the faces, and Orme-Campbell felt it necessary to explain.

'Well,' he said, 'we business men have to be like politicians. If we dish it out, we've got to take it. Isn't that right, Budd?'

'That's quite right. You chaps are a bit thin-skinned, Levenson. After all, it's you who want to run the whole show.'

'Yes—that's the idea,' said Levenson. 'I'm going to make it what it hasn't been for the last thirty years. I'm going to make it efficient.'

'And when you do that,' said Budd, his face flushed and interested, 'you're going to sack ten thousand men. You said so in *The Times*. I'll tell you one thing, Harry. If you ever want to go into politics, don't try and get a Midland seat.'

'It's not what I said, and I don't want to be in Parliament. What I did say was that O.C.E. are carrying over ten thousand redundant men on Government contracts who are being paid for out of public funds.'

'That's simply untrue,' said Orme-Campbell, his lips tightening with resentment.

'Even if it was true, it's not the point,' Budd broke in. 'The important thing—whether it's right or not—is that a take-over is going to make it tough for a lot of workers.'

'Oh, yes,' said Levenson, removing his glasses and shrugging. 'A lot of people will lose their jobs. I admit it. But it all depends on how you look at the industry. If you see it as a state-run charitable institution, then keep your ten thousand men on the pay-roll. But don't pretend that a firm run on that basis is efficient or that it's going to be competitive.' He waited for a comment, but when none came he went on. 'Do you want to know why the acceptances are rolling in? It's because the public are waking up to the fact that the Old Boy style of management is dead. All you want is Government subsidies,

33

and when they run out you go squealing for more with your begging-bowls to the press and your tame M.P.s.'

Orme-Campbell stood up, and there was a shuffle of chairs as the others at the table rose with him.

'I had hoped, Levenson,' he said, 'that we could have conducted our affairs without abuse. That's why we arranged this dinner tonight. I'm obliged to say that I don't like your—your style of discussion.'

Levenson looked satisfied.

'I'm just telling you the facts,' he said. 'Right, Lattner? You asked me here because you had something to tell me. I'm still waiting to hear it.'

Orme-Campbell rested his hands on the back of his chair, and said,

'I'd hoped to explain to you in a reasonable way why we're turning down your offer—why we have asked the major shareholders—the insurance companies—the union trusts—not to accept. I believe they'll take our advice.'

'You're quite sure?' said Levenson quickly.

'I know what you mean,' said Orme-Campbell. 'You're counting on the Alliance, but you're wrong. The Alliance Company will accept your offer only if they're satisfied that Mr. Budd, as Minister of Industrial Reconstruction—and I asked him specially to hear our discussion—undertakes not to veto your bid, as is his statutory right, as being against the public interest.'

'I would be surprised if he did veto it,' said Levenson. 'Budd'—speaking of him as if he weren't there—'knows perfectly well that if the bid doesn't go through, there won't just be ten thousand redundant in a year's time. There'll be a major collapse in the industry.'

'Mr. Budd,' said Orme-Campbell, 'takes a somewhat different view.'

Budd moved away from his side. He didn't like standing next to a man who was nearly a foot taller than himself.

'It might be better,' he said, 'if neither of you prejudged my views. I'd rather wait, Orme-Campbell, to hear the result of your own meeting tonight. I'll never understand why you boys don't get together and knock some sense into the industry. . . . Ten thousand redundant engineers! It's a hell of a lot for the country to carry—and pay for.'

He turned to Levenson.

'Frankly, Harry, there's another side to the coin. I don't know if the country will wear it if you get O.C.E. You're a bright fellow, all right. But I've got a feeling that Britain doesn't want bright fellows. The line between the bright boy and the wide boy is a very narrow one.' He watched with satisfaction the twitch in Levenson's jaw. 'Now if Orme-Campbell took you over, that would be very well received.'

There was a guffaw from the directors, who had been listening to him respectfully.

'No doubt,' said Levenson. He had quickly recovered from Budd's jibe. 'But the fact is that Orme-Campbell can't take me over—and I believe that if I take him over, I can make O.C.E. into a national asset, and not the national liability it is.'

'Very patriotic,' Hamblett interposed.

'Well, we'll have to see,' said Budd judicially. 'I'm going for a stroll in the grounds.'

'Just a minute,' said Levenson. His voice was sharp. 'I hope you'll give us a clear-cut answer tonight—one way or the other.'

Budd answered with an equal edge. 'Don't push me, Levenson. I'm an Englishman, you know. I don't like to be pushed.'

Chapter Three

IN the drawing-room, Isobel and Elaine Orme-Campbell were casting glances towards the white doors in the hope that the arrival of the men would release them from their exhausted conversation.

'They're taking a long time tonight,' said Isobel, sipping her coffee, now cold.

'Yes,' said Elaine in her throaty voice. 'I'm afraid we're just a couple of spare parts. I wouldn't dare interrupt.'

She paused and stroked the arm of the sofa, remembering the time when her hands were free from the brown maculae that she called her freckles. Through the open curtains, they could see that the dusk, dove-grey and flecked with pink, was beginning to darken the trees and brighten the lamps on the terrace. Apart from the mumble of voices and an occasional crash of laughter from the dining room, a stillness had fallen over the gardens, the woods and the house itself.

'I love this time on a summer evening,' said Elaine. 'Everything's so peaceful—if it weren't for all that!' She waved her hand towards the door. 'I must say I can't get passionately involved in these battles. I don't think Geoffrey can either. He isn't a natural business man. Finance bores him. What he likes most in the world are machines, horses and boats, in that order.'

Isobel smiled lamely.

'That wouldn't do at all for me,' she said. 'Horses frighten me—they've got so many teeth. And boats make me sea-sick, even on rivers. . . . I'm afraid that, try as he will, Harry has

36

never been able to explain a single machine to me. And, heaven knows I've walked through dozens of factories.'

'What about the companies? Do you understand anything about them?'

'No. . . . Do you?'

'Not very much. When I hear the word "shares" I close up. It's strange how some words have that effect. Technology's another one.'

'What about "students"?'

' "Students"?' said Elaine, opening wide her china-blue eyes with their careful make-up. 'They don't affect me that way. I like the young. When my two sons were up at Oxford, our house was always full of their friends. Emma too—but she got married when she was eighteen. I miss the noise they used to make.'

'How long ago was that?' Isobel asked.

'Oh, don't be unkind, Isobel—may I call you that?'

'Of course, I'm so sorry.'

Elaine put a reassuring hand on her arm.

'I'm not serious. Six or seven years ago I had a niece at Newnham—my sister's daughter. She was very tiresome—always talking about "not compromising".'

'What happened to her?'

'She compromised. She got married at St. Margaret's to a pompous young barrister, and she's got two children and lives happily in Knightsbridge. Emma lives in Chicago. He's a physicist. You've got to be tough not to compromise.'

'There's been a change in the last few years,' said Isobel thoughtfully. The image of Jonathan's friends standing gravely in front of the tapestry at the bottom of the staircase came into her mind. 'All those young people give themselves labels like syndico-anarchist or Trotskyist or General Protester. They cocoon themselves in vogue words. But it's all designed to hide some private complexity.'

'There's a lot of that about,' Elaine said, taking a cigarette from her gold snuff-box. 'You're very lucky having a husband like Harry.'

'Why?' Isobel asked. 'Why lucky?'

'I mean,' said Elaine, lighting her cigarette, 'he's so down to earth—so practical. He believes in efficiency and success. I like that.'

'Yes,' said Isobel. She spread the panels of her dress over the sofa and looked again towards the door, seeking a respite.

'He's got the common touch,' Elaine insisted. 'It must be very stimulating being married to someone who comes from a different background.'

Seeing Isobel's expression, she went on hurriedly,

'You may not know this, but Geoffrey and I are second cousins.'

'No,' said Isobel. 'I didn't know.'

'We hesitated about getting married—but that part of it worked out very well.'

'It must be very comforting.'

'There's a lot to be said for conventional husbands.'

'Yes, indeed.'

'Geoffrey's as normal as the next man. When he was younger, he used to be mad about polo.'

'Were you?'

'Not really. What about—?' She had forgotten Levenson's first name.

'Harry?'

'Yes—Harry.'

'He never played games as a boy, and he went to work when he was very young. But he's learning to shoot.'

'I saw something about it in the papers,' said Elaine. 'I do admire him. He's so dedicated and determined. Would you like to use the loo? It's through the Medal Room.'

As if in a pavan, she rose and preceded Isobel to an outer

room containing framed photographs and glass cases with silver trophies and medals, where she switched on the strip lighting.

'There's Geoffrey,' she said, 'when he was a young man—the second on the left when he won the Public School Racquets Championship at Queens. And that's him next to Lord Crainton when he captained his polo team—and that's his Military Cross—and that's one of him sailing—oh, we've got bags of pictures of Geoffrey winning things all over the place and looking very handsome.'

'That must have been fun,' Isobel said politely.

'Fun?' said Elaine. 'I don't really know. I seem to have spent a lot of my life shivering and clapping and yawning in grandstands.'

She moved on towards the staircase through the hall that was painted with huge caryatids in *trompe l'oeil*. Four pedestal lamps, throwing counter-shadows, deepened the sudden mystery of the Herculean figures with their arms raised as if to sustain the ceiling, and Isobel's eyes traversed the massive pectoral muscles of the brooding giants.

'When were these painted?' she asked.

'Oh, about fifteen years ago,' said Elaine. 'I call them Campbell's Follies.'

'They're superbly painted.'

'Yes—they were done by a young Italian—Galliano—we picked up in Positano that year. He came and stayed with us for nearly eighteen months. Geoffrey was mad about his work. He painted a frieze and the ceiling in his bedroom. Remind me to show it to you.'

Isobel touched the wall with her finger-tips, and examined the stippled surface.

'We liked this young man so much,' Elaine said unsmilingly. 'His permit ran out, and they sent him back for some reason. I never knew why. Look at those marvellous thighs! Look at the way it all seems to be bulging under the weight! . . . My

39

favourite Italian painting is the Atalanta and Hippomenes in Bologna. Have you seen it? It's a huge picture of two naked figures with Atalanta bending over and Hippomenes turning away.'

'No,' said Isobel. 'I don't know the Italians awfully well. What about your husband—does he like pictures?'

'Only Stubbs—and the family pictures, of course.'

'And your friend?'

'Geoffrey liked him as a craftsman more than anything else.'

'Does it matter very much—I mean him not sharing your enthusiasms?'

'Oh, we do share quite a few. But about my special ones, Geoffrey is wonderfully understanding. I think I told you I'm chairman of the Friends of Foreign Museums.'

'Yes, you did.'

'Well, that helps a lot. You must come on one of our expeditions, Isobel. Do you ever travel without your husband?'

'Not really—not much further than London to Marfield. I don't think Harry would like it. In any case, we both enjoy works of art, and we like to see them together. We collect in a small way, too.'

'What?'

'A few pictures—some porcelain—George II silver—Nymphenberg—not very much.'

'It takes two to make a collection,' said Elaine as they climbed the stairs. 'One to collect, the other to admire one's taste. Collecting alone is a kind of self-abuse. So I prefer to look at other people's collections. . . . Mind you, Geoffrey does get spasms—he once started a collection of old coaches that drove me potty. He even had a copy of the one in the Armoury Museum with the Boucher paintings. They took up about half an acre. Then he settled for something more specialized—what he calls The Coachman's Curiosa. . . . You go second on the right through my room.'

Broken into groups, the guests returned noisily to the drawing room from which an arc of light spread over the lawns towards the avenues, now in a penumbra.

'I'm sorry, Mrs. Levenson,' Orme-Campbell said above the din, advancing towards Isobel. 'This is a very ragged evening. It's kind of you to put up with us.'

'It's disgraceful of me to enjoy such a delicious dinner and run away.'

'So soon?'

'Yes—Jonathan's giving a party. Not that he wants me. On the other hand, I'm not really in favour of wives hanging round when their husbands are working.'

'No,' said Orme-Campbell, shaking his heavy head. 'I wouldn't want to inflict that on you, much as we would enjoy it.'

Levenson was standing with Lattner and Lord Hamblett. Budd was already seated, surrounded by a coterie whom he was lecturing in a dogmatic voice. And, to rest her eyes, Elaine Orme-Campbell had put on a blue pair of glasses fringed with brilliants, even though she didn't like wearing them.

'Let me at least monopolize you for the next few minutes,' said Orme-Campbell to Isobel. 'It's a very warm evening. Why don't we stroll outside?'

They walked on to the terrace, and he said, 'Be careful going down these steps. They're crumbling at the edges.'

He took her upper arm and Isobel felt his fingers, warm and slightly moist, enclosing it. She moved, but his grip tightened, and she decided to accept the polite intimacy with good grace.

'The place was built originally as a manor house and redesigned by George Hattersley,' he explained. 'You must see it properly soon.'

'Yes, we'd adore to see it in daylight,' said Isobel.

'When Harry and I have settled our tiresome little argument,' Orme-Campbell said, 'I hope you'll both come and

41

visit us. Over there on the right,' he went on, turning her round and still holding her arm, 'you see an early Victorian wing, added by great-great-grandfather Sir Auberon Campbell. Our Orme came later—part of a marriage settlement. He was an extraordinary old man—you know, a knight of the shires who turned his land over to sheep and then found coal. Coal, iron, engineering—that's how the cycle went, but it's petering out with a lot of other things. I know one can't really identify history till it's over, of course, but we're obviously at the beginning of a new phase in Britain's history.'

'What phase?'

'Well,' he said, 'I'd say that an expatriate returning to Britain after ten years would have some difficulty in recognizing the country he knew. It would be like returning to an old town that has been rebuilt with motorway and flyovers.'

'Isn't that a good thing?'

'Not entirely. You mustn't be angry with me.'

'I'm not. I just don't understand why you talk of change with such regret.'

'Well, it's obvious. To begin with, our old social structure is dead and gone.'

'I don't think I'm very sorry about that.'

'I am. There's nothing yet to take its place. The old system —even the Imperial order—was based on responsibility. The New Establishment is without roots and without responsibility.'

'You think that a man like my husband with nearly thirty thousand employees has no responsibility?'

'I was thinking at the moment,' Orme-Campbell said, 'of those terrible life peers. What social responsibility have they got?'

'You didn't answer my question,' said Isobel.

'About Harry?' Orme-Campbell said absent-mindedly. 'He has economic responsibility—yes. But, if you'll forgive me saying this, no roots.'

Isobel detached her arm from his hand, and said,
'I will not forgive you for saying that.'

They walked a few steps in silence, till Orme-Campbell said,

'Your husband wouldn't have been offended. He's far too much of a realist.'

*

On the other side of the drive Lady Orme-Campbell slowed the pace of her walk, and her companion adapted his step politely to hers.

'One always thinks in stereotypes,' she said, relentless in her attempt to provoke Levenson, who, so far, had replied with phrases like 'Very interesting', into a more personal conversation. 'I used to think of you as something out of the Times Business Supplement.'

Levenson said, 'I'm haunted by that damned photograph.'

'Why don't you change it?'

'Well, every photograph—even the best—is a caricature —whether it's in the boardroom or the street. They like taking me with my mouth open.'

'Yes,' said Elaine. 'That can be very disadvantageous. You're much nicer than I expected you to be. And Isobel's adorable.'

'We can agree on that,' said Levenson.

'You and she are such perfect counterparts—such contrasts. I was telling her about my travels in Russia—as chairman of the Friends of Foreign Museums. You know Russia, of course.'

'Not well. I went there last year with our trade delegation.' He described the purpose of his journey, his stay in Moscow and the difficulty of contacting the right officials.

'That's very interesting,' said Elaine absently, borrowing his previous tone and deciding that she had done her social duty. 'I see Isobel and Geoffrey approaching us in a clockwise direction. She's such a good listener and Geoffrey's such an

43

insistent talker. She must be a great asset to you in your business life.'

A rhododendron bush straggled across the path, and Levenson ducked to pass it.

'I've never thought of her in those terms,' he replied. 'Does your husband include you in his balance-sheet?'

'Rather foolishly, yes,' said Elaine. 'You're very prickly, Mr. Levenson.' She had decided to try again.

'Why not?' said Levenson. 'I have good reason to be.'

'Not with me. Let's get back to Russia. Do you speak the language? I tried to learn once, but it's so full of "shchtchi's" and the verbs have so many aspects, I gave it up.'

'It's a language you've got to be born with,' said Levenson.

'Were you born with it?' Elaine went on. 'Is it true you were born there?'

'No,' said Levenson calmly. 'That's the story put out by your husband's friends. But it's not so far out as some of them. My father was born at Plotsk, in Poland.'

'He's Polish!' said Elaine, as if making a great discovery. 'I love the Poles. They're so chivalrous and gallant. No wonder they did so well during the war.'

'They were overrun in a few days,' said Levenson.

'I meant in Edinburgh,' said Elaine. 'Do tell me—does your father still live in—where was it? Tomsk?'

'Plotsk.'

'Yes—Plotsk. Does he still live there?'

'No. He's dead. But my mother's alive. She lives alone with a housekeeper, bless her, and she's eighty-five.'

'Bless her indeed. She must be very proud of you.'

'Yes,' said Levenson. 'I think she is. She had a very hard life. My father was a cap-maker, you know, always working away late into the night. He earned in a year what I earn in a few hours.'

'I can only say—congrats!' said Elaine as if to herself, watching her husband approach.

'We've completed the circle,' said Isobel, greeting her.

'Actually, it's an oval,' Elaine replied. 'Things here are never quite what they seem. Your husband and I are worn out with exercise.'

'Only mental exercise,' said Levenson. 'Lady Orme-Campbell has been encouraging me to write my autobiography.'

'How far did you get?' Isobel asked.

'I sketched in a few family details,' said Levenson. 'We can expect a lot more in the next few days.'

*

Thirty-one rioters had been killed in Kuala Lumpur. The typhoid outbreak in Cardiff was under control. The strike at Fords, now in its second week, was likely to end on Monday, following a meeting between union officials and management in St. James's Square under the chairmanship of the Minister for Employment.

In the library where the directors' meeting was to be held, a group was gathered around the television set listening to the ten o'clock news and comment. The announcer shuffled his papers, stared at the telecaster, and went on:

'The future of O.C.E. in face of Mr. Levenson's bid still rests in the balance. At 7.30 Hurstcombe's issued an announcement on behalf of Mr. Levenson that over thirty-four per cent of acceptances had already been counted. If the proposal goes through, this will be one of the biggest successful take-over bids in the history of the engineering industry. Our economic correspondent reports increasing depression in the O.C.E. camp as the tide seems to be running for Mr. Harry Levenson against Sir Geoffrey Orme-Campbell.'

'Come off it,' said Hamblett, and everyone guffawed.

'. . . the crucially important international stake . . . a pronounced split . . . Alliance expected to accept . . .'

The announcer's voice penetrated the chatter.

'However, the attitude of Mr. Budd, Minister of Industrial

45

Reconstruction, remains enigmatic, and although the indications are that he will authorize the transaction despite the inconclusive reference to the Monopolies Commission, there is at present no certainty of Ministerial approval. . . . Cricket. At Old Trafford this afternoon, England made . . .'

Hamblett drew Howell into a corner of the room, where an elaborate figure of Psyche after Canova looked incongruously towards the television set and the directors gathered around it.

'Where's the Rt. Honourable Gentleman?'

'He's still in the drawing room,' said Hamblett. 'When I last saw him, he was busy examining his conscience—like a middle-aged Chinese confessing to the youth that he'd fallen below the standards of the cultural revolution.'

'Or a Methodist lay-preacher who's been accosted in the West End. What's the trouble now?' Howell asked.

'Oh, God knows,' said Hamblett. 'You never can tell with Alf. He was beating his chest and asking everyone if it was really suitable for him to be ringmaster in this take-over circus. He was also saying that as a Nonconformist he felt that money is overrated. And he also takes the view that there's a lot less in his Rt. Hon. friend Mr. Cranfield, the Leader of the House, than meets the eye.'

'That's familiar stuff,' said Howell. 'I hope he's not going to get too elevated. For a man who never drinks, Alf has a remarkable ability to get high.'

'That's all right,' said Hamblett. 'It's his blood pressure. He never gets tight—he may look tight—he may behave tight —but he always knows exactly what's going on.'

'What we want,' Howell said, lowering his voice and swivelling the brandy-glass that he had taken to the library, 'is a statement from Budd before midnight. It should be on the early news tomorrow morning, and in the second editions.'

He finished his brandy quickly, and said, 'Levenson wanted to have a word with me before our meeting.'

'Something interesting?'

46

'I don't know. He's a great brain-picker. The last time he asked me to see him privately, he offered me a job.'

'See if you can get me one too.'

'Funny fat pouches he's got under his eyes,' thought Howell, as Hamblett's laugh rolled up from his stomach and wobbled at his lower chin, only stopping at his eyes that remained watchful in the light of the green table-lamp.

'I'll put in a word for you,' said Howell. His smile sagged into his pale, cavernous cheeks, and disappeared.

*

Alone in Elaine's bedroom, Isobel listened to the conversation rising in gusts from below. She didn't know where Orme-Campbell had put her fur cape, and she sat on the counterpane unable to decide where she should begin to look for it. In the last few months she had noticed in herself a growing inability to make decisions, even small ones, and the problem of where to find her cape began to swell like a balloon inside her head. She got up and moved towards the door, and then returned to the bed as if to a sanctuary. The cape! The wardrobe fitted into the wall seemed a keyless, doorless ivory surface. The Buhl clock on the dressing table had lost both its hands and Isobel sat for a few minutes contemplating its blank face and umbilical centre. She put out her fingers and touched it, and it carilloned lightly at the disturbance. '*Sans amour et sans haine.*' Without love, without hate, without anything. The worst pain and not to know why. The familiar panic began to surge irresistibly, rising like water in a lock as she sat with her head bowed, waiting till she would drown beneath it and then emerge in a quivering resurrection.

Isobel put her forehead in her hands, and waited. The curtains were drawn and, eyes clenched, she fumbled to put out the light. Soon after her marriage she had told Harry about the nightmares that came to haunt her in daylight, and

47

he'd said, 'You'd better see someone about it,' and then he'd forgotten.

'Edward!' she said in the darkness, and his name was an amulet that she clung to as the dread closed around her. She could no longer conjure up his face in her mind, only his presence, his gaiety, the feeling of his neck above her as she clung to him, trying to keep herself from the hands that wanted to drag her into blackness. 'It's nothing, nothing at all,' she would say to herself. 'Don't be silly—it's nothing. It doesn't last. It'll go.' As a child she had climbed for a dare the outside ladder of a pit shaft, and in the strong wind her fingers had begun to lose their hold on the rungs made slippery with wet coal dust. That was how it seemed to her when the panic began to fill her, and her mind rushed from one fear to another in search of a grip to secure herself from the amorphous horror that blew around her. It was nothing—fantasy—but it returned, a presence that refused to be exorcized.

She thought of her son and his teasing expression, affectionate and relaxed, when they were alone. She remembered him introducing his friends as she and Harry said good-bye a generation away. The corsair. The boy with the dark hair and blue eyes and insolent manner. What was his name? Anthony? Adrian. Adrian when he dived in the sunlight, a corsair at night. He was very truculent, but young, hopeful; his voice was laughing, and his brown face was clear as a painting behind her eyelids. The image anchored her in reality.

She switched on the light again, picked up the telephone, and in a steady voice asked the operator for Avebury 371. 'The number's ringing,' the operator answered in a few seconds. Isobel listened. The burr-burr echoed her heart-beat. Each sound of the ringing tone as it rang into the emptiness of the three rooms at Marfield where it might have been heard confirmed her in her old fear that some disaster might have happened to Jonathan in her absence.

Yet as the fear became more precise, so the diffuse panic

evaporated. She flicked the receiver and said, 'Try that number on another line.' Again the burr-burr—five times in all, till an unfamiliar woman's voice said, 'Avebury 371.'

'Who's that?'

'Avebury 371—this is Henrietta.'

'This is Mrs. Levenson—Jonathan's mother.'

'Oh, yes.' The voice was laconic.

'I'd like to speak to him.'

'I'll see if I can find him.'

From the other end of the line, Isobel could hear the clamour of youthful voices overlaying the background music of the discothèque.

'Hello, mum.'

She controlled her voice.

'Hello, Jonathan darling. I'm still at Orme House. Having a good time?'

'Yes, marvellous, except that one of the fridges has gone.'

'That's too bad. You'll have to give them mulled Coca-Cola. Anything else?'

'No, everything's going very well. We've got the fountain working by the river—blue and white—it looks terrific. How are you?'

She hesitated. 'It's very boring here. I feel stifled. The English upper classes can be very spiteful. And besides, I miss you.'

'Well,' said Jonathan, 'why don't you come back? I'll fix you up with a man.'

'You're insufferable,' she said. 'I do wish I could get away. They've put my cape somewhere, and I don't know who to ask for it.'

'Tried the butler?'

'I'm upstairs. I don't want to get mixed up with all those grim-looking business men.'

'How's all that going? I heard something about it on the news.'

49

'I really don't know—don't want to know. What about my cape? Tell me what to do.'

There was a pause, and again the sound of the discothèque rose with its melancholy beat and plangent descant.

'It's a matter of elimination,' Jonathan said. 'Capes are always put in bedrooms. If they're not on beds, they're in large cupboards. I should start in the room you're in, then work leftwards.'

'I see,' she said meekly.

'And when you've got it,' Jonathan said, 'come and join us. I think I'd like to finish that dance with you.'

Isobel got off the bed and began to open the cupboards. Her cape wasn't there, and she went into Orme-Campbell's room next door. The room was lit by a standing candelabrum, and the frieze, painted with what seemed to her a heavy emulsion, faced the bed from the wall like a strip cartoon. Against a cobalt sky and a mountain range tipped with white, an athletic contest was taking place—lithe runners, muscular wrestlers, discus throwers and swimmers, with a centrepiece of the Victor Ludorum, a naked youth being crowned by Apollo. Opposite the bed, surrounded by sporting prints, was an eighteenth-century closed cabinet with an ornate handle of twined silver cherubs. She turned it, and the doors opened. She stared, stared again and closed it quickly.

'Christ!' she said aloud. 'The Coachman's Curiosa!'

Her cape was lying on a chair, and she picked it up and ran downstairs to where Levenson was standing, earnestly addressed by a white-faced Howell at the curve of the balustrade.

'I'm going, darling,' she said.

'I'll see you to your car,' said Levenson.

'What on earth have you been doing to that poor fellow?' she asked, as they walked towards the drive.

'Nothing much,' said Levenson, looking her straight in the eyes. 'I've just been asking him a few questions.'

Chapter Four

FROM her balcony at Marfield an hour later, Isobel could see through the trees the glow of the barbecue, darkened from time to time by the silhouette of Jonathan's friends. The discothèque on the edge of the dance floor thumped its music, and every now and again laughter floated up irrelevantly, like applause from a radio in an empty room. She felt tired and awake, indecisive after her solitary return, a stranger walking through a house where the guests with their excited young faces and preoccupied indifference were more at home than she was.

A few had noticed her as she climbed the stairs to her room, and had greeted her as 'Mrs. Levenson'. Twenty—twenty-one years? A hundred years between. 'Hello, Mrs. Levenson. It's a lovely party—and it's barely begun. Going to bed?'

Mrs. Levenson is going to bed. Mrs. Levenson is going to bed alone. Down below, they are playing a French song, '*Etreins-moi, mon amour . . .*', and along the lantern-lit walk leading to the marquee, blue-and-white striped in a floodlight, there is a stir of slow and happy footsteps. Isobel Levenson is turning her back on the balcony, and is going to bed with her sleeping pills in her hand.

She removed the bottle from the drawer on the other side of the room, where she kept them for fear that absent-mindedly in the night she might take too many, and counted three tablets into her left hand. She would sleep through the party, through Harry's return and the sudden brawling of birds in

51

the early summer dawn. And she would wake at nine, and try it all once again. Again and again till she was old and passive.

Before she began to take off her make-up, she unzipped her long dress and stepped out of it as it fell to the floor. In the looking-glass, her arms and her shoulders were brown, but at the embroidered rose-bud between the cups of her brassière, the tan faded as in a vignette into the white of her breasts. Releasing the hook, she examined herself, first directly and then in profile, passing her hands over her body to feel its texture. Then she said aloud to her reflection, 'I'm very nice.' And added, 'What for?' She lay on the bed, still looking at her half-naked image in the mirror, and repeated, 'What for?' For all the days and months and years that stretched ahead, the changing and unchanging of clothes for cocktail parties and dinner parties, for the great perspective of nothing. Willing time away. The desultory phone-calls, the gossip of the night before, *The Times*, menus, the odious television, the London flat, his friends, Oh God, his business friends, the galleries and the servants. What for? The question fixed itself in her mind, a moaning needle in a groove.

*

'What for?' Not for Harry's acquaintances whom he brings to dinner in London. The tall men with the watchful, well-massaged faces and the well-coiffured hair who speak quietly and listen respectfully to Harry, and then, when he moves to the other end of the room, relax and look at her as if to say, 'What for—when you are one of us and not of him?'

And three or four times they had asked if they might telephone her, and she had answered, 'Why not ring my husband? We'd love to see you again.'

And then there was the doctor—Fisher, Frobisher, Farquhar, Foster?—she couldn't remember the name—she wanted to forget it—whom she had gone to see in Welbeck

Street about her insomnia and headaches. It had been winter, and she had to wait for nearly a half-hour opposite an unhappy middle-aged man who sat with his head bowed in a catatonic trance while his companion, who looked like a nurse in day-dress, turned the pages of an old copy of *Punch* and the *Illustrated London News*, in front of a large wall-mirror over the fireplace, where a pair of rearing bronze horses harmonized with the Victorian seascapes around her.

Fisher-Frobisher-Foster-Frisby was a well-dressed middle-aged man with white teeth and a deliberate manner. When he shook hands with her he faced her at eye-level, but when he sat and put on his bi-focal glasses to make notes, she felt reduced, a suppliant.

She began to speak, and he interrupted her and asked her full name. She started again, and he asked her her age and her medical history. And when he had finished his preliminary questioning, he leant back at last and asked her to tell him her problem, and she couldn't speak.

That was the first time.

But the second time, she had been more confident. He listened, and she wanted to speak. And it seemed to her as if, sitting against the light, he was some god to whom she was bringing a sacrifice of all that was most secret and private in her feelings about Edward and Harry and Jonathan and her father, even her mother who had died when she herself was fourteen. And he had asked her only about Harry and what she felt afterwards.

And then, eyes shut, exposed on the couch with the woman receptionist on the other side of the screen, the close palpation and Frobisher-Farquhar's accompanying *obbligato* about winter sports, the hands, dwelling and returning, the commentary, 'That's good,' 'Excellent,' something about the Suvretta, the talk of symmetry, the exclusion of secondaries, and all the time the hands kneading, till at last the shaming, stifled, response.

With the curtains drawn he had examined her eyes with an ophthalmoscope, and she sat still listening to the click of the ratchet as Foster-Fisher-Frobisher travelled over the circumference of her eyes with his face close to hers, so that she could see his pale eye-ball and inhale the scent of the after-shave lotion and feel his nostril breath on her own cheek.

Then he had sent the receptionist away and gone to the other side of the table, and written a prescription while she read an incomprehensible advertising brochure from a pharmaceutical company on the table and studied the photographs of the doctor's wife and two children. Afterwards, he stood up, and she rose too. He walked around the table, and she noticed that his face had become very pale and that the pouches under his eyes had darkened. He was sweating slightly, and when he tried to smile his face went into a tic. He stood in front of her, and she saw that the prescription was fluttering in his hand as if it was being blown by an electric fan.

'I wonder,' he said—still the tic—'if I might see you again.'

'Thank you so much, Doctor Foster. (Frobisher—Farquhar —Frisby—the memory lay beneath a thousand tons of rubble.) If I feel no better—'

'Oh, you will be (*tic, tic*)—I really meant—(*the hands are reaching for her shoulders, her face*)—I meant perhaps—(*I hope he isn't going to drop dead*)—perhaps away from these consulting rooms?'

'Oh, that would be very unwise,' said Isobel. 'You're much too attractive.' (*Spare his feelings.*)

A smile, backing towards the door. Dr. Frobisher, or whatever his name is, squares his shoulders. He remembers, and is afraid. He presses the bell, and the woman receptionist comes in like a bullet. 'Mrs. Levenson is leaving. Thank you so much.' Shakes hands. The hand is sweating.

That was three years ago. Mrs. Levenson is very nice. But not for that—not for Dr. Farquhar. Not for Dr. Frinchley.

In the open drawer where she kept her sleeping pills, she

could see a silver bracelet, given to her by her father when she was a schoolgirl, which she had stopped wearing long ago, and now kept as an amulet. She remembered her father, tall and fair in his uniform, the admiration of her friends when he visited her at school, though he never became the brigadier that he told her he was going to be and that she, in turn, had bragged about to the others. And at the end of the war, without his uniform, he seemed bewildered, like an unfrocked monk coming out of a monastery into a bright light. He became an unsuccessful investor, his last speculation a scheme for the nation-wide promotion of orchards; and when Isobel got married for the second time, his capital was gone. Then he lost a diamond brooch, pawned and re-pawned, belonging to his dead wife. After the claim had been paid, a porter at the United Services Club told the insurance company that he had seen Canley-Mills secreting it in a suitcase that he had left there. Her father had wept in front of her, but it was all right, because Levenson, a large shareholder in the insurance company, repaid the £3,000. Now her father lived on what was euphemistically called a pension which Levenson paid him through a bank.

'Poor daddy!' Isobel said, and her childhood endearment defied the recollection of the half-closed door, of her husband in persuasive conversation with the Chief Assessor and a director of the insurance company, and the contemptuous words, 'Canley-Mills—poor old sod!' Remembering, she suddenly wanted to hear his voice, to be compassionate and forgiven for her anger, and to ease her own loneliness. She dialled his number in Rottingdean.

'Yes! Canley-Mills here!'

The voice groaned, a caricature of the brisk, hectoring tone of Colonel Canley-Mills, O.B.E.

'It's Isobel, father.'

'Who?'

'Isobel—your daughter Isobel.'

55

'Yes.'

There was a pause.

'It's very late, Isobel.'

'Yes, father. I hope I didn't wake you.'

'No.' A long pause. 'You know I never sleep.'

She tried to laugh it off.

'No one's sleeping nowadays. . . . I just wanted to say "hello". All the family's busy. Jonathan's giving a party.'

'Glad you can afford it. I can't afford more than one double whisky.'

'Are you well, father?'

'No. How do you expect me to be well with my arthritis? My legs are killing me.'

'I'm so sorry. You know when we went to see Dr. Raeburn.'

'That quack. There must be someone better. You promised, Isobel—'

'Yes. I'll ask Dr. Sanders if he knows anyone who might help. I'll try and come down next week.'

'Oh, I shouldn't do that.' The voice was ponderous, ironic. 'Why should you come all the way to—Rottingdean.' And in the place-name he put all his disgust. 'I don't want to disturb your social life. Besides, isn't Harry in the middle of a big take-over? I heard something about it tonight on TV.'

'Yes.'

'Well, perhaps he'll keep a block of shares for me.'

'You'll have to talk to him.'

'Those fellows never give anything away.'

Isobel felt her hand tighten on the telephone.

'He isn't ungenerous,' she said mildly.

'Don't talk to me like that, Isobel,' Canley-Mills replied. His old voice had become firm. 'It's a pretty bad show having to take anything from Harry. It isn't for you to rub it in.'

'But, father—'

'I can assure you, Isobel, I'm keeping a very careful account

56

of what Harry's advanced me. And I plan to pay him six per cent interest. Or isn't that enough?'

'You know he doesn't want anything back from you.'

'Doesn't he? Then why did he get you to phone me and taunt me?'

'Oh, please, daddy—don't be absurd.'

'Yes—that's it. That's what I am—absurd. All right, Isobel. I shouldn't worry. You won't have to put up with me for long.'

'What do you mean?'

Again the savouring pause at the other end.

'Nothing!' said Canley-Mills.

'You mean your health?'

She could feel the anxious quickening of her heart.

'Thank you for phoning, Isobel. Thank you very much.'

The instrument purred in Isobel's hands as he disconnected the line. Oh, to hell with him, said Isobel. To hell with him. To hell with him. I'll go and see him tomorrow afternoon.

Having decided to do so, she put on a short print dress, spread her hair over her shoulders, and went to find Jonathan.

*

Although only forty guests had originally been invited, the party had swarmed with friends of friends, and after its subdued and self-conscious beginning had become relaxed. Jonathan himself was in charge of the bar, and as Isobel approached, he said,

'Champagne?'

'No, thanks,' said Isobel. 'What else have you got?'

'Whisky.'

'Oh! I didn't think—'

'It's all right,' said Jonathan. 'Some of them brought their own bottles—and I've got a private store.'

'I'll have a whisky and soda,' said Isobel.

'It isn't a very lady-like drink,' said Jonathan.

'So much the better. Is everything going well?'

'No one's fallen in the pool, or drawn blood, or got raped, if that's what you mean. The Upminstrels have turned up, and Mark hasn't.'

'Are you pleased?'

'Yes,' he said. 'So's Henrietta.'

He looked around for her among the groups that had gathered under the yew trees by the braziers, and said,

'You ought to get to know her. She's very nice.'

'She's very pretty—certainly. What does she do?'

'She works in the House of Commons' library.'

'That sounds very exciting.'

'I don't think it is. Fetching and carrying for a lot of crumbling politicians in arm-chairs.'

He handed her a glass, and said,

'What time's he coming back?'

Isobel shrugged her shoulders.

'I've no idea. These negotiations are very complicated.'

'I bet they are,' said Jonathan. A brazier suddenly flared up, and there was an excited rush from the bar towards the flaming twigs on the yew trees. Jonathan said,

'It's perfectly all right.' Then, following his earlier thoughts, he added, 'You know, there hasn't really been much change since the 1820s. In those days, they bought and sold plantations, complete with slaves. Nowadays, they take over factories. You can be working for one man one day, and overnight you find someone else has bought you.'

'Oh, come on, Jonathan,' said Isobel. 'Nowadays if you don't like your boss, you can change your job.'

'Ever tried it?' asked Jonathan.

'Yes,' she said, 'I have.'

'It's different for working people,' he persisted. 'They go with the factory in single-plant areas. Their homes are a bus fare away. If Harry's bid comes off, a lot of them are going to feel pretty sick tomorrow.'

'It's far from being decided,' Isobel said. 'The Minister's got the last word.'

'Everyone knows Alf Budd,' said Jonathan.

'What do you mean?'

'Nothing special. I just mean that everyone knows about Budd. And if you don't, darling, I can only imagine Harry doesn't tell you quite everything. Let's dance.'

The discothèque in the marquee was playing again 'Etreins-moi, mon amour', and Isobel danced with Jonathan to the slow Blues tune, watching over his shoulder the scarcely perceptible movement of the other couples, crushed together in an absorbed embrace, touching every now and again a bare arm, feeling an alien hip pressed against hers, the privileged intimacy of the dance floor. And as the music went on, endlessly it seemed to her, she wanted it to stop so that she could go back to her room and feel her separation from the unfamiliar guests.

'Do you mind if we stop?' Jonathan asked. 'I don't want Henrietta to think I ditched her.'

'No,' said Isobel, relieved. 'Let's fight our way back.'

Henrietta was waiting on the edge of the dance floor to greet them. She was smiling, and Isobel said,

'He couldn't get rid of me soon enough.'

'Oh, rubbish,' said Jonathan.

'He dances very smoochily. I thought he'd picked up a girl-friend,' said Henrietta. 'I was terribly jealous.'

'So you should be,' said Jonathan. 'Pretty—my mum—don't you think?'

'Absolutely beautiful,' said Henrietta. 'It isn't fair. I hope when I'm—'

Isobel laughed, flattered but unwilling to be patronized.

'I always know when Jonathan wants something,' she said.

They walked down the Italian steps where each of the ornamental fountains had been lit from beneath so that the waters sprayed in a white haze.

'Henrietta's coming to Avdat,' said Jonathan.

'Avdat?' said Isobel. 'Where is it?'

Henrietta waited for Jonathan to reply.

'You've got a frightful memory,' said Jonathan. 'Advat's in the Negev. They're excavating a Nabatean temple. I told you—I'm going to work there for two months.'

Isobel turned away to look at the statue of the boy struggling with a dolphin from whose mouth gushed a high jet of water that fell back in a delicate spiral into the basin.

'Two months,' she said, 'is a very long time. I didn't think you were serious.'

'Of course I'm serious,' said Jonathan. 'You know I've always wanted to go to Israel and see what it's all about.'

'And you, Henrietta. Why are you thinking of going to Israel? You're not Jewish, are you?'

'Not ethnically—so to speak,' said Henrietta. 'But Jews interest me. Would you like me to cook you a banger or two on the barbecue, Mrs. Levenson?'

'Yes, please,' said Isobel. 'It'll be awfully hot in Israel in August and September. You'll need to take anti-dysentery tablets.'

'I've got a stock of those,' said Henrietta calmly.

'We were plagued by sandflies in Beersheba.'

'That must have been ages ago,' said Henrietta. 'They've had an anti-fly campaign since then. It's stamped them all out. . . . And I know about El Fatah.'

'And when did you arrange all this?' Isobel asked her.

'Oh—just in the last half-hour,' she replied coolly.

Isobel smiled to Henrietta, deciding that she didn't like her.

'Oh, well,' she said, 'I hope you have a wonderful time.'

*

A wonderful time. Around the dance floor and by the braziers, the figures formed and re-formed in changing shapes, dissolving and fusing in clouds of colour as in an optical-machine.

She paused at the deserted swimming pool, and looked down. Now the party was far away, the voices and the music deadened. She thought of her husband, a self-confident hostage among strangers. He was self-confident, and she was afraid. And she knew that his self-confidence gave her security, and that without him she too was a hostage among strangers, but in fear.

'Hello, Mrs. Levenson.'

The voice came from behind the glow of a cigarette in a wicker chaise-longue. She stared into the darkness, and a form uncurled itself and said,

'It's me.'

'Oh, it's you,' she said, and she felt the pleasure of someone who has waited a long time at a rendezvous, and after giving up hope sees a familiar person approaching.

'Why aren't you dancing?'

'I hate dancing,' said Adrian. Having disposed of the matter, he began to walk by her side.

'And what have you been doing?' he asked. The question was perfunctory, but as Isobel glanced at him she saw that he was waiting for an explicit answer.

'Oh, we dined with a lot of business men, and I came back alone because I wanted to go to bed early. These things drag on. And then I phoned my father. The old are very sad.'

'Sadder than the young?'

'I think so. They're sad because they know there's nothing much to look forward to.'

'Yes, I can understand that,' said Adrian. In the light that went on in a window of the house, she saw the grave expression on his face. 'That's why they live so greedily.'

'You're not very charitable,' she said.

'I can never understand,' he replied, 'why the young should be charitable to the old. It should be the other way about. They've got it made.'

He hesitated, and said,

'Were you on your way somewhere? I feel as if I hi-jacked you.'

'No,' she said. 'I just thought I'd wander towards the party, and say "good-night" to Jonathan. Would you like to go back to your friends?'

'I'm not in a very sociable mood,' said Adrian. 'I'm feeling black and aggressive. It comes of dressing up as a corsair.'

'Well, shall we walk down to the lake?' Isobel asked.

'If we can dodge all the noise,' he replied.

'Oh, yes, please,' said Isobel. 'There's a path by the water-gardens. Where are your people?'

'My people?'

He gave her an incomprehending glance.

'Your parents.'

'I'm so sorry,' he said. 'I thought you were asking me a metaphysical question. . . . My father's in the Foreign Service, and they're in Lima. Do you know it?'

'No.'

'It's a very clammy place. . . . Having a father in the Foreign Service gives one an excellent knowledge of weather and cooking. Ever since I was at school, my parents' letters have been full of both.'

'But you see them?'

Adrian took her hand to help her over a broken step, and said,

'We visit each other. It's very strange growing up as a visitor to one's parents. I imagine that's how Royal bastards get to feel. Not exactly acknowledged and not exactly repudi-ated. Mind you,' he went on, 'it's rather splendid not having a fixed address. It gives one a great sense of freedom. I'm always surprised when I read in the papers of somebody who's been hauled up in front of the magistrates for being of "no fixed abode" and having "no visible means of subsistence". They ought to be congratulated, not punished. Treated the way they treat loonies in the East—with respect, because they've got the divine touch.'

62

'But freedom means not being dependent on others. Do you really feel free?'

'Yes,' said Adrian. 'I feel very free tonight. I've spent my grant. I'm wearing just a shirt and trousers. I'm sponging on Jonathan, but I'm not *dependent* on him. Dependence is a state of mind. He's much more dependent on me than I am on him because, rather absurdly, he feels responsible for me. Have you got a cigarette?'

'Yes, I have,' said Isobel. 'They're cork-tipped, I'm afraid.'

'They'll do,' said Adrian.

He took a cigarette from the gold case that was a present from Harry, and said,

'This is very arch-ducal.'

'Harry—my husband—bought it at Christie's last year,' she replied.

Adrian took it from her hand, looked at the crest, and handed it back to her.

'Vorontsov,' he said.

'Yes,' said Isobel. 'It's come down in the world.'

He stopped walking, and as he faced her she could see that the mocking expression was gone.

'It's very beautiful,' he said, 'and it goes very well with you.'

She saw in the half-darkness his pupils with a bluish arc of light beneath them, and she answered,

'That's very flattering.'

'But not excessively,' said Adrian. 'I don't believe in exaggerating my enthusiasms.

"*Folles amours font les gens bestes;*
Bien est eureux qui rien n'y a."

'Ronsard?' she asked.

'No, Villon. He and Apollinaire are my two favourite poets —both highly disreputable.'

'I like Apollinaire,' said Isobel. 'I used to think his poems were like a long love-letter. A happy one.'

They walked through the darkness without speaking, though

she wanted to question him and find out something about his life, thinking that all she knew of the sombre young man who walked at her side was the little that Jonathan had told her of their acquaintance at school and Cambridge.

'You lived in France, didn't you?'

'With my parents. When my father was at the Embassy. Then I spent a few months there last year.'

'Do you know Carcassonne?' she asked.

'Why do you ask?'

'I don't know. It came into my mind—those lovely mediaeval towers and battlements.'

Adrian's face had suddenly become sulky, and he pushed back the black fringe that fell diagonally over his forehead.

'Is anything wrong?'

'No—except that you'll ask me in a few moments where I'm spending the hols.'

'I don't have to ask you,' she replied. 'I know. Jonathan told me you're going to stay with friends in Sardinia. I wish he was, instead of digging in the desert.'

'He's got this Jewish thing,' said Adrian. 'He believes that everyone should be rooted in institutions, even when they change their form. That's his definition of identity.'

'He's very ambivalent about it.'

'I know,' said Adrian.

'But he shouldn't be,' said Isobel. 'He's old enough to make a decision.'

They were approaching the lake, the path guarded at the end by two broken columns, silhouetted against the sky's afterglow. A single lamp in the island, a hundred yards from the shore, reddened the azaleas and the tips of the water-lilies. On the other side, the cornice of the temple gleamed out of the mauve-black trees.

'It's peaceful here,' said Isobel.

'I dislike institutions,' Adrian said challengingly. 'I've never needed them like Jonathan. The difference between us is that he always wants to say "yes" and I want to say "no".'

'They've protected you,' said Isobel. 'They still protect you.'

'Well, battery hens are protected too,' said Adrian. 'In just the same way. Everything in our industrial society is designed to protect, then to exploit and destroy. Do you know what youth is today?'

'What it was yesterday, I imagine.'

'No. It's changed. It's become a market for old men.'

'Such as—?'

'You ought to know—you live in that world. It's the world where everything turns to money, and the men who work the dream-factories of TV sell poison. The chaps who ban pot and push cancerous fags. The men who organize our consumer society to create waste while others starve.'

She looked at his angry face, and said timidly,

'Are you a Communist?'

'Communist?' His face was baffled. 'Communist? The very opposite. The great Communist aim is to do what the capitalists are doing. But as they are less self-confident, they're less tolerant. They're less experienced; so they're less efficient. There's nothing that capitalism can do that Communism can't do worse.'

'Well, what *are* you?'

'What *am* I?' he echoed her words, and she thought his face had become child-like and insecure after the dogmatic certainties. 'Do I have to be catalogued and filed?'

'No,' she said, and she took his arm as they walked over the stones at the rim of the lake. 'It's just that only hermits can exist in isolation. Everyone else has to have some relationship with those around them. Do you take any part in politics?'

'None. I told you, I'm against organizations. I know them too well.'

They came to the columns at the bottom of the narrow path, and Isobel leaned against the eroded marble while, with his arms folded, Adrian stood close to her, listening to the mutter of the miniature cascades in the garden and the intermittent tremble on the water like the opening of lips as a fish stirred.

'Aren't you cold?' Isobel asked.

He lounged against the pillar, and his upper arm rested lightly against her breast. She didn't move, seeking at once to retain the stir of pleasure that it gave her, yet affecting to be unaware of it.

'Haven't you noticed?' he replied. 'It's a very warm night.'

He drew away from her to light a cigarette from a packet that he found in his hip pocket, and her breast felt deprived of his arm, widowed of its closeness. She looked at his face in the steady light of the match, and it appeared to her as if it had changed again. His firm dark eyebrows were pursed; his eyes absorbed in the act of lighting the cigarette.

'You've been asking me about myself,' he said. 'Tell me about yourself. You've got everything. Does it make you feel free?'

Her answer was impersonal.

'I agree it's impossible to be completely free in a modern industrial society,' said Isobel. 'You have to make some sort of contribution to it—even passively by accepting what it makes—from tinned peaches to nylon stockings.'

'In that case,' said Adrian, 'let's stop pretending to be free. Let's recognize that everywhere—in Britain and France and America and the Soviet Union—the Machine Men have got us by the throat—the managers and the generals and the bureaucrats and the whole court that surrounds them. Some know what they're doing; some do it instinctively. They've taken what Ford said one stage further. You get it black but they call it white. . . . You know, Mrs. Levenson, the people who are suffering from this aren't the working classes. All they want is a bigger share. They don't mind about the lies that advertise the product. They'll swallow them as long as they get a bit more. More—more! It's what the Communists and the Socialists and the Tories trade on. Nowadays it isn't religion that's the opium of the people. It's the New Materialism of our industrial society, pre-packaged by the ad-men and the politicians.'

He paused to take breath, and Isobel smiled to him.

'That was a good speech.'

Adrian shrugged his shoulders, and said, 'I'm sorry. All I was trying to tell you is that the youth protest that everyone's been yammering about isn't a working-class protest at all. When we marched from the Sorbonne to the sit-in strikers at Renault, they simply couldn't understand what we were talking about. We offered them ideas, and all they wanted was Gauloises.'

'You can't really blame them,' said Isobel. 'Wouldn't you in that situation?'

'I'm not blaming them,' said Adrian irritably. 'I'm just reporting. They were asking for a twelve per cent rise. We were asking for something—' he groped for the word.

'Transcendental?' she suggested. He accepted the word grudgingly.

'You can call it that. I was going to say "truthful".'

Isobel's face had become serious.

'You enjoyed the Revolution.'

'Yes. We'd turned the tables on the examiners. *We* started asking the questions.'

'In the university that others had built. You had an immunity that belonged to another age.'

'Which one?'

'The twelfth century—the immunity of Ecclesiastical Law. And when it was all over, your friends went home to their sports cars and smart apartments in the Avenue Foch or wherever, and the workers went back to their tenements in Belleville. You make different demands; but you must admit you've got different problems.'

67

'That's what I said all along. . . . I happen to think that struggling to tell the truth is on the whole a better way of living than trying to do a more favourable deal with the liars.'

'How would you define what you're protesting about?'

'Protest itself is a definition—it's a definition of what you don't want.'

'And can you say what you do want?'

'Not yet,' he answered.

'That at least I can understand,' said Isobel. She thought of him in the Sorbonne and was curious about his environment there.

'Were there many women in the Sorbonne?' she asked.

'Quite a few,' he answered.

'That must have been very cosy.'

'Yes,' he said, unaffected. 'It was very cosy. I was living at the time with a woman anthropologist.'

Isobel felt an impulse of jealousy, and she wanted to ask him who the woman was, whether he still saw her, whether she was French, and she visualized the Sorbonne, the students sleeping in corridors and the amphitheatre, and Adrian and this woman, locked and enclosed against the world. And the thought churned within her in a thwarted excitement, as if she was watching a play in which she identified herself with the exhibition. His eyes under his dark eyebrows became a deeper blue in a passing light.

'Are *you* free?' he asked again. 'I mean personally.'

'Of course I am,' she answered. Then she added, 'At any rate, I am tonight. Tell me more about the Sorbonne. I suppose you were one of the rioters.'

'We weren't rioters,' he said. 'We were a manifesto in action. If I hit a policeman, it was an impersonal act that affirmed my right to be a person in face of the system he stood for.'

'Perhaps I'm very simple,' said Isobel. 'I just see a policeman as someone who defends my right to be private.'

Adrian looked gloomy. 'You're not simple,' he said, 'but you do have some naïve views.'

He was standing a few feet from her, and Isobel said,

'Let's have a pact. We won't quarrel over our political—'

'Sociological—'

'All right, sociological views. Why don't you go back to the party and those lovely young girls?'

'Thank you, Mrs. Levenson—'

'Isobel.'

'Isabeau. Isobel, Queen of France. It's a lovely name.'

'I always wanted to be called Candida or Serena—something with a soft, feminine "a".'

'You don't need it. May I stay here with you?'

She hesitated.

'I think we should go back.'

He stretched himself, and she could see the muscles of his arms tightening against the white shirt.

'Would you like me to row you to the island?' he asked.

'I think,' she said, 'it's a bit late.'

'How would you like me to row you to the island?' he repeated, in exactly the same tone.

'I think,' she said, 'I'd like it very much.'

'Mrs. Levenson—Mrs. Levenson.'

The voice came in a wail from the top of the garden.

'Mrs. Levenson—Mrs. Levenson.'

It came nearer, and she called, 'Yes, Luigi?'

'Mrs. Levenson—it's Mister—he wants you at the telephone.'

'Tell him I'm coming. I'll be a minute or two.'

She turned to Adrian in regret. 'I'm sorry, Adrian—I'm afraid our boat trip is off.'

'I'll wait for you.'

'Will you?'

'Yes, I will.'

The thought delighted her. They glanced at each other and

69

smiled, and she walked quickly up the path, following Luigi with his bandy-legged, hopping gait.

At her bedside the telephone lay like an abandoned child, complaining. A distorted, squawking, 'Hello, hello,' came from the instrument as Isobel raised it.

'Hello,' she said easily.

'Where the devil have you been?' Levenson said from the other end.

'I was seeing how they were getting on,' she answered. 'Anything wrong in that?'

'Why don't you let them get on with it?'

'That's just what I was doing. But you said yourself—you didn't want them smashing the place up.'

'Yes, that's all right. I'm sorry, Isobel. It's not easy here. I can't talk very well.'

'What's going on?'

'Well, at the moment I'm playing gin-rummy with the Rt. Hon. Alf Budd, M.P., and Lady Orme-Campbell, and Lattner.'

'That's jolly.'

'I just stepped out for a few minutes. I'm trying to get Budd alone for a bit, but she's squatting there. Probably been told to. At any rate, I've got to talk to Budd and Howell and Orme-Campbell within the next half-hour. What are you doing?'

'Me?' The question made her feel guilty. 'Oh, I'm taking off my make-up. Then I'm going to bed.'

'O.K., darling.'

Her reply had cheered him as if he had established one fixed point, a secure base in the unpredictable night. 'O.K.,' he repeated. 'Listen, I've got to go now. I'll ring you in half an hour.'

'Half an hour? I'll be asleep.'

He was in a hurry to ring off.

'All right, then, a quarter of an hour. 'Bye, darling.'

She put the telephone down, and sat restless and exasperated that she was now imprisoned in the bedroom till her husband telephoned her again. She kicked off her shoes and walked across to the dressing-table, where she examined and improved her make-up. She turned off the bright light over the looking-glass because it cast downward shadows on her face, and studied her profile in the wing-glasses, stretching her chin to tighten its slackness. Then she turned and watched the silent telephone as if it was an enemy. Outside, the music kept up its emphatic beat, and she stood for a few moments, dancing alone in front of the looking-glass till the shouting harmonies ended with a clang, and she laughed at her image with her arm extended and her hips out-thrust. She picked up the telephone, and as it purred she slammed it back into its cradle.

'I hate you,' she said.

After that, she stretched herself on the bed, thinking that if the call didn't come within twenty minutes she would say the following day that she couldn't sleep because of the noise, and had gone downstairs to read.

The phone rang.

'Is that you, baby?'

'Hello, Harry.'

'I haven't time to talk. Just wanted to say good-night.'

'Well, don't work too hard.'

'No. I may wake you up when I get back.'

'Good-night, Harry.'

So that was that. She put on her shoes, brushed her hair twice, and went back to the marquee.

Chapter Five

LEVENSON was thinking. And his thoughts in the Medal Room as he sat in front of the card-table marched in and out of each other like troops at a tournament. He was thinking of Lady Orme-Campbell who was looking closely, though sideways, at Budd's cards, of Budd slumped and half-hidden behind his cigar-smoke, of Lattner, quietly winning, of Isobel and Jonathan, and of the need for a Securities and Exchange Commission like the one in New York. Skulduggery. When countering Levenson's bid circular, Orme-Campbell and his bankers had made a forecast of profits which he was certain was 'cooked'. 'Optimism isn't a sin—even under the take-over panel code,' old Hurstcombe had said. It wasn't a sin; it was a lie, and he was waiting to tell Orme-Campbell at the right time. There was small cheating like Elaine's and big cheating by business men. Connivance and inside deals in the course of take-overs and mergers. Yes. What was needed was something like the U.S. Securities and Exchange Commission, staffed with independent lawyers, trustworthy, men like Lattner—expert, patient, analytical, systematic men who never lost.

'Gin!' said Lattner, and there was a sigh of disappointment from Elaine.

'You really have too much luck,' she said, groping for the cards with her thin fingers.

After all this was over, Levenson thought, he would take Isobel to New York, where he had to talk to Mannheim about the automat deal. The price was right, and the Financial Secretary wouldn't find it hard to get Treasury sanction. The dollar argument never failed with orthodox Socialists, even if Left-Wing M.P.s started howling. Except for her constant worries about Jonathan, Isobel was at her most comfortable with him when they travelled. Osaka, Nara, Kyoto, San Francisco, Hong Kong, Rome—he could map their happiness. But Jonathan. Good God, when he was Jonathan's age, he'd been at work for at least five years. Half his wages had gone to his parents, who lived in Hackney Road. But he didn't want to remember that, nor his mother with her melancholy eyes and worn hands, lined with dried washing soda. Even now, thirty, thirty-five years later, the racking pity came back.

He wanted to be free from pity, free from anxiety about others. Waiting in hotel suites abroad for Isobel's telephone calls to Jonathan to come through, they had spent hours in which her self-inflicted anguishes and his rage mounted together. Not that he disliked Jonathan. He just had nothing to say to him. When they were left alone in a room, each felt an acute unease, hoping that Isobel or someone else would come in so that they had no further obligation to try and communicate. Every question he put to Jonathan led to the dead-end of 'yes' or 'no'. And even in those replies, Levenson felt an arrogant undertone of 'You wouldn't understand, even if I explained.' Yet he wanted Jonathan to like him, and in their rare moments of contact, like those, years before, when he had bought him some camping equipment at the Army and Navy stores, he had felt briefly that his unspoken nostalgia for a son might have been fulfilled in him. But that was quickly over. Now Jonathan was a tall and cold competitor in the household, disturbing his own relationship with Isobel, and one whom he could wish out of the way.

Levenson watched Budd turn up a card, and their eyes met. This was a different kind of antipathy, deep and murderous. Budd was the clever boy of the primary school, quick with his fists and his jibes, the one who pretended never to do his homework but always did, the ringleader who became a

73

political boss, the austere climber who nevertheless marked his advance with the changing make of his cars. In London or Chicago they were all the same. Alf Budd, the lovable politician with the rolling voice, the ginger hair, the albino eyelashes and the randy manner. Good old Alf. Alf the open-hearted, with his secrets and dark anxieties.

'Well, that's enough,' said Budd, averting his glance and his cards on the table. 'Lattner—you've done all right. *You'd* have done better, Elaine, if you'd kept your eyes on your own hand.'

'Oh, really, Alf,' said Elaine, 'you've only lost—let's see—fifteen shillings.'

'I don't mind losing,' said Budd. 'It's how you lose that matters. Isn't that right, Lattner?'

Lattner gave a quick glance at Levenson, and Budd, intercepting it and fastening on a suitable recipient for his chagrin, said,

'Can't you bloody well have an opinion of your own, Lattner, without permission? How do you pay this man, Levenson? By the headshake? By the measured nod? Steward'—he called to the butler—'another tonic water, please.'

Lattner and Levenson laughed uncomfortably, and Elaine said,

'I think I'd better have a word with Geoffrey. Their meeting is due to begin.'

'Don't jolly me along,' said Budd, the freckles standing out on his sweating forehead, 'I really want to know how these fellows signal their bids to each other. It's a bit naughty of you, Elaine, to interfere.'

'Oh, really, Alf,' Elaine began.

'Don't change the subject,' Budd said heavily.

Elaine's eyes filled with tears, and she rose and left.

'What is the subject?' Levenson asked calmly.

'The subject,' said Budd, 'is your intentions. . . . I wanted to get rid of that bitch. I don't know how Geoffrey can put up with her.'

74

'You were pretty rough with her.'

'Why shouldn't I be?' said Budd. 'I'm not here because she wants my company. Do you think she'd give me a tumble if I weren't Minister of Industrial Reconstruction? Or you—if she wasn't after something?'

'No,' said Levenson. And his gaze traversed the sparse red hair, the exophthalmic eyes, the cupid lips and the crab-apple chin.

'On the whole,' said Levenson, 'people want us not for what we are, but for what we can give them.'

'That's right,' said Budd dolefully. 'That's the trouble. Mind you, it's all right for you. You've got a base. Every year, your base gets safer. A few hundred thousand here. A few hundred thousand there. My job depends on men who hate my guts.'

'But the P.M. himself—' said Levenson. 'After all, Alf—you represent something in the Movement. He's—'

'Trevor's all right,' Budd said. 'It's the gang around him.'

'If you don't mind,' said Lattner, 'I'll go and phone London.'

As he left, Budd's eyes followed him moodily.

'Why do you want that fellow hanging around all the time? I get rid of my officials whenever I can, like tonight. I told them I didn't need them.'

'He's very efficient.'

'I suppose he's done well out of you.'

'Yes. . . . And I've done well out of him.'

Budd shook the ice in his glass for a few seconds, and said,

'It's a deadly life—being a dogsbody. You know, Levenson, three years ago I could have had the leadership.'

'Why didn't you?'

'I chose not to stand against him. He was a friend of mine. I wouldn't do it. The unions, the Parliamentary Party—they were all on my side. I'd already brought in the Industrial Partnership Act.'

'That was a mistake.'

'You may think so. But I didn't and don't. Nor did the Party. I know you boys at Embankment House didn't like it, but everyone else did. I was being pressed inside the Party to change my mind. I discussed it with Betty. She said to me, "I don't want to be the Prime Minister's wife. Why should you want to be Prime Minister, Alf?" '

'That's a very good question. Why should you?'

'The truth of the matter is, Harry, that by the time I got around to answering the question, things had moved on—the trade balance was almost right, the new U.S. tariff cuts came just in time for him, along with the old sleight of hand at the Party meeting. And then, on the advice of that bastard Cranfield, he reorganized the Treasury and the Board of Trade—and here I am in the outfield. . . . Now, as a business man, Harry—imagine yourself being crowded out—bit by bit —to the edge. How would you tackle the situation?'

Levenson brooded for a few moments, toying with the deck of cards.

'I'd sit tight,' he said. 'Railton—you know him, he's on our Board—he says, "If you're under fire, don't run, freeze." It seems good advice.'

'That's all very well,' said Budd. 'But it isn't like that. What Cranfield's been making him do is chip me to bits—bit by bit. It's death by the thousand cuts and Trevor doesn't even realize that it's happening.' His voice rose angrily. 'Only yesterday, just by accident, I saw in the Cabinet minutes—oh, well, never mind. . . .'

'I'd sit tight,' Levenson repeated. 'At least until you've got somewhere else to go.'

'Where?' said Budd. 'The back benches? It's a slag-heap, chum. You start off with the feeling that you're going to make the P.M. sit up by making a speech from the third row below the gangway. You make it. Everybody listens. "Alf is still on form", "Alf is off form". When you've spoken five times, nobody notices any more. Then you start attending less regularly. And then, if you're lucky, you're in the Lords, and if you're unlucky, you're in the tea-room, humouring your prostate, or in the Terrace Bar watching your pals getting cirrhosis of the liver.'

Levenson rose and patted him on the back.

'Don't get gloomy, Alf. Have you ever thought of leaving politics?'

'That's a long way off,' said Budd. 'Sit down, old chap. There's no hurry.'

They could still hear the sound of general conversation from outside.

'Nothing much is going to happen,' he said, 'till Orme-Campbell talks to me. And I'm not ready to talk to him yet.'

'He's confident,' said Levenson, sitting down again.

'Why shouldn't he be?' Budd asked provocatively.

A manservant offered Levenson another glass of whisky.

'No, thanks,' said Levenson. 'I've had enough.'

Budd finished his glass of tonic water and said,

'I admire your fraternity. You don't really drink. You just sit there working out the figures.'

His tone was goading and Levenson didn't answer.

'You know,' Budd went on, 'even the ones who hate your guts have to hand it to you.'

'Do they?'

'Yes. But they'd take a different view of you if you landed in the Old Bailey.'

Levenson looked across the card-table at Budd's red mouth encircling a spiteful smile, and he wanted to slam his fist against it so that the small teeth disintegrated in a mush of blood and pain. He picked up the deck of cards and tapped it lightly against the baize.

'I don't think that's very likely, Alf,' he said calmly. 'But you should be very careful yourself.'

77

Budd held his empty glass suspended as he said,

'What do you mean?'

'What I say,' said Levenson, rising. 'You're a very able fellow, Alf, but not a very discreet one.'

Budd rose.

'Who the hell do you think you're lecturing, Mr. Bloody Levenson? I'm beginning to think—'

'Don't think, Alf,' said Levenson. 'Not yet at any rate. And don't think of threatening me about our bid.'

He was calm now, and went over to a show-case where Elaine Orme-Campbell kept her collection of eighteenth-century fans and bonbonnières.

'I'm not going to have you talking to me like that,' Budd said to Levenson's back.

'Beautiful—this ivory work,' said Levenson without turning. 'It's a view of the Grand Canal in Venice. How well do you know Howell?'

'What's that got to do with you?'

Orme-Campbell, followed by Howell, Henderson-Kerr and a few others talking loudly, came into the Medal Room.

'Hello, Levenson,' he said. 'Admiring the fans? That one's supposed to have belonged to Madame de Maintenon, and that's a later one from the collection of the Empress Eugénie.'

'They're very fine,' said Levenson. 'What time's your meeting? It's getting on.'

'I'm sorry,' said Orme-Campbell. 'The agenda's a short one. I hope we can get everything through by midnight, and have a press conference which you're invited to attend—if you want to. . . . I don't want to embarrass you, Levenson. Besides, you know what the Press is like. I can see the opening sentence in the *Economist*—"Not since the slaughter of the Mamelukes has supper been followed so promptly by massacre."'

'We'll have to see who are the Mamelukes,' said Levenson, 'and who's the Sultan.'

'Well,' said Hamblett in his booming voice, 'we're all Levantines now.'

Levenson turned away, and Henderson-Kerr, approaching him from the other side of the room, said, panting slightly,

'I'm sorry about that. You're in jungle country, you know.'

Levenson smiled at his good-natured, apologetic face, and said,

'I'm used to it. I travel armed.'

Orme-Campbell turned to Howell and, lowering his voice, said,

'Any news of Stapleton? When I spoke to him last night, he said he'd be here in the early evening.'

'I phoned BOAC half an hour ago,' Howell said. 'His plane was due in from Montreal at about 8.30, but the last they heard it was delayed.'

'That's a bloody nuisance,' said Orme-Campbell. 'I want him there when we start the meeting.'

'I've got Dawson down at Heathrow waiting with a car, and I've arranged for Stapleton to get a quick clearance.'

'Good!' Orme-Campbell said, dismissing the subject.

'I thought you'd like to see this piece about him in today's *Telegraph*.'

Frowning, Orme-Campbell took the cutting, but Howell quickly reassured him.

'It's O.K. All it says is that as President of one of the biggest engineering corporations in Canada, Gregory Stapleton's speech to the Montreal Chamber of Commerce on Anglo-Canadian cooperation—'

'That's all right.'

The interruption was abrupt as if to silence a possible indiscretion and Orme-Campbell, turning his back, asked the others in a loud voice,

'Anyone see Hilditch at Lord's this afternoon?'

'Guilty,' said Lord Hamblett. 'It was worth it, though, just for that catch. About two feet from the boundary.

He did a sort of backward jump and rolled over twice. But he definitely caught it before it went over the line. I saw it.'

'The umpire disagreed.'

'I disagreed with him—so did the crowd.'

'Well, the difference between hitting a six and being caught out is just the matter of a line.'

'Or of perspective,' said Hamblett.

'Yes—it's chastening,' said Orme-Campbell.

Levenson had joined the group, and stood silently by as his host continued,

'Extraordinary family of athletes, the Hilditches. His father was in my House. He could make a ball do anything. Another drink?'

'When do we start?' Hamblett asked. 'What with cricket and company meetings, I'm in danger of losing my wife if I don't get back by three.'

Orme-Campbell laughed.

'Nothing to worry about, Fred,' he said. 'Our meeting shouldn't take too long. But I don't want to start till everyone's here.'

'I don't see anyone missing. Aren't we all here?'

Orme-Campbell didn't answer. Instead, he beckoned the the manservant carrying a tray of drinks, and waved him towards his guests.

'You a cricketer, Levenson?' he asked, taking notice of him at last.

'No,' Levenson answered.

'No,' Orme-Campbell echoed in a melancholy tone that was a condolence.

'What is our programme?' Levenson asked.

'Well, it's up to you, old chap. You'd better stick around till we've met. Just make yourself at home.'

'I may need a phone.'

Orme-Campbell looked around vaguely.

'You'll find one at the end of the lower corridor. Or use the phone in the drawing-room. It'll be all yours in half an hour.'

The corner of Levenson's mouth contracted, and Orme-Campbell, noticing the inward smile, hurried to add,

'Metaphorically speaking. . . . Come on, Alf, let's go and talk somewhere. I've postponed the board meeting till 11.30.'

'All right, chaps,' said Budd cheerfully. As he stood grinning, he felt himself filling the image which innumerable political commentators had imposed on him. Like an actor before going on stage, he glanced at himself in a looking-glass over the fireplace, squared the shoulders that a few moments earlier had drooped dejectedly, and organized his face into the mode of one accustomed to acknowledge applause. Good old Alf! Up and down the country, at public meetings where the faces were a haze of love, he had stood at the centre of the platform, the authentic champion of a great movement, invoking the heroic struggle of the Party and the Socialist saints, and conjuring up the future triumphs of the Second Industrial Revolution. Alf Budd—courageous, frank, sometimes extravagant in language, giving the Tories as good as he got.

Good old Alf! After meetings, he would lie awake, excited by the roaring, by his own skill in touching the nerve that produced it, by the hands and the faces glowing and steaming in the act of political love. And there he was in the looking-glass, side by side with Orme-Campbell. Good old Alf! He could still do it.

'See you later, old chap,' he said to Lord Hamblett. They were being careful, he thought. Afraid to say anything that might provoke him. Hamblett hated his guts; he knew it. The Minister of Power had once reported to him in detail what Hamblett had said of him at a Livery dinner. A Parliamentary Free-loader. That was eight years ago. And Henderson-Kerr— thin-faced with distinguished grey hair that he surreptitiously combed from time to time—Henderson-Kerr, who was playing a double game, was in favour of accepting Levenson's bid. He was nearly sixty, and wanted to sell out. Then there was Howell. He liked Howell. Howell had done it the hard way. Orme-Campbell and his friends tried to push Howell around, and Budd liked the way he stood up to them, quietly and without complaining, but getting on with the job. And, come to think of it, that had been the basis of his own success. He had always done his homework. It was one of Budd's favourite phrases in debate, public and private. At Party and trade union meetings, he had always read the last minutes; studied the agenda; carried a resolution or two already drafted in his pocket; knew Standing Orders by heart.

The others could shout their heads off. They guessed. Budd knew. Later, there'd be a lot of loud argument in the clubs, and Alf would be in the thick of it, waving his pint that he never touched and shouting over the voices of the best of them. But in his pocket were the resolutions he'd drafted, and the delegations that he'd picked.

He winked at Howell, and Howell gave him a friendly jerk of the head. They knew each other well. They didn't have to pretend.

'Let's go down to the breakfast room,' said Orme-Campbell. 'It's cooler there. God, it's a hot night. My jacket's sticking to my back.'

Tall and deliberate, he walked in front of Budd who, leaving his audience behind, shambled in his host's track.

'Take care,' said Orme-Campbell. 'These stone stairs are very slippery. You'd better hold on to the rail.'

Spontaneously, Budd gripped the balustrade and followed him one step at a time.

Orme-Campbell switched on the lights in the breakfast room, which Elaine had designed in the form of a monastery refectory. The tessellated floor and the bare oak table echoed in their design the Gothic windows, protected by wrought-iron grilles.

'I like this,' said Budd. 'Reminds me of Waltham Abbey.'

'Oh, yes,' said his host absently. 'Why don't we sit down and talk? It's very comfortable.'

'I used to go there for a retreat sometimes,' said Budd. 'I'm a non-conformist, you know, but there's a lot to be said for the monastic life.' He chuckled. 'A man's got to get away sometimes.'

'No one's ever thought of you as a monk,' said Orme-Campbell.

'No—that's more in your line,' said Budd. ('O.K., you old sod,' he said to himself, 'if you want to play it that way, let's start.')

Orme-Campbell became quickly appeasing.

'I don't think either of us is ready to go into Holy Orders. Let me get you something, Alf.'

He went to a sideboard, poured out a whisky and a soft drink and brought them back.

'Everyone knows your deep religious feelings, Alf, but I didn't know how far you went—oecumenically speaking.'

'A long way,' said Budd. 'My wife's a Roman Catholic.'

'Interesting—these mixed marriages,' said Orme-Campbell. 'I believe Levenson's wife's an Anglican. They often work out very well.'

'Mine's involved a lot of strain.'

'Yes.'

'For me as well as her.'

'It cuts both ways, naturally. How about your children?'

'I never interfered,' said Budd. 'My wife had them brought up as Catholics.'

'Well, that's straightened them out,' said Orme-Campbell.

There was a pause as the two men sipped their drinks, waiting for the other to speak.

'It involves a lot of strain,' Budd repeated at last. 'My wife never really liked politics. She's a very quiet woman by nature.'

83

'It must be very difficult,' said Orme-Campbell, 'for a business man or a diplomat or a politician when their wives don't like society.'

'Betty's very sociable,' said Budd. 'Don't get me wrong. It's just that she likes her own crowd. She's a simple girl— she likes her home and her family and her friends. But she never caught up with all the bull-shit of politics.'

'That's very much to her credit. I think I met her at Lancaster House with you a few years ago. But I haven't seen her around lately.'

'No,' said Budd. He examined morosely his finger marks on the condensation around his glass. 'It's a hell of a problem.'

His eyes prickled with tears.

'Let me open a window,' said Orme-Campbell. 'These basement rooms are splendid except that one never gets a decent stream of air.'

'It's a hell of a problem,' Budd said again. 'I've got to make a decision.'

Orme-Campbell stood at the window, assessing Budd's last sentence and trying to relate it to the context of their discussion. He wasn't sure if Budd had begun to talk about Levenson's bid, or whether he was involved in one of the private and lachrymose self-torments that, according to the gossip-writers, affected him from time to time. He waited.

'I've been married for years,' said Budd.

His host didn't answer.

'I've had to make a lot of decisions in my time,' said Budd. 'I've always found it easier to help others than to help myself.'

Orme-Campbell wanted to distract him from his self-pity.

'You haven't done so badly—what are you in the set-up— Number Two, Three?'

'God knows,' said Budd. 'About sixth in the official list. But that's not the point.'

He emphasized his words by slapping the oak table as if it

was the Despatch Box, till the decanter and the glasses rattled and shook.

'I should have stood against him. I would have won.'

'Well, that's all history now, Alf. The real question is what you're going to do tomorrow.'

'It was hard with Betty,' said Budd, fixed on his course. 'She didn't like politics—didn't like the people in it. She was working at Marks and Spencer when I met her. The trouble was, she didn't grow. I back-pedalled for a bit, but it couldn't work that way. I had to make it on my own.'

'It's not easy being a politician's wife.'

'Well, she had the kids, and they were a bind. She lived in the constituency—I had to be away a lot—Parliamentary visits, speeches up and down the country. She didn't grow. That was the trouble.'

'How could she when you were away such a lot?'

'I thought she was happy. Then there was the problem of religion, I suppose—her flopping on her knees every five minutes, and rushing off to the priest.'

'Perhaps she was lonely.'

'She had the kids.'

'Is that enough?'

'No,' said Budd, and taking up the other's words, 'It isn't easy being a politician's wife. I'm surprised we don't have more divorces in the House than we do.'

'There are quite a few, aren't there? Perhaps there ought to be more.'

'Perhaps there should—perhaps there should. You see, Geoffrey, it's as lonely for a man in politics as it is for his wife. Most of the time you go along with the crowd, but when you get down to bedrock, you're on your own. They're trying to squeeze me out, you know.'

'That's what they've been saying.'

'All those stories,' said Budd. 'All those leaks about me in Cabinet—who d'you think started them?'

'I can guess.'

'I *know*. Cranfield did. But I've still got a few shots in my locker.'

Budd fumbled with his tie.

'I sometimes think, though, I'd be happier out of politics.'

'Oh, come on, Alf,' said Orme-Campbell. 'You were born a politician. You'd be miserable if you left the House.'

'I'm not so sure,' said Budd. 'Tell me, Geoffrey—and tell me frankly.'

Orme-Campbell looked at Budd's lips, the vein at the side of his forehead and his thick fingers drumming on the table, and waited for the question.

'Do you think,' asked Budd, 'that it's absurd for a man of my age to fall in love?'

'In love?' Orme-Campbell asked, startled. The phrase 'To a wart-hog there is nothing so beautiful as a female wart-hog' leapt into his mind and remained there.

'Love?' Orme-Campbell repeated, temporizing. He didn't want to spurn Budd's sentimentalities or to be drawn into a homespun analysis of love. They had already been sitting together for a quarter of an hour.

'Yes—love,' said Budd defiantly. 'Too old to fall in love?'

'Why should you be?' said Orme-Campbell warily. 'There are all sorts of ages—chronological age, physiological age and psychological age. If you fall in love, you're the right age for it.'

'Yes,' said Budd, leaning back against his chair. 'That's the hell of it.'

Orme-Campbell, impatient, curious and contemptuous, examined him with an amiable smile.

'Well, tell me all about it,' he said. 'We've been friends a long time.'

Budd put his hands in his pockets and didn't answer. At last he said,

'It's nothing very special. She works at the House—the secretary of one of our committees. It's the usual thing—when you work together with someone, you develop interests.'

'It all started in the back of your Ministerial car, I suppose—one night when you drove her home after working late. You took her hand under your raincoat.'

'For Christ's sake, how did you know?'

Orme-Campbell laughed.

'They're big cars with glass partitions. And she has a husband.'

'Yes.'

'It happens all the time,' said Orme-Campbell.

'Not like this.'

Orme-Campbell opened his mouth to say, 'Just like that,' but stopped. 'You're not thinking of getting a divorce.'

'I'm thinking of it,' said Budd. 'But it isn't easy. Betty's a Catholic. I doubt if she'll ever agree. She wouldn't take the pill and wouldn't do it without it. We're virtually living apart as it is.'

'And the other girl? Does her husband know?'

'Not exactly.'

Orme-Campbell stood up and walked to the window. Suddenly the fact that a podgy, middle-aged man had fallen in love with a young secretary had become important to O.C.E. and to himself. Not only was Budd involved in a public decision about O.C.E., but Orme-Campbell was involved in the personal decisions of Budd.

'Do you think, Alf,' he asked, 'that you'd feel—how shall I put it—more secure, better based, better equipped to deal with your problem, if you left the House?'

'Yes,' said Budd from the table. 'I'm sure of it.'

The tall clock struck eleven, hurriedly, as if urging them to finish their final sentences. Orme-Campbell made up his mind abruptly.

'If you left politics, Alf, would you consider going into business—the City, banking, industry?'

87

'Industry maybe,' said Budd. 'I've spent my life in it—on the other side of the table.'

'How would it be,' said Orme-Campbell, 'if, say, six months after you left the House, you had an invitation to join our Board?'

Having invited the question, Budd hesitated.

'That would present problems,' he said. 'You know there's a Private Member's Bill before the House at this very time trying to prevent resigning Ministers from going into industries that they've dealt with departmentally.'

'That's nonsense.'

'I agree—but it's the mood it creates—the public discussion. There was a TV programme about it the other night.'

Orme-Campbell returned to the table, and sat facing Budd.

'Listen, Alf,' he said, 'there isn't much time to talk about these matters now. If you decide your—your personal happiness is more important to you than politics, well, jolly good luck. . . . We've known each other a number of years. I don't have to put it into writing. With your background and experience, there's an enormous amount you could do in an organization like ours. Assuming, of course, we continue as we've been doing.'

'I'm sure there is,' said Budd. 'I'm sure there is.'

'But I don't think you should quit in a hurry. Don't let Cranfield think he's won. You ought to go, Alf, at a time of your own choosing, on an issue that's important.'

'It's the timing,' said Budd.

'Yes,' said Orme-Campbell. He stood again, feeling at an advantage.

'You've got to show authority, Alf—get the decks clear.'

'Yes—that's true.'

'So that whatever happens, you will know that when you leave the House, you'll be slipping into a position that's really worthy of you.'

'That's right.'

'It would be too early to talk of salaries. But if I tell you that Howell's been getting £20,000 and expenses for the last three years—'

'I know. I've seen the figures.'

'In that case, I needn't go on. . . . There should be an interval because, after all, Alf, you are making an important decision in connection with the bid. I wouldn't like you to be compromised or feel vulnerable just because you backed us against Levenson.'

Budd pushed his chair back and stood facing Orme-Campbell, contriving by his square stance in front of the taller man to present a figure of determination.

'I wouldn't like to think,' he said deliberately, 'that you're mixing one thing up with the other.'

'Good God, no,' said Orme-Campbell, waving the thought away with his hands.

'I imagined so,' said Budd. 'All I can tell you is that I've got to have another talk with Levenson before I make my final decision about the bid.'

'May I ask,' Orme-Campbell said, 'what are the considerations—'

Budd's cheeks wobbled with self-satisfaction.

'Oh, you know,' he said, 'a few questions of fact—forecasts—all that sort of thing. I hope it won't be long before I can give you a firm decision.'

'Tonight, I take it. You don't need to talk again to the Permanent Secretary?'

'No—he's my Permanent Secretary. I'm not his. I'll tell you definitely tonight. I've got an early Cabinet tomorrow. Yes—tonight. Let's go back to the others.'

Orme-Campbell didn't move.

'We are counting on your support, Alf,' he said, and his mouth was tight. 'You don't want our industry to fall into the hands of the Jews.'

'I see your point of view,' said Budd. With his hand on the door-knob, he said to Orme-Campbell,

'Incidentally—those personal ruminations of mine—you won't take them too seriously.'

Orme-Campbell patted him on the shoulder as they walked up the stone stairs.

'Of course not,' he said. 'We were just thinking aloud.'

Chapter Six

THE music had stopped and Isobel laughed as she ran past the swimming pool towards the water-garden, the interval of silence quickly replaced by a cotton-wool roar, an underground tumult, the rumour of a distant crowd with which she had no connection. From the hedges there blew a privet scent and, running, she snatched a handful of the pale flowers, crushing the granules between her thumb and forefinger.

'Good evening, Mrs. Levenson,' a Byron and Lady Blessington said together.

'Hello, Robert,' she answered. 'Hello, Céleste.' And without stopping, she called over her shoulder, 'Having a good time?'

The wind blew back to her a diminishing chorus,

'Oh yes—absolutely marvellous.'

At the water-garden Isobel, breathless, slowed down to a walk. The path that led to the lake was paved, the footing uneven. The only light came from the lanterns, the braziers under the yew trees and the reflection of the thin moon on the scaling statues, the broken-nosed senators, Graeco-Roman huntresses, slender ephebes with shapely buttocks and mutilated Aphrodites, marking the avenue. As the noise of the party became more remote, the ripple of water over the steps grew into a cascade, accompanying her on her journey to the pillar by the shore. She remembered the pressure of Adrian's bare arm on her breast, and it was a secret that excited her and she leant for a moment against the statue of a Diana with a fawning dog. His arm had small fair hairs bleached by the sun, inviting her to touch it, to feel its hardening and the movement of its sinews, while his face mocked and lacerated the world. And that was what her phantasy wanted—to see everything that surrounded her destroyed and discarded, everything that had ever happened since Edward to be wished away, the American, the other man she'd forgotten, the accumulating possessions, the people who came and went, to say 'Good-bye' and perhaps to be reborn mature, purged of everything that had been wrong or foolish or unfortunate in her youth.

She smiled into the night because she could see Adrian's white shirt by the stone pillar.

'Hello, Adrian,' she called out. 'So sorry to have left you. I had—'

She stopped as the figure casually leaning against the stonework brushed the hair from his forehead and said, straightening his glasses,

'Michael Hornsby—I'm afraid we all look rather alike this evening.'

'Yes,' she said. 'So many Byrons. I was looking for my son—and Adrian Sinclair. You haven't seen them, have you?'

He pondered for a moment.

'As a matter of fact, I have. Jonathan was trying to get the barbecue going again. I think it ran out of fuel.'

'You haven't seen Adrian?'

'I have,' said a girl in a long white directoire dress who had joined them.

'Where?' said Isobel. Her heart had begun to accelerate, and she could hear its beat in her ears almost as loud as the voices.

'As a matter of fact,' said the girl, and she stressed each syllable to indicate that her report was significant, 'I saw him about ten minutes ago.'

'Where?' Isobel repeated.

The girl waved vaguely.

'Oh, somewhere up there. He seemed to be looking for someone.'

Isobel turned her back on them, and began to run with the girl's voice drifting after her.

'What's eating her?' And almost simultaneously the man's voice,

'We'll never know, lovey.' And then the giggles, receding into nothing while the sounds of the waterfalls swelled and faded beneath the uproar of laughter and talk from the groups around the tightly-packed dance floor. Isobel's back was clammy with the effort of running, and she could hear her breath, heavy in her ear as if she were accompanied by another person.

At the head of the stone steps she paused, and said aloud,

'No stop—stop. Pull yourself together. He waited for you— you didn't turn up. He's gone to look for you. Don't get panicky. Don't run!'

And in time with her exhortation to herself, she ran, stumbling and panting, across the lawns towards the yew trees, her heels catching in the grass, afraid that she might miss him, that he might have missed her, that what had unexpectedly been given to her might cruelly be taken away.

'Adrian!' she called out. 'Adrian.' A night breeze puffed across the grass, and she felt the sweat on her print dress chilling her shoulders, and she stopped again.

In sight of the lanterns, the young men and the girls' black and white dresses, she felt easier, less isolated. Her heart beat slowed. She was sure that one of the youths in the ruffled shirts must be him. It was like a dream she often had in which Edward was still alive, and she wanted to telephone him, but she had forgotten the number. But now the thought of Edward himself was an intrusion. He was dead, and belonged to a past that was unhappiness as well as joy.

She walked towards the bar where Jonathan was standing with a glass in his hand.

'I've resigned from the job of barman,' he said. 'The

responsibility of measuring doubles was too much for me.'

'I hope you're not testing them too much on yourself.'

He put his arm around her shoulders, and she pulled away. Jonathan looked surprised for a second, and Isobel, unwilling to hurt him by her rejection, said,

'I'm all sticky, darling.'

'Yes, you are,' said Jonathan. 'Have you been dancing?'

'No,' she said. 'It's a very warm night.'

'You'll be my last customer,' said Jonathan. 'What can I get you to drink?'

'A double vodka.'

'You're joking. Gin and tonic?'

'No,' she said. 'A double vodka without ice. That's exactly what I want.'

Jonathan hesitated. Then he said, 'All right, mum. I'll have the same.'

While Jonathan bent behind the bar to get the vodka from his private store, Isobel scanned the dancers. The Upminstrels were now playing a somnolent Blues, and some of the guests were dancing with both arms tightly held around the back of their partners, eyes closed, in a shifting embrace, like a nest of turtles heaving and enclosed in their slow rhythm. She took the glass from Jonathan and drained it. Then, still holding the empty glass, she walked, with him following, to the edge of the dance floor.

'Like to dance?' he asked.

'Yes,' she said.

They danced without speaking. She tripped over his feet, and he apologized.

'Where's Henrietta?' Isobel asked.

'I don't know,' Jonathan said detachedly. 'I think I saw her dancing a few minutes ago.'

'And your friend Adrian?'

'He's about somewhere. Why don't you like him?'

94

'What makes you think I don't?'

'Oh, I know you don't. He's very nice when you get to know him.'

'He seems a very ordinary person.'

'No, he's not. I don't agree with a lot of what he says. He's an anarchist.'

'I imagined he was. He seems to hate everybody and everything.'

'You've got it wrong. He's a philosophical anarchist. He loves everybody, and hates the State.'

'He gets his university grant from it.'

'Well, of course he does. We're all involved in our environment, and we've got to live with it till we can change it.'

'Isn't that rather hypocritical?'

'I don't think so,' Jonathan said. 'Did you know that Adrian got beaten up by the police in the anti-colonial protest outside the Portuguese Embassy?'

'No, I didn't,' said Isobel. Then she added quickly, 'Did they hurt him?'

'Yes, he had concussion. He was pretty groggy for a long time.'

'He's got a very provocative manner.'

'That's just another way of saying he isn't afraid to tell the truth. I hope you get to know him. You'll like him and he'd like you.'

'Why would he like me?'

Jonathan paused to consider his reply.

'Well,' he said, 'we like a lot of the same things, even though we disagree on others. It's hard to get to grips with him. He's a dedicated refuser.'

Isobel took her hand from his shoulder and waved it in the air till the lights flashed on the square-cut diamond on her ring and the sapphires on her bracelet. A girl whose face was drooping over her partner's shoulder in an expression of dulled ecstasy caught the sudden glitter, and momentarily her eyes widened. Jonathan greeted her, and the corners of her mouth jerked before she relapsed into browsing contemplation.

'I wouldn't like to compete for your attention with all these Regency beauties,' said Isobel.

Jonathan frowned.

'Don't be absurd, mother, I don't think in those terms. You're different. . . . There's Henrietta—over there.'

Isobel looked around but Henrietta was already hidden by the surge of the other dancers. She was confused, unwilling to leave Jonathan in his superior posture.

'In what way would you say *you*'re different from Adrian?'

'Well, politically, I'm a reformer. I believe that institutions are social instruments that can be adapted. Adrian believes they have to be wiped out in each generation, and that new social relationships have to be built from scratch.'

'Do you believe that?'

'I don't,' Jonathan said. 'What is important is to test their validity, and I am a traditionalist, a conservative, because I don't think that everything in the past is worthless. Tomorrow we will be in the past—all of us. To say the past is useless is to disown ourselves.'

Isobel, cautiously feeling her way into Jonathan's reasoning, said, 'Perhaps Adrian does take that line. Perhaps he's just stoical.'

'That's just what he is,' said Jonathan. 'It's what I've got against his ideas. There's a kind of pessimism—*accidie*—in everything he does. I'm an optimist. I think I must have a lot of Jew in me, after all.'

'Why?' she asked, 'and what is *accidie*—despair?' The double bass, the altos, the violins—*Etreins-moi, mon amour*, they were playing it again. She wanted the earth to open in some Biblical disaster that would swallow her together with her insatiable longing for hope.

'Why?' she asked again.

'Well,' he answered, 'look up their history—our history—

no, not yours, our history. If the Jews weren't optimists, how could they have put up with it? Kicked, insulted, massacred, pillaged, burned, gassed—and yet, we're still around. And Harry's still trying to put one over on O.C.E.'

'No, he's not,' said Isobel. 'He's buying them at a fair price.'

'Except that they don't want to sell.'

'That's quite right. That's Harry's optimism.'

They both laughed, and Jonathan called out,

'Adrian, where've you been hiding?'

The music stopped, and Adrian appeared, holding Henrietta at arm's length. He said,

'We were jammed against the pillar over there in the far corner and couldn't budge.'

'Like something in Donne,' said Henrietta.

'That's it,' said Adrian.

' "And whilst our souls negotiate there,

We like sepulchral statues lay;

All day the same our postures were,

And we said nothing all the day." '

'Not quite like that,' said Henrietta. 'More like animated commercials—twist, squiggle and jerk.'

'We couldn't move,' said Adrian, 'so we took it in turn to have our backs to the pillar.'

Everyone except Isobel laughed.

'I think I'll say good-night,' she said.

The Upminstrels were playing again. Jonathan asked Henrietta to dance.

'Let's see if we can find that pillar,' he said.

'Would you like to dance?' Adrian asked Isobel.

'No, thank you,' Isobel answered. 'I thought you didn't like dancing.'

'I dance,' said Adrian. 'But usually I hate it. I would have liked it with you.'

She picked up her petit-point handbag from a chair and said,

97

'Good-night, Adrian. I was sorry to have missed you.'

He looked at her with the challenging smile gone from his mouth, though it remained in his eyes.

'I waited,' he said. 'It was lonely by the lake, and I thought you weren't coming. So I came to look for you. Then I danced with Henrietta to pass the time.'

Isobel didn't return the glance.

'That must have been very agreeable. She's a very attractive girl.'

'Rather heavy, I think. She spends too much of her time with politicians. Can I see you back?'

She was still unreconciled.

'I don't want to take you away from the party.'

Without answering, he began to walk at her side towards the house that now lay in darkness except for the lights in the hall.

'The aftermath of every all-night party that I've ever been to,' he said, 'is pneumonia. People sweat, then they feel cold, then they get pneumonia.'

'Are you cold?' she asked, with her face turned to his, and she wanted to protect him as he walked by her side with his sleeves rolled down and crumpled, and his shirt dark with patches of moisture.

'I'll lend you one of Jonathan's sports shirts,' she said. 'He won't mind.'

She expected him to resist, but instead he said,

'Thank you very much. I got bored with the Regency uniform after ten minutes.'

'It suited you. You should have lived in 1820.'

'Only if I were Byron—or perhaps Disraeli.'

'Why Disraeli—that old Tory?'

'He was a Tory by convenience—a radical by conviction. I can understand that. I'm sorry he came to a bad end.'

As they walked side by side to the house, they heard footsteps hurrying behind them, and Isobel turned to find Jonathan holding her scarf.

The three of them stood uncertainly, and Jonathan looked from Adrian to Isobel and the silhouette of the building in a slight bewilderment.

'Your scarf,' he said without smiling. 'You left it on a chair.'

'Thank you,' said Isobel.

Adrian watched them with a detached expression as if he was waiting for them to unravel their thoughts before he continued his talk with Isobel.

'Going to bed?' Jonathan asked.

'Not just yet,' said Isobel. She wanted to invent an explanation, a lie, but the enquiry in Jonathan's eyes was an accusing doubt. And for the first time, she felt anger against him, not the anger that she had felt when he had misbehaved as a child but anger against him as a parasitic adult who sapped her capacity to breathe and grow. She wanted to reject the feeling as unfitting, but Jonathan, standing indeterminate after he gave her the scarf, was an exasperating irrelevance that she wanted to be delivered of.

'You'd better go back to your guests, Jonathan,' she said. 'Don't worry about me. Adrian's promised to look after me.'

Jonathan groped for some flippancy in reply, but he could find neither the words nor the smile. He turned away awkwardly and the sound of their footsteps, separating, faded in each other's ears as Jonathan walked downwards to the party and Isobel and Adrian walked up the steps to the house.

'He didn't like that,' Adrian said.

'No,' she answered. 'He must have felt snubbed.'

'He looked surprised.'

'What at?'

'At you—me.'

She didn't answer, but walked ahead of him into the house, switching on lights.

'I'm afraid of the dark,' she said. 'I can never sleep with the curtains closed.'

'That's interesting,' said Adrian. 'I like them closed. Where are all your staff?'

'They've gone to bed—they have the small house to themselves on the other side of the lawns. Will you wait for me while I change in my dressing-room?'

'Yes,' said Adrian. 'You can throw me a shirt.'

She walked up the carpeted stairs, and he followed her with his hands in his pockets, watching the wave of her hips, the darkness of her shoulder blades through her dress, and her hair, softened by the night air, falling on her shoulders.

'How long do you think this party's going on, Adrian?' she asked, talking in front of her. 'Do you know how many of your friends are going to stay the night? I hope they won't be too noisy after two o'clock. Harry doesn't take very kindly to noise, and he hates pop-music. He likes Hindemith. What about the discothèque?'

She asked her questions in succession without waiting for his answers, and when she was out of breath she stopped on the landings and took in her hand one of the fat tassels hanging from the heavily brocaded curtain.

'I'm going to strap-hang for a moment,' she said. 'I'm tired.'

'I don't know about the others,' Adrian said, 'but when the party's over, I'm driving back to London. Jonathan's lending me the Triumph.'

He leaned against the balustrade, and they looked at each other without moving.

'I hope you'll come and see us often,' she said.

He half-smiled. 'I don't think so.'

'Why not?' she asked quickly.

He watched her fluted fingers slowly passing over the thickly plaited cord, encircling the tassel then nervously returning to stroke the velvet in a compulsive, rotatory motion.

'Let's open the curtains,' he said, and she pulled the cord, creaking on its rail as the grounds, stippled with lights, appeared.

Still holding the tassel in her hand, and laying it against her cheek, she turned her back to him and said,

'I've never seen the gardens look so beautiful. We've lived here for years, and it's never seemed so gay and happy.'

He stood pressed against her, and said,

'I think I'd like to stay here—just here—all the time without moving, like the couple in Donne's poem, till the party ends.'

She didn't answer, but putting a hand behind her, took his left hand and drew it on to her breast so that his mouth lay against her hair, while his fingers moved slowly, exploring and cautious.

After a few moments, she said in a matter of fact voice, 'I must change. Let me get you another shirt,' and she moved quickly ahead of him to the bedroom.

Adrian picked up a small photograph of an officer in uniform on the dressing table, and asked,

'Who is that?'

She took the photograph from his hands, and said,

'It's Edward—my first husband. He was killed.'

'In the war?'

'No.'

She studied the portrait unmoved; it was shadow and light on cardboard, unrelated to feeling or memory.

'He looks very neat,' said Adrian. 'Strange how they wore those tidy little moustaches in those days.'

'Yes,' said Isobel, and her agreement echoed like a betrayal in her mind as he put the photograph back.

'Doesn't your husband—Harry—mind these monuments?' Adrian asked.

'Why should he?' said Isobel, opening a drawer and taking out a sports shirt.

'Here you are,' she said. 'Try this one. It's easier than going up to Jonathan's room—I've got no idea where he throws his stuff. . . .' And, returning to Adrian's question, 'Harry knows everything that ever happened to me. There's nothing for him to mind.'

'Well, you change your dress,' said Adrian. 'I'll try this.'

She chose a sleeveless linen dress from the wardrobe, and carried it into the dressing room. Adrian drew off his shirt and put on Harry's blue check shirt in its place.

'How is it?' Isobel asked, coming back from her dressing room.

'That's a nice colour,' he said, admiring the delicate pink of the dress she had put on.

'How's the shirt?' she asked.

'Fine,' Adrian answered, 'except that the laundry has taken off all the buttons.'

She laughed, and came near him, as he stood beside the bed, and said,

'You *are* silly. You're wearing it inside out.'

Looking down on her head, he felt her fingers fumbling with the buttons, and said,

'Perhaps it might be simpler if I took it off and started again.'

She sat on the bed, watching the movement of his brown muscles with the lighter flesh beneath them as he slid her husband's shirt from his chest. He came nearer, and she put her arms around his hips. Tired, she would have liked to have melted into that position, indefinitely and undisturbed, tremulously feeling the great, invading poignancy that marched through the valleys of her body; but he drew her up and she rose, slowly, reluctant to leave the anonymity of the figure before her closed eyes and afraid to confront the face that was familiar and strange while the hands forced her head towards him, cupping it with his fingers in her hair.

'Hello,' he said quietly, looking down at her. It was a murmur of greeting and recognition.

'Hello,' she answered, and she wanted to smile but couldn't, and tried to twist her head from his hands.

'No,' she said.

Carmella had laid out her husband's pyjamas on the bed, together with a pale mauve nightdress with its bodice gathered and its skirt spread out like a fan. The pyjamas were a presence, an occupation, a flag marking a possession.

'No,' she said, and tried to turn her mouth away, but Adrian moved his hand to enclose her chin, and as her lips opened he filled them with his mouth, till their tongues were engaged like wrestlers rolling together, reversing their postures and separating only to take breath. She looked at him, observing his frown, and then at the ceiling as she fell back on the bed, and at his naked shoulders glistening above her, and the plaster mouldings, garlands of flowers and urns and drapings, the tendrils, the scenery of a death.

'No,' she said again. And her voice sounded in her own ears like a groan before her mouth was again enclosed, and the nightmare weight of her recurring dream straddled her again, but this time the dream was a reality that she felt in the firm back where her fingers were clenched, and in the hand fumbling at the zip-fastener behind her dress.

He half-pulled her towards him, and she heard the fastener's hiss as it opened and the dress fell from her shoulder. Then the mouth groping, and the sudden ringing of the telephone that went on and on, anaphrodisiac and separating.

'I must answer,' she gasped. He pulled his face away from her for a second.

'No,' he ordered. 'Let it ring.'

The sound accumulated in her ears.

'I must answer,' she said, struggling away from him. 'I *must* answer. It rings through to Luigi's and if I don't answer at this hour he'll come and find out why.'

Adrian, scowling, heaved himself over Harry's pyjamas to reach the instrument and handed it to Isobel.

'Hello,' her husband said. The voice was apologetic. 'Did I wake you up?'

She lay with her head resting on Adrian's chest, and said, 'No—well, not exactly.'

'You sound out of breath. Anything wrong?'

'No. Everything's fine. I was in the bathroom, and I rushed. How are you? Will you be long?'

'It's going to be longer than I thought. Budd's being difficult, and I've got to deal with a couple of Orme-Campbell's hatchet-men. Some of them aren't what they seem.'

'No,' she said, and she tried to push Adrian away 'It's what I've always thought. Is anything—?'

'No.'

Adrian's arm had tightened around her shoulders, and he was stroking her hair with his other hand.

'Are you sure you're all right?' Levenson said.

'Yes—why?'

'You sound—I don't know. You sound different.'

'It's only because I'm lying down.'

There was a silence at the other end.

'Do you want anything special?' she asked.

'You sound different,' he repeated. 'What's the matter?'

She raised herself on her elbow. 'Nothing,' she said in irritation. 'For heaven's sake, darling—this is your third call in an hour.'

'I know,' he said. 'I miss you—that's all there is to it.'

'You mustn't be silly,' she said. And more quietly, 'You mustn't be silly.'

'No,' said Levenson. 'Go to sleep, angel. I'll be another couple of hours. Good-night.'

'Good-night, darling,' said Isobel. She put the phone down, and Adrian smiled to her, triumphantly. She put her arms around him and kissed his mouth, his neck and his chest. She felt happy, delivered. He began to draw her back to the bed, but she released herself from him.

'Luigi might come,' she said. 'Let's go back and dance. And then, afterwards, we can take the boat and go to the island.'

Chapter Seven

'WHAT is Right Wing?' Jonathan asked. Henrietta, stretched out on the bench under the arch overlooking the lake, disregarded his question.

'I suppose,' she said sleepily, 'this is what the Victorians called an Eminence, and this is where couples rested when they took their Sunday afternoon strolls. Why don't you have mutton-chop whiskers like Peter Watson? It would go very well with the gazebo.'

'My step-father built this,' said Jonathan. 'Everything here is strictly fake.'

'All the same,' she replied, 'it's very pretty. It's strange how quickly one can get away from all that din. I like watching the reeds. Right Wing, I suppose, is anything opposed to liberty and consent. Or is that Left Wing now?'

'Lately,' Jonathan said gloomily, 'all the labels have become meaningless—except for abuse. There are only two parties—the ones who believe in personal rights and the others who don't.'

Henrietta had kicked off her shoes, and lay with her back against the arm of the bench and her legs over his thighs. Jonathan took her feet in his hands, and she said,

'You know, Jonathan, you don't look at all Jewish.'

'Should I genuflect?' he asked, stroking her toes. 'Anyhow, what does it mean?'

She was embarrassed, and said,

'Well—dark and Mediterranean—'

'Like my step-father.'

'Yes—I'd say he was Jewish-looking. You're fair and quite tall, and you've got light-coloured eyes. I imagine you get all that from your mother.'

'I doubt it,' Jonathan replied. 'I've an idea that she's rather dark underneath all those rinses. My father was fair. Lots of Jews are.'

'You've never told me much about your father.'

'He died when I was ten, but I remember him very well. He was a tremendously good-looking man—very tall—and always laughing. He was a major in the RAMC. I can never think of him without a picture in my mind of him and mother laughing together . . . and our holidays . . . the last one was in Cervia . . . miles and miles of sea. We swam every day . . . we stayed at a hotel that had an enormous buffet that seemed to go on all the time.'

'You're making me hungry,' said Henrietta, curling her toes.

'Then he got killed.'

In the moonlight reflected from the lake, Henrietta saw that his face was closed and unhappy, and she wanted to change the subject.

'Let's go and dance,' she said.

'No,' he answered. 'I like remembering my father. He's somehow much more real to me than Harry. To begin with, I used to see him nearly all the time. We had a big house, and he practised nearby. He was one of the best endocrinologists in Europe—somebody wrote that in *The Times*. My step-father's a kind of myth—a sort of King Claudius who's got no right to be there at all.'

'And Queen Gertrude?'

Jonathan shrugged his shoulders.

'I don't know. It's strange. In one way, I know her very well. But when I see their bedroom door close behind them, I feel she's unrelated to me.'

'You're very fond of her, all the same.'

'Oh yes—of course I am, and after father died we just stuck around together all the time. We lived in a one-room flat for nearly a year, but I liked it. We had very little money, and grandfather was a problem. Always sponging.'

'I'm going to turn round,' said Henrietta, and she squirmed herself into a reversed position so that her head rested on his chest and her feet lay over the arm of the bench. 'Go on,' she said. 'I like hearing about your family. What happened to Claudius? I've forgotten.'

'He got bumped off,' said Jonathan moodily. 'That's how I sometimes feel about Harry.'

'Sweetie,' said Henrietta, kissing him under the chin, 'you couldn't expect your mother to become a Vestal Virgin after your father died. She was quite young—not much older than I am now. Imagine if she hadn't got married. She would probably have lived from time to time with all sorts of men—'

'Oh, rubbish,' said Jonathan. 'You don't know her. She's frightfully prudish really.'

'Is she?' asked Henrietta, deciding not to pursue the matter. 'I've often noticed you've got a special style with her.'

'What sort of style?'

'Well, it's private—as if you're not letting anyone else in on the secret. And then it's—you won't be offended, darling—it's a bit schoolboyish, as if she wanted you to be fifteen for ever.'

'O.K.,' Jonathan said, stroking her long hair, 'I *am* offended.'

'Well, don't be,' she answered. 'You're very nice with your mother. But she hates the sight of me.'

'I'm not surprised,' said Jonathan. 'You're her only competitor.'

'In that case,' she said, 'kiss me.'

He kissed her, fumbling his hand through the ruffles of her blouse till it reached her breast. Underneath his palm the nipple rose, sentient and firm, and his fingers felt their way delicately over its texture, pressing and releasing it as she clung to him in a quivering delight, unwilling for him to speak.

She drew away from him at last, and said,

'I like that. Why can't we put up a tent and stay here always?'

'I'll give you a few guesses,' Jonathan said. 'Anyhow, your parents would want to visit us, and there'd be very little room.'

'You'd like my parents,' said Henrietta.

'I'm prejudiced,' said Jonathan. 'What does your father do?'

'He runs a copying and drawing office at Colchester—very ordinary—that's probably why I'm dressed up as Lady Blessington.'

'What will they say about your coming to Avdat with me?'

'Nothing,' said Henrietta with a slight frown. 'They've got used to me sharing a flat in London and being on my own. I go and see them whenever I can.'

'Will they mind you going on a Jewish archaeological expedition?'

'Oh, no,' she said in her clear and singing voice. 'Not a bit. Daddy's—how can I say it without it sounding prissy? He's a Christian. It's the only way I can put it. He believes in goodness and charity in its real sense of love.'

'What about you?' Jonathan asked.

'Well, of course, I do,' said Henrietta. 'It's just that we all approach it from different directions. It's a kind of pilgrimage in which we all converge. And then we find we are all looking for the same thing. It isn't just oecumenicism. That's all to do with churches and what not. It's more a discovery of things that you feel are universal and eternal.'

She had disengaged herself from Jonathan, and was looking at the dark mass of the island as she spoke.

'Do you go to church—I mean to synagogue?'

'No,' he answered. 'The last time I went to synagogue was to say prayers for my father. It's strange. Although he was a scientist, he was rather orthodox and he had faith. He used to like all the rituals, and we went on the Jewish holy days to a synagogue near Marble Arch—a huge, neo-classical temple. What I remember most about it were the women up in the gallery, all wearing very smart hats like a Tory Women's Conference, and I waved to mummy from down below. . . . Then there was the choir. That was terrific. It was hidden away behind a screen, and they had a tremendous *basso profundo*. And every now and again they'd open the Ark—'

'Very Old Testament.'

'It's where they keep the Scrolls of the Law with silver breast-plates and bells—rather tribal, but somehow, looking back on it, vivid and real. I never wanted to go back after father died—it went with him—but now—perhaps in Israel— I feel I'd like to know more about it.'

'Adrian's violently anti-Zionist.'

'Adrian's violently anti-everything that he can't understand. What I want is to link up with my own history—with all those scrolls and bells.'

'What about me?' Henrietta asked. Her expression was half-playful, half-serious.

'You have your own—lots of it,' Jonathan answered.

'Well, couldn't I perhaps come along for the ride?'

He held her by the shoulders, kissed her mouth quickly, and said,

'Perhaps—we could try it.'

*

The music had stopped, and the mass of dancers who had crowded the marquee now fragmented itself into a coming and going of faces along the paths and over the lawns, fusing with the obscure bushes or sharply defined under the lanterns before disappearing into the interstices of darkness. After the beat of the drums and the electric guitar clanging over the absorbed and jerking bodies, the silence, except for the talk at the buffet and around the barbecue, the laughter and the footsteps.

Jonathan and Henrietta walked hand in hand along the path skirting a thicket that led back to the marquee. Henrietta, short-sighted, suddenly pulled back as they heard a moan from a clearing close by. Jonathan put his arm around her shoulders and her head against his chest, and walked firmly past.

'What was it?' she asked without looking up.

'Just the two-backed beast,' said Jonathan. 'Starts prowling around about now.'

'It sounded rather horrible,' she said with her head down. Jonathan glanced back at the pale, involved figures on the grass, hardly moving and zebra-ed by the branches.

'Yes,' he said. He paused and took both her hands in his, and kissed her again. 'I wish,' he said, 'sex had been invented exclusively for us.'

'Don't you think sex in other people is revolting?'

'Quite repulsive,' said Jonathan.

Henrietta laughed, and said,

'I suppose there's enough for everyone. We mustn't be greedy.'

Near the circular rose garden they heard a guitar being played, and they walked hand in hand towards the sundial in the middle where, propped against it, a fair-bearded, broken-nosed man of about thirty was accompanying himself in a French song, '*Regarde ce qui va se passer*'. His voice was harsh and unmelodious, but he sang aggressively and rhythmically so that the group lying close to him, a white-faced girl in a cowboy hat who had undone the front buttons of her blouse, and two shirtless men in jeans, observing him in an entranced respect, set a standard of appreciation to which other bystanders who had drifted up to hear him felt it proper to conform.

'He's terrific,' said Rawson, sidling up with Venetia Cohen, his girl-friend, to Jonathan and Henrietta as they stood watching the singer. Jonathan looked distastefully at Rawson's wiry figure, his wavy hair, drooping over his ears, and his thick spectacles. He had come across him for the first time earlier in the summer in the large flat in Highbury where Rawson was living with Venetia, whom he had met at Oxford. All that he knew about him was that he had read P.P.E. and started a thesis on the Cuban and Algerian revolutions which he never finished. Venetia, about two inches taller than Rawson, had worn a long, clumsy plait falling to her waist, and wrangled the whole evening with him about Left Wing sectarianism. Jonathan had met them a second time at a demonstration in Belgrave Square where he had seen Rawson, timid in the face of private bullying, urging on his comrades with a loud hailer in a high-pitched voice, while Venetia, whenever the heaving of the crowd separated them, kept calling in a plaintive and anxious voice, 'Alan—where's Alan?'

He had invited Rawson and Venetia to the party, and they had turned up with about ten others. Not that he had minded. They all had strangely white faces, moved spasmodically, and wherever their aimless strolling took them, in the grounds or in the house itself, stood or sat, handing each other cigarettes with an abstracted air.

'He's terrific,' Rawson repeated.

'Marvellous!' said Venetia enthusiastically.

'Who is he?' Jonathan asked, finding it hard to join in the general reverence.

'I don't know his name,' said Venetia. 'They call him the Katangan. His first name's Bill.'

'He fought in Africa,' said Rawson. 'Splendid chap in a demonstration! You should have seen him outside the Greek Embassy. He picked up a flower-box, and went through the police line like a bull through a gang of picadors.'

'Marvellous!' Venetia repeated, clinging to Rawson's arm. 'You remember at Tarifa last year. There was that matador with a pike on a white horse, and all those beastly people up in the box—those horrid women cheering him on. And that superb bull, coughing up black blood, suddenly turned and unseated him. Do you remember, Alan?' She turned to him to support her memory.

'Yes,' said Rawson. 'It was very spectacular. I can't understand why the Spaniards never take the side of the bull.'

'Not *never*,' Venetia protested. 'They're all for the bull provided it doesn't win.'

'Like the English with the fox,' said Rawson.

'It's horrid,' said Henrietta, who had followed their recollections with distaste. 'What were you doing in Spain anyway?'

Together they began to explain their visit to Spain. They were on the way home from Tangier; it was the cheapest route they could find—they didn't think it necessary to penalize the Spaniards just because they disapproved of dictators; and besides, though he didn't actually succeed, Alan had hoped to make contact with the Barcelona syndicalists, the Basque separatists, and the Catalan anarchists. Patiently, Jonathan listened to them as they multiplied their justifications.

'But we didn't really *want* to go to Spain,' Venetia said.

'You don't have to explain to me,' Jonathan said. 'You must explain it to yourself. I'm all for everyone doing whatever they want to.'

Bill had stopped playing, and the girl in the cowboy hat brought him an opened bottle of wine and a plate of sausages. His audience waited respectfully as he drank, the wine gurgling down his muscular throat. When he put the bottle down, Jonathan noticed that it was a Château Talbot.

'Well,' he said to Henrietta, 'he's got one thing in common with Harry.'

'What's that?' she asked.

'A taste in wine. It's Harry's favourite claret. I wonder where our friend Bill got it.'

'Would you like to meet Bill?' Venetia asked, as if she were

113

a court chamberlain arranging for a presentation to the monarch, now lying with his head on the cowgirl's lap while another favourite was fingering the charm hanging from the gold chain around his neck.

'Wouldn't we be disturbing him?' Henrietta asked.

'Oh, that's all right,' said Venetia. 'He's marvellously sweet-natured. After all he's been through, it's extraordïnary. Do come and say "hello".'

She took Henrietta by the arm with Jonathan following reluctantly behind, and led her over to Bill.

'Bill,' she said, 'this is Henrietta, and this is Jonathan Levenson, our host.'

'Hello,' said Bill, without moving. 'Say "hello", Liz.'

'Hello,' said the cowgirl, looking up through her blue-circled eyes and her false eyelashes.

'I hear you were in Africa,' said Jonathan.

Bill moved his head as if a fly had alighted on it.

'Yup,' he said.

'Whereabout?' Jonathan asked.

'Here and there,' said Bill. 'What is this—the dock?'

There was a bay of laughter from those surrounding him as if he'd spoken a witticism. Bill hoisted himself up and took another swig of the Château Talbot, coiling his arm around the cowgirl's neck, with the light from a lantern glinting on the oblong wrist-watch.

'I wish they'd all bugger off,' said the cowgirl in a clearly articulated voice.

'Liz was at Somerville,' Venetia explained. 'For about two terms.'

Henrietta laughed, and said,

'We must have missed each other. Come on, Jonathan, let's go and dance.'

'Yes, go and dance,' said Bill dismissively. He was drunk, satisfied with his admirers, and didn't want to enlarge his court.

On the way to the marquee, Jonathan stopped and said to Henrietta,

'Do you know, darling, I think that Katangan fellow was wearing Harry's wrist-watch.'

'Don't be absurd,' she said. 'How could he be?'

Jonathan looked back over his shoulder to the group in the rose-garden and said,

'I saw him in the house earlier on. I must say I resent them swigging the Château Talbot as if it was Coca-Cola.'

She took his arm and led him onwards.

'It's no good getting fussed,' she said. 'You know these people. They've got no respect for anything that belongs to anyone else. You've got to expect them to behave like that.'

Jonathan walked on for a few paces. Then he stopped again, and said, 'I'm sure that's my father's watch.' And he spoke naturally of Levenson as his father, allying himself with him as if he and Levenson had a common interest which was being attacked from outside. 'I recognize the Longines face and the crocodile strap. They were all prowling about the house.'

The party had suddenly become darkened for him by the presence of Bill, the cowgirl and their friends, squatting around the sundial and staring unseeing in front of them, in a dulled hebetude, passing their cigarettes from mouth to mouth, gracelessly trespassing and abusing his tolerance. He half-turned, and said,

'I'm going back, Henrietta, to talk to that fellow.'

'No, Jonathan,' said Henrietta, and he could see her frightened eyes. 'He's a nasty character—he really is—you know, one of those people de Gaulle calls *la pègre*.'

'He looks a sod in English or French,' said Jonathan.

'Let's dance first,' Henrietta begged him. 'Perhaps they'll settle down or go away or something.'

'The watch—'

'Oh, blast the watch. I'm sure the insurance will pay if it's stolen.'

115

'That's not the point. It's a matter of principle. I don't want him to imagine he can walk in and walk off with something that belongs to my father.'

'Yes, sweetie, but you must consider the balance of advantage. After all, perhaps it's not your father's watch. And if you ask, there's bound to be a bust-up. It would be such a shame to spoil this lovely party.'

'All right,' said Jonathan sullenly. 'I'll think it over.'

*

In the marquee where the Upminstrels were playing again, most of the dancers had surged around the dais and were clapping in time to the beat. Clutching the microphone like a fetish, a strangulated singer was ascending a scale in a diapason with an electric organ and straining upwards, engorged in a hoarse and sweating effort. 'Up—up—up—that's where I want you.' And the streaming foreheads, the damp shoulders of the girls, the clapping hands and the moving elbows formed a hedge around the Group, hiding them except for the singer who from time to time leapt into the air, holding the microphone on its long lead. 'Up—up—up. . . .' The cymbals and the hands crashed together.

'This is fun,' said Henrietta, tugging Jonathan by the hand.

Cut off in an enclave in front of the Upminstrels, a few couples, Isobel and Adrian among them, were dancing, facing each other with solemn, inward-looking expressions, yet jerking ritually like mating birds in the Galapagos Islands. 'Up—up—up.' The singer's eyes were shut tight, and his lips bared back so that his blue gums and mauve gullet dominated his features. Up—up—up—jerk—up—twitch. The onlookers clapped, jerked and twitched with the singer as conductor, till they seemed a single, bisexual, self-propagating body, active and passive, giving and receiving, with the music as its powerful heartbeat. Still holding on to Jonathan, Henrietta pushed her way through the crowd from the darkened back of the marquee to the brilliantly-lit front. He spoke to her through the din, and she called back over her shoulder, 'Sorry! Can't hear you.'

Then she smiled at him, and beckoned. Two of the couples had become tired and withdrew among the spectators, leaving only Adrian and Isobel. As if they had a long experience of each other, they approached, detached themselves, their faces close and impassive, their bodies separate, moving restlessly, their hips in counterpart, their hands groping the air in a simulacrum of touch, while the singer sang the verses and the recurring chorus, 'Up—up—up—that's where I want you.'

And now the clapping was continuous, encouraging the dancers. Jonathan, holding Henrietta's hand as she watched Adrian and Isobel with a half-delighted, half-amused expression, could feel his own hand contracting with misery and distaste at the sight of his mother under the bright lights above the dais.

'Adrian's marvellous,' said Henrietta. 'But so's your mother. Where on earth did she learn?'

'In her bathroom, I imagine,' Jonathan said.

From the darkness behind them, a woman's voice said crisply, 'The great thing about it is that you've got to keep your upper part straight and do all the work from the belly downwards.'

'Well, she's doing that all right,' a man replied, and there was a guffaw. Jonathan turned angrily, but the crowd had re-formed behind him, and almost in the same moment the music stopped and the bystanders clapped, cheered and whistled.

'Hello, Jonathan, that was wonderful,' said Isobel, catching sight of her son. She had drawn up her hair in a pony-tail, and her face was flushed and her eyes glittered. 'He's a super dancer. Isn't he, Henrietta?'

'Not bad,' said Henrietta. 'Adrian gets enough flattery.'

Jonathan drew his mother away.

'What's the matter?' she asked.

'Nothing,' he said.

'You look strange,' she went on. 'Anyone been upsetting you?'

'No—well, not really. There's a chap out there who, I think, has pinched Harry's gold wrist-watch. Did he leave it behind?'

'Yes,' she said at once. 'He never wears it with his dinner jacket.'

'I'll have to get it back.'

Isobel put her hand on his arm, and smiled.

'No, darling, it's not worth having a scene and spoiling your party. It's really not. If it's been stolen, tell the police tomorrow. Anyhow, it's not all that valuable.'

'That's not the point,' Jonathan said stubbornly. 'I object to him walking off with—the point is I have some responsibility to Harry for looking after things.'

She glanced towards Adrian, who was chatting with Henrietta.

"Well,' she said in a languid voice, 'you'd better look after your girl-friend first, or you'll lose her. Adrian and I are going to get something to eat.'

She turned to rejoin Adrian, but Jonathan called after her sharply,

'Oh, mother!'

She knew what he was going to say, and her eyes met his defiantly.

'What is it, Jonathan?'

He looked at the floor, and scraped it with his toe.

'I don't like to say this, but—'

'—but you're going to.'

'Yes.'

'Well, say it.'

He paused, and said, 'I wonder if you'd do something for me.'

'What's that?'

'I'd rather you didn't dance again tonight.'

She faced him coldly.

'No? Why not?'

'Well—this is a party of my friends. They're really not your contemporaries.'

'Do you object to my dancing with Adrian?'

'Not object—I just feel it's—I don't know—not dignified.'

'I see,' said Isobel. 'Anything else?'

'No,' said Jonathan, still avoiding her glance.

'Well, don't worry,' said Isobel. 'I won't dance again tonight.'

'I'm sorry, mum. I didn't mean—'

'Of course you did. But it doesn't matter.'

He began to explain again that he hadn't wanted to wound her feelings. She walked away.

'Oh, for God's sake,' he burst out. 'Do you have to make a fool of yourself?'

She paused, and then said deliberately, 'You know, Jonathan, I sometimes think you were born old.'

She didn't turn her head, the Group was playing a quiet tune, and Henrietta came rushing back to Jonathan.

'You, please!' she said, laying her face against his and holding him closely.

'I've decided I don't like your friend Adrian,' she said in his ear as they danced.

'Why?'

'He tried to make a date with me.'

'That must have flattered you,' he said morosely.

'Not really. I told him I only make dates with Mr. Jonathan Levenson.'

'It sounds like a roll of drums.'

'Nice ones. They give me a lovely sensation.'

*

After a few minutes, Jonathan took Henrietta by the arm and led her off the dance floor. She looked at him enquiringly, and he said,

'I'm going back to have a word with Bill. You stay here.'

The night breeze blew her hair in her face, and she waved it away.

'For God's sake, what for?' she said. 'He'll kill you.'

'No, he won't,' said Jonathan. 'I was rather a good boxer at school.'

'You were always beaten,' she said. 'You told me. Don't get involved.'

'You stay here.'

'No, I'm coming with you.'

Bill was still sitting against the sundial when they arrived, and he interrupted his anecdote briefly to glance at Jonathan and ignore him.

'. . . so there they were—six Belgians and Urumbu with a Bren gun . . . was giving them cover . . . just for. . . .'

'Can you tell me the time?' Jonathan said, standing in front of him.

The Katangan hesitated, then grinned.

'Sure!' he said, supporting himself on the shoulders of the two girls he was addressing, and heaving himself to his feet. 'Sure I can.'

Around him the smiling, respectful faces took on a new look of curiosity.

'It's exactly—let me see—' He held the watch to the light. 'It's exactly . . . hard to read this fancy watch, for Christ's sake . . . it's exactly . . . oh, take a look yourself.'

'Thank you,' said Jonathan, cautiously watching Bill's grinning face. 'Perhaps you'll let me have it back now as you're leaving.'

'Sure,' said Bill, still grinning. 'We were just leaving. Get the guitar, Liz. Here you are, sonny. Take it off my wrist.'

Around them, the onlookers had become silent, and two or three had moved off. Jonathan looked at the bored girls behind Bill, and from them to Henrietta's anxious face. He hesitated.

'Come on, sonny,' Bill said. 'Take it off.'

He held up his hairy arm with the slim watch tightly strapped around its wrist, and Jonathan put out his hand gingerly to undo the strap.

'It's a good fit,' said Bill, his lips turned back in the shape of a smile. 'You'll need two hands.'

As Jonathan bent over the watch with his fingers fumbling, he felt a stunning blow on the back of his neck, and fell on his knees. Then darkness, the smell of grass and the earth stuffed in his mouth; a winch pulling him to his feet, a vicious stroke, and Henrietta's voice screaming, 'Leave him alone! Leave him alone!' A movement of shapes, the thud of blows, his world spinning, a sudden dissolution and a reluctant, vertiginous return.

'Go away!'

The voice was becoming clearer.

'Please—do please go away! Give him some air!'

Clearer still.

'I'll look after him.'

The voice and the image were clear. He tried to stand up, but his knees were faint, soggy, as they had been when he was knocked out in the under-18s at school.

'You'll be all right soon, darling,' said Henrietta. 'Andrew and the others hustled them off. What a ghastly thug that man is!'

Jonathan forced himself to stand, and leaned on the sundial till Henrietta's blurred face returned into complete focus.

'Where are the others?' he asked.

'I told them to go away. Does it hurt?'

'Only when I bend my neck. What happened?'

'You went to get the watch, and he hit you.'

She was holding the watch in her hand, and he said, trying to smile,

'Well, anyway, I got the watch.'

'Yes,' she said, handing it to him. 'He trod on it.'

Jonathan took the watch, fingered it, then put its smashed face to his ear.

'It's ticking,' he said. 'Listen.' He held it to her ear, and watched her slow delight.

'So it is,' she said. 'Despite Bill.'

'Yes,' he echoed. 'Despite Bill. . . .' The earth was still in his mouth, and he said, 'I'd better get washed.'

'Yes,' said Henrietta. Then she kissed his muddied face, and said, 'You were pretty good.'

Chapter Eight

'HARRY would like to see you,' Lattner said to Howell, intercepting him in a corridor.

'It's very late,' said Howell.

'Up to you,' said Lattner. 'I'm only giving you his message. He said he wants a chat with you.'

Howell hesitated, remembering Levenson's questions earlier in the evening.

'Where is he?'

'Playing two hundred up—God help him—with Lady Orme-Campbell in the billiard room. Sir Geoffrey is helping us pass the time till sentence.'

'How often are visitors allowed?' said Howell, entering glumly into Lattner's imagery, and studying his even-tempered face to see what he intended.

'I'd guess,' said Lattner with a short laugh, 'most visitors would find once is enough.'

Still cautious, Howell asked, 'What does he want to see me for?'

'I'd rather he told you himself. D'you know where we can go to be private?'

'Most of the rooms are in use.'

'Well, perhaps you can think of somewhere.'

'I can't stay away too long,' said Howell.

'I shouldn't think he would want to delay you,' said Lattner. 'Harry puts his points pretty succinctly—what he calls the old one-two.'

Howell straightened himself like a man who, committed to danger, decides to put a good face on it.

'The old one-two doesn't always work,' he said.

'It usually does,' said Lattner, retaining his untroubled expression. 'Let's see what he's up to.'

★

As they opened the door of the billiard room Levenson was about to try a cannon off the red from the bottom of the table and Elaine put her finger to her lips for silence. It was a difficult shot, but measuring it with happy concentration, his shirt sleeves resting on the table and his cue poised in a practised control, Levenson looked more relaxed than at any time during the evening.

He hit the red but missed the cannon, and his ball came spinning back from the cushion to the base. Scowling at Lattner, Levenson began hurriedly to chalk another cue.

'B-bad luck,' said Elaine, stuttering slightly as she turned to address Lattner and Howell. 'You see he's left me nothing. He gave me a fifty start, and I thought he was being generous. Not a bit. He began with a break of thirty-nine.'

'It's just a trick,' said Levenson. 'You've got to get them bunched over the pocket. You can then roll off the cannons.'

'Where did you learn that?' she asked. 'It's something father forgot to explain to me.'

'I learnt it at our Boys' Club in the East End,' he said. 'I practised it every day for about two years.'

'I do so envy you,' she said, bending over the table to aim the cue, her arm stringy with the effort. 'This is dreadful. I can't reach it.'

'Try using the rest,' said Levenson.

She stretched her hand for the cue-rest, and the polished staves clashed clumsily together.

'I can never hold them both. One or the other always slips.'

'All right,' said Levenson chivalrously. 'I'll hold it for you.'

He put the rest into position, and Elaine took aim.

'A bit more bias,' said Levenson. She looked up at him and murmured, 'Not *too* much.'

She struck the ball jerkily and mis-cued.

'It's no good,' she said, watching it feebly roll in the wrong direction, 'I'll never catch up with the years I wasted hunting instead of playing billiards.'

Levenson smiled again.

'We all have to take our exercise the way we can. I'll give you the game.'

'But you were leading by thirty-three.'

'Forty-three,' said Levenson. 'It adds to the pleasure.'

Elaine put her cue on the baize and said, 'Let's call it a draw.'

'That's fair,' said Howell.

'What do *you* do for exercise?' Lattner asked him.

'Nothing much,' he replied, watching Levenson replace his cue in the rack. 'I sail a bit.'

'I'm allergic to boats,' said Lattner. 'The last time I was in a boat was at Dunkirk nearly thirty years ago. I'd just got in when a bomb blew me out. That's where I smashed my leg. Funny thing—it only hurts in the summer. A sort of anniversary pain.'

'Come on,' said Elaine to Howell. 'You take over from me.'

'No, thanks,' he replied. 'I've got to do some work.'

'In that case,' she said, 'bless you all and good-night.'

After she had gone, Levenson carefully put the balls in the pockets, restored the cue-rests to their place, and said 'All set?'

'Howell says the only private place at Orme House is the squash court,' said Lattner. 'Do we have to go there? All these games are killing me,' he added.

'What's that?' Levenson said sharply. He wasn't in the mood for jokes.

'Nothing,' said Lattner. 'I think the squash court's a very good idea. We can talk in the spectators' gallery.'

'Come on,' said Levenson.

'It's a little bit musty, I have to warn you.' Howell's broad accent had returned.

'The situation itself is a bit musty,' said Lattner. 'You'd better lead the way.'

They walked in single file from the house to the ivy-covered squash court that lay on the far side of the walled garden, treading carefully over the uneven flagstoned path.

'Where are the lights?' Lattner called out to Howell when they pushed past the flush outer door.

'They're here,' he said, fumbling in the darkness at the side of the door jamb. The six switches were separate, and as each one clicked, the squash court itself flooded with an accumulating yellow light that threw shadows over the spectators' gallery. The door closed itself on a spring behind them, and they climbed the stairs to the bleak wooden benches overlooking the court.

'Chilly!' said Levenson. 'Is it ever used?'

'Not now,' said Howell. 'Not since the boys have been away. And Sir Geoffrey doesn't play any more.'

'Very wise,' said Lattner. 'Middle-aged men on squash courts are the undertaker's delight.'

Levenson took a seat in the second row resting his chin on the palm of his hand while the others sat in front.

'Did you get down to Portofino this year?' he asked Howell amiably.

'Yes,' Howell replied. 'We edged our way along the coast, taking it rather slowly. I've got quite a good fellow looks after the boat. A Portuguese—settled in Genoa—emigrated from there to Nice.'

'They're very good, the Portuguese,' said Levenson, talking easily as if they were still at the dinner table. 'We had a first-class Portuguese couple in Grosvenor Square.'

'Very good sailors too,' said Howell. He was observing Levenson warily as he circled around him with his conversational feints and passes.

126

'I saw your boat tied up at Cannes.'

'Antibes.'

'Was that it? Oh, yes, Antibes. . . . Yes . . . the *Dolphin*.'

'No, the *Triton*.'

'I wouldn't mind getting something for myself next year,' said Levenson. 'You must advise me.'

'Delighted,' said Howell. There was a pause as he waited for Levenson to continue.

'I really wanted to ask you about property down there,' Levenson said.

'It's not easy,' Howell replied. 'The Banque de Paris is very helpful, but even if you can borrow locally, the Bank of England, as you know, has first option on any surplus foreign exchange if you sell the assets. Then there's capital gains tax. It's not a very encouraging prospect.'

He was wondering if, after all, Levenson wanted to pick his brains rather than go on with his inquisition.

'I like to get these things right,' said Levenson, crossing his legs between the uncomfortable benches.

Howell took out his pipe and lit it.

'Always good to get things right.'

'Yes,' said Levenson. 'Let's get back to what I was asking you earlier on . . . remember? There's something about you, Howell, that puzzles me. You're an eminent chap—financial director of the company for the last five years—trusted right-hand man of Orme-Campbell, respected in industry, pal of Alf Budd, member of half a dozen Government advisory committees, C.B.E.—right?'

'That's it,' said Howell, forcing a confident note into his voice. 'I have no secrets from *Who's Who*.'

'No,' said Levenson. 'I would say that your integrity is above question—or at any rate, that no one would question it.'

'I hope not,' said Howell. The squash court with its anti-septic yellow surface and the brick walls behind them imprisoned him.

'Nobody,' Levenson went on, 'except an irreverent fellow like Lattner who's been going through your accounts.'

'My accounts?'

'O.C.E.'s accounts. This year's unpublished accounts.'

Howell sucked at his pipe with a popping sound before he replied.

'Leaving aside the insolence, I can't imagine that anybody outside our companies has the data—'

'Would you agree, Lattner?' Levenson interrupted, looking down at Lattner who was listening with his eyes shut.

'With what?' he asked.

'With my summing-up of Mr. Howell.'

'Yes and no,' said Lattner, opening his eyes and turning them on Howell's uneasy face. 'You see, I've been interested over the last three years in your O.C.E. *Société Anonyme* registered in Paris. And very well it does too. O.C.E. (S.A.) has a very interesting structure. You've got property, commercial radio, automobile interests, even publishing, as well as machines. Isn't that so, Howell?'

'That's right,' Howell answered. Now he felt more at ease, and his pipe was drawing nicely.

'I imagine,' Lattner went on, 'your French company gives you more elbow room for Treasury permission to export investment capital.'

'Naturally,' said Howell. He didn't like Lattner, but he had regard for his precise mind that expressed itself in a financial and economic language that he could understand.

'I suppose you go there and back quite a lot,' said Lattner.

'Yes—why?'

'To Paris?'

'Yes.'

Howell's eyes moved from Lattner to Levenson as if he were following the flight of a ball in the squash court below. The simple game needed his close attention.

'And Antibes—of course,' Lattner went on.

'Yes,' said Howell. 'I have a villa there—a very nice one too.'

He had said it defiantly, and immediately regretted it.

'That's just what I was saying,' said Levenson. 'Its market value is over £150,000.'

'I'm delighted to hear it,' said Howell.

'Budd's got a good eye for property,' said Lattner. 'I've always thought he chooses his friends by the size of their villas. He told me the Villa Howell is one of the finest on the Côte d'Azur.'

'What are you getting at?' Howell asked angrily. 'I resent these questions about my private affairs.'

'They're about public affairs,' said Levenson, taking over from Lattner. He stood up, a heavy shadow in the gallery, and his voice changed. 'You know very well what I'm getting at. Five years ago, O.C.E. got Treasury permission to transfer £200,000's worth of investment capital to the French firm— to build an administrative block. You might have raised the money on the French market, but someone—perhaps Budd— persuaded the Treasury to give permission. At any rate—you can correct me if I'm wrong—a lot of that advance went into building your villa.'

'That's a lie,' said Howell.

Levenson opened the brief-case that Lattner handed him, and laid a file on his knees.

'No, it's not a lie,' he said. 'The property company attached to O.C.E. (S.A.) built the villa, the Villa Howell. They then sold it to you for five million francs—about £48,000 or so— which you, in turn, borrowed from the firm at $2\frac{1}{2}$ per cent interest. An exceptionally low rate. Right?'

'I'm not answering questions. You're giving me information,' said Howell.

'Yes,' said Levenson. 'But it's old hat for you. You worked the whole deal.'

A bird nesting in the eaves and disturbed by the unfamiliar

light fluttered across the court with a flapping of wings that momentarily distracted the three men from their discussion.

'Is that the lot?' Howell asked, glancing from one of his inquisitors to the other.

'For the moment,' said Levenson.

'All right then,' Howell said flatly. He felt safer now that he knew the charge. 'In that case, you can have a few more facts. In the first place—' and he spoke the explosive consonants with venom—'the Treasury sanctioned the transfer of funds for property development.' With a self-congratulatory chuckle, he added, 'I saw to that myself. It's perfectly true that Budd helped. He happened to be Financial Secretary to the Treasury at the time so he had to sanction it. Anything wrong in that? We asked for permission to finance the building of a combined Head Office and rest house for our European administration. Budd O.K.'d it. What's wrong with that?'

'But then you took it over,' said Lattner. 'It's your property.'

'Now it is,' said Howell calmly. 'It was badly sited—access and communications were difficult. So I bought it—personally —and took it off the firm's hands. We—the Board—made a misjudgment.'

'I wish I could make such misjudgments,' said Levenson.

'Come off it,' said Howell. 'You make them all the time. But you know that these things can go wrong. . . . Believe me, I'm not the sort of chap who needs a villa in the South of France. For me, it's a white elephant.'

Lattner and Levenson looked quickly at each other.

'Who's responsible for looking after this white elephant?' Lattner asked. 'The Group?'

'Of course,' said Howell. 'They still use it. It's at their disposal. What are you getting at?'

'I'm getting at one simple point that affects you, Howell,'

said Levenson slowly. 'I'm saying that you as Financial Director haven't been running the Group in its best interests, and that, in at least one case, you've made use of it to do a deal that has brought you personally a capital benefit of something like £100,000. You will agree, that's nice going.'

Howell took his pipe from his mouth and cleared his throat.

'I don't see any reason,' he said, 'why I or any of us shouldn't benefit from good luck—or even insight.'

'That wasn't luck,' said Levenson coldly. 'Your horse was past the post when you betted. You betted with hindsight, not insight. You had access to the books. You fixed the deal. I'd say you've been milking the company.'

Howell stood up uncomfortably in the narrow space between the benches so that he was almost touching Levenson and Lattner. His right hand held the ash-hot bowl of his pipe, but he wasn't conscious of it. In front of him was Levenson, waiting for the counter to his insult, wary and determined, while Lattner studied the worn leather of the balustrade, apparently examining a brown tear that left the padding exposed.

'That's a very serious charge,' Howell said, listening to the booming of his own heart.

'Very serious,' said Levenson. Howell, he could see, was temporizing, searching for a formula that would answer the insult without deepening it. 'I don't think your shareholders would be very happy to have it spelled out for them.'

'I've done nothing without the approval of the Board,' said Howell defiantly.

'You mean Orme-Campbell's approval, as chairman and managing director. . . . He's incompetent,' said Levenson contemptuously, 'and getting worse in the last three years. Spends too much time on other matters.'

'I'm not concerned with his private affairs,' said Howell, waving the thought away with his right hand.

'How often was he at the Villa Howell last year with his young friends?' Levenson asked.

Howell didn't answer.

'Wouldn't I be right in saying, Howell, that you've been running the show for the last year or so?'

Howell took a step towards the exit.

'If I were you, Howell,' Levenson said sadly, 'I wouldn't leave yet. You see, your three-card-trick in connection with the villa is unimportant compared with another matter that Lattner wants to ask you about.'

'I'm not really interested in his police-court stuff,' said Howell, hesitating. 'Look here, Lattner. You and I have got two things in common—we're both provincials and we both know what the score is. I'm not on a charge, boy, and I've no intention of being on one.'

'No,' said Lattner. 'I can see that. But I just wanted to clear up one point with you. In the chairman's letter to shareholders advising them against our bid—and with the backing of your merchant bankers you forecast a profit of £5 million.'

'That's quite right,' said Howell.

Levenson shook his head.

'No, it's not quite right. Lattner and I have been having a look at those figures. You've put in the forecast £6 million of Government cash advance under the pre-production payments scheme for machine tool stock—and you've added £6 million for the stock itself.'

'What's wrong with that?'

'Oh, come off it, for God's sake. The Government subsidy is a repayable advance to encourage stock-holding in the slack season. It's not a fixed subsidy. And you damn well know it.'

Howell hesitated.

'Of course it's a subsidy. It's just a political fiction to call it a repayable advance. Everyone knows it's a disguised subsidy.'

'Not everyone,' said Levenson. 'I don't for one. You've deliberately fudged the picture.' His voice became savage. 'You claim you're going to make a £5 million profit on the basis of a Government subsidy. You're promising to pay dividends out of a subsidy—except that you don't let on it's a subsidy. I told you the truth at dinner, and you and Orme-Campbell know it. Tell him, Lattner. What's our projection for O.C.E.?'

'A £5 million *loss* this year,' said Lattner. 'Next year, £6 million.'

'So,' said Levenson, 'to hold off our bid, you and Orme-Campbell have put out a bloody great lie. You're on the way to a loss, and you call it a profit.'

' 'Our bankers—'

'To hell with that,' Levenson said in a rising voice. 'They go by the figures you give them. You've made a crooked forecast so that you can keep O.C.E. all cosy with everything ticking over as before, the capital assets dwindling, the closures postponed by a Government advance here and there, Orme-Campbell drawing his £35,000 a year plus benefits, and you doing very nicely thank-you-very-much in the middle. Is that a fair picture?'

'No,' said Howell.

'I'm not asking you,' said Levenson. 'Is that a fair picture, Lattner?'

'Fair?' said Lattner. 'It's more than fair. It's generous.'

'I'm not sure what you're getting at,' said Howell. He looked helplessly at Levenson. 'What—?'

'I'm not getting at anything,' said Levenson. 'I'm hoping that when we finish our talk you'll see for yourself what's got to be done. The Villa Howell—'

'My wife hates Antibes. She's a very unpretentious girl. Doesn't even speak the language—except what she's picked up—hasn't got any real friends—doesn't like the cooking—'

133

Levenson interrupted impatieutly, discarding the subject.

'I know all that. I don't care whether she likes bouillabaisse or roast beef. That's your affair. My affair begins when we talk about management.'

Howell's pipe had gone out, and he tried twice to relight it, but the tobacco wouldn't kindle.

'I'm not blaming you for the fraudulent prospectus.'

Levenson spoke as if the fact was established.

'You mustn't say that,' Howell said, shaking his head. 'That's defamatory.'

'It may be,' said Lattner, 'but it's true. You and Orme-Campbell hoped the cash advance would get lost among the figures. That was a bit optimistic. Now listen, Howell. I know you're in a jam.'

Howell opened his mouth to speak, but he felt a choking sensation at the back of his throat that prevented him from articulating. Levenson intervened, turning to Lattner as if Howell wasn't present, and said,

'It's no good putting all the weight on Howell. As financial director he's had to do a job for the Board and Orme-Campbell. When you get down to it, it's a question of management. Orme-Campbell imagined that because O.C.E. has run for a hundred years, it could run another hundred on its own momentum. It can't. It's run out of steam, like a lot else in British industry. The trouble with the Orme-Campbells is that they take too much for granted. They think the taxpayer owes them not just a living but their dividends as well.' He reflected. 'It's all out of date. We all know it. What's Orme-Campbell been doing over the last three years? Every other week, he issues a statement on Government policy. Oh, yes, Sir Geoffrey can't manage his own business, but he can run the country. Better than the Prime Minister, better than the Cabinet. Is there a crisis? Put Sir Geoffrey and Lord Hamblett and Lord Mayland on the telly with all the other boys from

"Renewal". He'll sit up there with his bloody supercilious smirk telling the whole world how it ought to be done. The trouble is he can't do it himself. You know what, Lattner? It's time someone told him.'

'How do you mean?' Howell asked, asserting himself into the conversation. In the darkness of the gallery, he had managed to recompose his face.

'I mean,' said Levenson sharply, 'it's time Orme-Campbell was told to go.'

'Go?'

'Yes, go—resign.'

'Resign?'

Howell repeated the word like an obscenity rejected by every convention, yet exciting in its utterance, a fantasy that had hitherto existed only for private and secret conversation, a paraphilia to be gloated over but not avowed, yet, once admitted, to be relished.

'That's it,' said Levenson. 'Go—resign—or be sacked.'

'It's impossible,' said Howell, and his judgment was a sigh, a renunciation. 'The whole firm has grown around the Orme-Campbells.'

'It stopped growing five years ago,' said Levenson, dismissing the tribute that had become traditional at every Board meeting of O.C.E. 'It's become stagnant. It's decaying. You've got to get rid of Orme-Campbell.'

'I could never do it,' said Howell, shaking his head. 'Never. He's been a very good friend to me, Levenson. It's out of the question.'

'Nothing's out of the question. The company's articles of association are explicit. Orme-Campbell only owns 12 per cent You have the right and power to get rid of him.'

'I can't do it,' said Howell, his voice rising. 'I've grown up in the firm. Sir Geoffrey helped me all the way. He's the god-father of my boys. Can't you see?' He fumbled with his pipe, discarded it, and shouted, as if he was shouting at his own temptation, 'I can't do it!'

Levenson shrugged his shoulders.

'O.K., it's up to you. But if you don't get rid of Orme-Campbell, someone else will.'

'Who?' Howell asked, quick and suspicious. 'Who?'

'Henderson-Kerr and Hamblett. They know my view. I'm seeing them together as soon as you leave us. If you're not with them, you're out.'

'It won't do you any good,' Howell said in a dull voice. 'Not a ha'porth of good. Budd's still in your way.'

'Is he?'

'Yes,' said Howell. 'He told Sir Geoffrey—'

'Let's leave that for later,' said Levenson. 'I can deal with Mr. Budd myself. This is *your* problem.'

'No, it's not my problem,' said Howell. 'It isn't in my hands.'

'You're not doing yourself justice,' said Levenson.

Howell raised his head and stared Levenson directly in the face.

'Look here,' he said. 'You're oversimplifying. O.E.C.'s got more than one defence. How would it be if someone came along tomorrow, say, and got enough voting shares—one way or the other—by a swap?'

Lattner put his leg over the wooden back of the seat, and laughed.

'Greg Stapleton? That Canadian fellow? It's a pipe-dream.'

Howell opened his mouth and closed it again.

'Who told you about Stapleton?' he said at last.

'Your fellow Dawson,' said Lattner coolly. 'He told Harry's chauffeur when he brought the documents over this afternoon. Strange how these things get about.'

'I shouldn't rely on Greg Stapleton,' Levenson added. 'I've known him a long time. He can't put up the cash.'

'He can put up shares,' said Howell. 'Orme-Campbell—'

'Orme-Campbell's dreaming,' said Levenson. 'Stapleton's looking for someone to bail *him* out. He approached us last week. . . . Oh, yes, he did. We said "No". They've got a big loss and a Government investigation coming up.'

'Is that a fact?'

'It's a fact. It's hopeless.'

'Yes,' said Howell, his face crumbling. 'That makes it look different.'

'When's he due?'

'Tonight—his plane's been delayed.'

'It'll be a sad sight,' said Lattner, grinning. 'Two con men trying to borrow money from each other.'

'All right, Lattner,' Levenson said harshly. 'That's enough of that. What I'm saying, Howell, is that if Orme-Campbell's relying on Stapleton, he hasn't a hope in hell. Look here. There isn't a lot of time to waste. Before I leave his house tonight, I want to be sure the deal's on.'

'What if Orme-Campbell could be persuaded to accept?'

Howell's voice was diffident, like that of a condemned man asking for a reprieve that he knew he would be denied.

'He won't,' Levenson said emphatically. 'He wants to die his own way. . . . Well, what's the position, Howell?'

Without looking at him, Howell said,

'I don't know. I don't know what to say. How would it be if you had a word first with Hamblett and Henderson-Kerr— let me know what they say—'

'They'll say,' said Levenson, 'what they've told me already. If you're in with them they're prepared to see Orme-Campbell off.'

'You mean we should ask him tonight?'

'That's it,' said Lattner, picking up his files and standing. 'Tonight.'

Surreptitiously, Howell wiped away a rivulet of sweat

137

which, despite the chilly air of the squash court, was trickling from his temple to his chin.

'I'm not promising anything,' he said.

'No,' said Levenson, looking at him with indifference. 'Neither am I. Lattner, see that all the lights are turned off.'

Chapter Nine

MISS Morgan, Orme-Campbell's secretary, slipped into the room and stood patiently waiting for Budd to turn his head. Surrounded and reflected by the ten Chinese mirror paintings framed in carved giltwood, he had fallen asleep with an illustrated book on his knees, his mouth open with a dribble of saliva at the corner, his arm swinging over the side of his chair as if with a single indignant movement it might destroy the vitrine and the fragile miniatures behind it.

A clock sounded the half-hour with a single ping, and he started up and, seeing her, said, 'Good Lord, what's the time? I dropped off.'

'It's pretty late,' she answered. 'The journalists want to know if there's likely to be a statement tonight. They're getting restless.'

'What does your boss say?'

'I haven't been able to get an answer from him. But I think they want to talk to you, not him. The TV people are down at the Orangery. Richmond and Parker are there too.'

In her pearl necklace, her hair neatly tied behind her head and her black dress, she looked as unruffled as if she had just reported for duty.

'How long have you been working for Orme-Campbell?' Budd asked her, standing.

'Eighteen years next November,' she replied, and her expression behind her glasses was detached, statistical.

'That's a long time,' said Budd.

'Yes,' she said, 'he's a very good employer and a very pleasant man.'

'Nice thing, that,' said Budd, pointing to a statuette of two ivory horsemen decorated with enamelled gold. Miss Morgan turned, and Budd put his arm around her shoulders.

'Not that one, love,' he said. 'That one over there.'

'Yes,' she said. 'They're very interesting—they were made by an eighteenth-century goldsmith called Dinglinger.'

'Dinglinger,' Budd echoed, smiling. 'That's a good name. Dinglinger! I take it you're an expert.'

'No,' said Miss Morgan. 'I know the house fairly well. I did the inventory a few years ago.'

Budd studied her for a second, and said, 'He's very lucky to have you. How is it that a pretty lass like you has escaped matrimony?'

Miss Morgan reddened, and said, 'Not everyone wants to get married.'

'You're dead right,' said Budd. 'How're you getting back to London?'

'I have my car,' she said.

'Well, that's all right, love. I was going to offer you a lift.'

He put his hand on her arm, and she stayed immobile, eyeing him steadily.

'What about the journalists?' she asked.

He withdrew his hand quickly, and said,

'O.K. Let's go and find them.'

*

The journalists in the sheltered patio outside the Orangery stood chatting in groups, interspersed between the myrtle tubs which had been brought out for the summer. Miss Morgan had arranged drinks for their long wait, and the TV team, drinking beer, talked together by the stone wall, while the men from the daily and financial papers were gathered by the path.

When Budd appeared with Miss Morgan, the conversation halted and the TV men turned on their lights which absorbed the yellow lamps of the Orangery in their incandescence, while the cameramen, having rushed up to Budd, marched backward in slow step as he advanced, their lenses steady as the rifle barrels of a firing squad. He waved his hands deprecatingly.

'Don't get excited, boys,' he said. 'I haven't got anything to tell you yet. This is just a social call.'

Parker, the sad-eyed correspondent of a Sunday paper who had known Budd for twenty years, said,

'Hello, Alf. How are things going?'

Budd grimaced.

'It isn't up to me,' he said. 'Not at this stage.'

Parker insisted. 'But if Levenson—'

'Well,' said Budd, and he drew Parker aside, 'the position, Jim, is this. Orme-Campbell's going to say "no". That's the simple fact that the Board will confirm. But if Levenson picks up the shares he's looking for, it's still going to be "no", because that's what I'm going to say.'

'How're you going to justify it?' said Parker.

'It's all there,' said Budd. 'A take-over at this stage would be against the public interest, and that's that.'

Parker insisted again.

'But that's not what the Prime Minister was saying yesterday in Norwich. He said mergers that increase the scale of production and competitiveness of industry are in the public interest. Do you think, Alf, that was a crack at you? After all, it's only three days since you made your own speech on the importance of medium-sized firms.'

He asked the question and made his comment with a sympathetic air, like a doctor explaining to a patient the nature of his malady. Budd thought for a moment, and said,

'I wouldn't be surprised, Jim. I wouldn't be surprised. It's a cut-throat game. All this is on lobby terms, of course?'

'Of course,' said Parker.

'Well,' said Budd reflectively, 'I don't need to spell it out for you.'

'No,' said Parker.

141

'Cranfield's been waiting for the opportunity to have a go at me.'

'Levenson's pretty close to him,' said Parker. 'Cranfield went out of his way to praise him at the Chequers industrial conference. I don't know if it's true—there's some talk about him getting a knighthood for export services.'

Budd frowned.

'It's possible,' he said. 'Anything to put my nose out of joint.'

'Why should he want to do that?' Parker asked, edging still further away from his fellow-journalists who were contemplating his intimate talk with bridled displeasure.

Budd chuckled.

'You ought to know by now, Jim. Cranfield doesn't like competitors. If there's a chance of putting in a bad word for me with the P.M., he will.'

Parker offered him a cigarette, and took one himself. As he lit it, he said,

'What time did you get here? Were you in the House this afternoon?'

'No,' said Budd. 'I left straight after lunch.'

There had been a diversion, an interval, a suburban distraction, when Westminster and Whitehall and Orme House had been as remote as the other side of the moon, and yesterday and tomorrow an inconceivable chronology, and Betty a name without content. Hidden from the afternoon sun in the crook of an arm, he had extinguished the midnight fears till the protective voice had said, 'I'll get you a cup of tea. The car's coming at six.' And that was a life ago.

'Anything new?' he said.

'I don't think so,' Parker said reflectively. 'Just one of those periodical buzzes about Government reshuffles and sackings.'

Budd stretched himself, and yawned so that his mouth looked like a choirboy's in song.

'It's the first I've heard about it. Who're they talking about?

'To begin with—you,' said Parker, carefully watching Budd's reaction.

'They always begin with me,' said Budd coolly. 'Let's get back to the chaps.'

Seeing that he had detached himself from Parker's monopolization, the other journalists surged back around him, and Budd singled out for special attention a surprised young lobby-man whom he had met at a regional conference. It was his way of establishing his easy connection with the press. During the young man's stutterings of pleasure, it also gave him a chance to think about the rumours.

*

At Question Time the previous week, it had been generally noticed that when a backbencher had asked the Prime Minister a provocative 'supplementary' about the 'energies dispersed by the Minister of Industrial Reconstruction in attendance at public banquets', the Prime Minister, instead of slapping him down, had replied that his Rt. Hon. Friend was perfectly capable of looking after his own gastronomic arrangements', a retort that seemed at once disowning and derogatory and had been greeted with a howl of approbation and delight from the whole House, though leaving the Chamber, Trevor had given him a reassuring and friendly smile. But after Budd had made a major speech on 'Technology and Change', which the General Secretary of the T.U.C. had publicly commended, Trevor had sent him a note, not of congratulation but of rebuke for encroaching on the territory of the Minister of Technology without clearing the speech with him first.

That had both surprised and hurt.

The general strategy that Cranfield, as number two, had been dictating was becoming clear. As the older members of the Government disappeared through illness or political decrepitude, so he recommended his personal favourites to the P.M., shuffling them into the higher echelons where, in turn, they crowded out the survivors of the old dispensation. And now, all who remained of the post-election period when the Prime Minister had found it necessary to placate the interests with an internal coalition based on geography and affiliations, were Haworth, Burgess, Jones, Lidgard and Botteril. They were a rag-bag. It was a sentence Budd often used to himself when he contemplated the difficulties of change. 'Europeans', 'Atlanticists', 'Expansionists', 'Restrictionists'—they covered the whole spectrum of conflicting political thought.

Cranfield wanted Trevor to extinguish the succession, and Budd had long learnt how to identify the graph of his own political fortunes. It wasn't by public opinion polls or even by press comment. They were usually a week or two out of date. When he was in favour, he observed that his colleagues greeted him with a special enthusiasm in the corridors or in the Smoking Room. When he was in trouble, they would sniff, then draw away, like dogs that circle and abandon an animal lying sick. And in the last few days, Budd had noticed that the salutes of his colleagues in the Government had become more perfunctory. They didn't dawdle.

In a way, it didn't matter. In the two years that he had been Minister of Industrial Reconstruction, he had made many connections in industry and the City. He could always rely on Orme-Campbell. But there were others too—Lord Mayland, Frobisher, Harley-White, Carrick.

Below the treble of the journalists' chatter, Budd was thinking in a contrapuntal bass that if he left the Government, a new freedom would open up for him. In the City, he could earn £20,000—perhaps even £30,000. Of course, he would provide for Betty—and generously. Perhaps they would live in the country. Perhaps he would go to the Lords—but only after Betty gave him a divorce.

Once upon a time, he had wanted power. But after getting power, he found that its satisfactions, though many, were almost exhausted. It would be pleasant to be a private person again, to have friends for the gratification of their company and not for their potential use, to travel where and when he liked. How much longer could all this continue? The nightly battles, the daily resurrections. He could scarcely count the years in politics that lay behind him, and they had all dissolved and disappeared, and he could scarcely remember what had happened or what he had achieved. Others had grown old and died. And the register grew longer of former Ministers, moving in a pallid decline from the front benches to the back benches, metamorphosed sometimes into peers, but in the end fading like shadows in the sunlight of their successors.

But he wasn't going to be pushed out. If he went, he'd go in his own time. Despite himself, Budd was disturbed by Parker's gossip, although he had become used to the recurring press reports of breaches between himself and the Prime Minister, which usually had no basis except in some disagreement resolved after a few sulky days. Besides, the Prime Minister, not to mention Cranfield, had more to fear from him than he from the Prime Minister. He'd be an awkward man to have on the back benches.

'Would you be in favour, Alf, of a new Trades Union Disputes Act that would bring the unions up to date?'

The young journalist was becoming familiar. Budd turned his back on him. The journalist repeated his question.

'Use your loaf, man!' Budd said to the startled face.

He strolled to one of the myrtle trees, and breathed deeply and wanted the night to be over so that he could get back to London and have it out with the Prime Minister. The Levenson bid was the sticking-point, and he wondered why Trevor had chosen to quarrel with him on an unpopular issue. The unions would oppose the bid, and he knew that his own strength had always lain in going along with the unions. Whenever there had been a national labour dispute, the P.M. had always sheltered behind him. It was the reason Budd had felt secure.

And yet his confidence was threaded with anxiety. For several days, he had received no direct word from the Prime Minister. Instead, there had been the story, obviously leaked to at least two papers, that the Cabinet was divided on its mergers policy, and that Budd had decided to challenge the Prime Minister on the Levenson bid. At the time, it hadn't been true, but imperceptibly he had found himself nudged towards a position in which to have retreated from his support of Orme-Campbell would have been publicly interpreted as a humiliating failure and a cause for resignation. He had asked Grayforth, Jones and Porson what they thought the P.M. and Cranfield were up to. But they had been bland, and that was the end of it.

*

He came face to face with Levenson in the lime avenue.

'Hello, dear boy,' he said cheerfully. 'I thought you'd gone home.'

Levenson paused, observing Budd's face in the half-light that reached through the trees from the Orangery.

'Oh, no,' he said easily. 'When I begin something, I like to see it through.'

'Well, as far as I'm concerned,' said Budd, 'if they don't get a move on, I'm going home myself. I don't like waiting on the doorstep.'

'It's a pleasant doorstep,' said Levenson, gazing at the house which, with its brilliantly lit windows, was like a great liner in a calm sea. 'I've often waited on others—much less attractive.'

'What's new?' Budd asked.

Levenson took a cigar from his pocket, prepared it, and carefully lit it.

'There's a certain amount of movement,' he said in between puffs. 'A certain amount of interviewing and so on.'

146

'To hell with that,' said Budd. 'I'm going straight in to see Orme-Campbell, and I'm going to tell him that if he doesn't get a move on, I'm going back to London.'

'You can't hurry these things,' said Levenson. 'I'm not in a hurry.'

Budd glanced at him suspiciously.

'What's got into you, old chap?' he asked. 'You look as if you've been at the cream.'

'What cream?' Levenson asked. Then changing from his bantering manner into a direct challenge, he said, 'Look here, Alf. Why don't you chuck it? You're just leading Orme-Campbell into the ditch.'

'I don't know what you mean.'

'I'll spell it out for you,' said Levenson. 'You know—or if you don't you ought to know—that O.C.E. can't go on without a complete overhaul—a new injection of capital—the lot.'

Budd stopped walking, pulled himself up, and said,

'That's not my information. It isn't the advice my people have given me. Their forecast is a thumping great profit and a substantial dividend next year.'

'Out of capital,' said Levenson.

The Ministerial expression that Budd had assumed, stiffened.

'That's an unpleasant slander,' he said. 'I don't think, Levenson, we ought to continue.'

'On the contrary,' said Levenson, 'I think we ought to.' His voice became hard. 'You see, you may have a few disagreeable surprises coming to you.'

'For example?' Budd asked watchfully.

'You may find in the next hour or so that I'm not alone in my view.'

'Would you be prepared to repeat to Orme-Campbell what you just said?'

'Certainly not. I'm just warning you that if Orme-Campbell paid a "substantial dividend"—those were your words—he could only do so out of capital. Because there's nothing else he could pay it out of. Not a damn thing. Listen, Budd, I know that firm inside out. I'm advising you not to get into a mess.'

'Why do you think Orme-Campbell's fighting you?'

'Why? I'll tell you. It isn't for money. God knows, he's not a poor man—and besides, he's got a lot of other things on his plate.'

'Well, if it isn't for money, you tell me what it's all about.'

'It's for prestige—pride—stubbornness—it's to keep his hand on something that belongs to his family. . . . It's to prove he's as good a man as his father and all the rest of the Campbells, and much better than the Levensons.'

'What's wrong with that?'

'Everything. It doesn't make sense for a hundred thousand workers who want to keep their jobs—who are in the hands of an old-fashioned, clapped-out absentee management.'

'Absentee?'

'Yes—I've calculated that in the last three years, Orme-Campbell has spent an average five months of the year abroad. But that isn't the main point. I want to give you this warning, Budd—and I'm giving it to you now not in your interest, but in Orme-Campbell's. And if you think of him as a friend, you'll take it to heart. . . . If you go on advising him against our offer—'

'I don't like sentences that begin with "if".'

'—if you go on advising him against our offer, I tell you he won't last another six weeks at O.C.E.'

They walked on for a few paces, till Budd said,

'We've been talking about Orme-Campbell. Tell me, Levenson, why are you so keen on getting O.C.E.?—Altruism?'

'No.'

'Because you think it'll make both firms more efficient?'

'Partly—yes.'

148

'You like the idea of power.'

'I like to have it. It isn't everything.'

'Well, tell me what else there is. Why should a chap like you who's already doing better than in his wildest dreams twenty years ago—why should you want to take on a fight like this? Do you like punch-ups?'

'No,' said Levenson. 'I was last pushed into a fight when I was fourteen. Look, that's when I got my broken nose. It was my last year at school in Hackney. They had me against a wall. Mind you, Budd, they taught us a bit about boxing at the Boys' Club. We needed it.'

'Well, if you're not taking on Orme-Campbell for exercise, why the hell are you doing it? No, don't tell me. I'll tell you.'

Levenson watched him with curiosity as Budd puckered his eyebrows and said deliberately,

'You're doing it for the wife.'

Levenson thought for a moment.

'That's an interesting point, Budd. You know, my wife—I've never said this to anyone—perhaps I'm telling it to you because it's the middle of the night—but since I got married, I've measured everything I've done by what Isobel would think of it—whether she'd approve. I don't mean the practical part of doing things. I mean the result.'

'You're very lucky,' said Budd. 'It's a great help.'

'It's more than a help,' said Levenson. 'It's a purpose. You see, we haven't had any children. You've got—?'

'Three.'

'Three. That must be very satisfying. On the other hand, not having children has thrown us very much together. It's made us share our experiences in every possible way.'

'Your wife's a very lovely woman,' said Budd. 'You're lucky.'

'Oh, it's a case of choosing my luck,' said Levenson comfortably. 'I had to chase her for months.'

'It shows she's fastidious.'

'I like to think so,' said Levenson. 'It's what I admire most in her. The way she keeps them off.'

'She must be a great asset to you,' said Budd. 'Entertaining —all that. You haven't been married very long?'

'A few years,' said Levenson. 'I married quite late in life. I wanted to be sure.'

'And you are.'

'Absolutely.'

'Well,' said Budd, 'most men would envy you. You've done very well for yourself—you've got a beautiful wife—you've got everything. . . . Just don't be too hard on Orme-Campbell.'

He was silent for a few moments. Then he smiled amiably to Levenson and went on, 'You know, old chap, what it says in the Old Testament—I take it you know your Bible.'

'I know it well,' Levenson said. 'Not quite so well as I used to—but pretty well.'

'You remember—"he that diggeth a pit for others" . . . .' He had become stern and evangelical.

'Yes,' said Levenson easily. 'It's a passage that I keep carefully in the front of my mind.'

Their conversation was interrupted by Girling, Orme-Campbell's manservant, who approached, hobbling urgently from the main entrance, and gabbling his message before he reached them.

'There's a telephone call,' he said. 'For you, Mr. Budd.'

'Who is it?' Budd asked curtly.

'It's from Number Ten Downing Street,' Girling said, lowering his voice.

'I see,' said Budd. His face became thoughtful, and then he smiled.

'I shouldn't keep him waiting,' said Levenson.

Budd straightened his jacket, and hurried off.

*

'Darling Isobel,

'I've just been talking about you. And you wouldn't guess who to. Please don't be angry. It was to Budd. And the reason I was talking about you to Budd was that it's halfway through the night—early morning, I suppose—and he was there and there was no one else I could talk to.'

Alone in the waiting-room, Levenson passed his fingers over the embossed heading, and thought that he would like to have a similar stamp for Marfield. Then he went on.

'I feel rather guilty writing to you on Orme-Campbell's paper. It's a bit like being a bailiff's man, and using the domestic crockery. As at this moment, the O.C.E. chaps are scattered all over the place in huddles. This house is huge. I don't think, somehow, you'd like to run it. There's something creepy about it tonight, as if everyone's died off and disappeared for one reason or another. Even Elaine's got something peculiar about her. I don't mean just her little stutter and that particular brand of smart sarcasm that she and her friends specialize in. I mean you get the feeling all the time that she and Orme-Campbell aren't really a married couple. They're more like conspirators. I know you'll think that strange, but that's how they strike me.

'Do you know why I'm writing to you now? It's because I'm feeling lonely. I've sent Lew off because I want him to get things fixed up for tomorrow. At the moment, I'm sure the Budd-Orme-Campbell alliance can't last. I've got a hunch that Budd is in big trouble with the Prime Minister. It's the last round between him and Cranfield, and the P.M. is at last going to come down on Cranfield's side. As for Orme-Campbell and Budd, they're like two sick men leaning on each other.

'But I didn't sit down to write about Budd. I'm staying here because I want to see things through. The reason I'm writing to you is to tell you what I always want to tell you when I am with you alone but can't quite get the words out. I want you to know that I love you, Isobel. More than anything I've ever known. More than my mother and father, or even my sister who died. And when I look at myself in a looking-glass, I always think, "How could that beautiful girl love an ugly brute like me?" Because at night, when you turn to me, half-asleep, you sometimes say, "I love you," and I'm afraid to answer in case it isn't me you mean.

'I never wanted to be married before I met you. I loved my family, and was all tied up with my responsibilities. There were all sorts of girl-friends who passed through my life, and then there was you, your face that I could never open, your head that was filled with so much that I could never know, and your body that made me wish that I had never had anyone else and could start all over again.

'I don't believe a woman can be seduced. A woman can only be taken if she *gives* herself. And I like to think that you gave yourself to me, and that is what is important in my life. All the money in the world would be no compensation if I were to lose you. And if I am greedy about you, it's because I'm afraid.

'Yes, I'm afraid. Not of people—not of the Orme-Campbells, the politicians or the hard men I meet every day. I'm only afraid that you might one day disappear from my life acci-dentally, like the way you came into it.

'Well, darling, that's enough for this hour in the morning. I can hear movement outside, and I'd better stop. I just wanted you to know that in the middle of all this, I'm thinking of you and loving you. I send you lots and lots of kisses.'

Levenson blotted the letter, re-read it, frowned, then tore it gravely into small pieces.

Chapter Ten

As the three men entered, Orme-Campbell at the mahogany desk went on writing, his forehead glistening under the single light of the green table lamp that left the rest of the study in shadow. They stood in front of him, waiting for him to finish the sentence he was writing in the foliate calligraphy which he had cultivated as a schoolboy and never abandoned.

'Won't be a minute,' he said, without looking up. 'I'm drafting a press statement we might use later.'

He finished the sentence and leaned back in the studded red leather swivel chair that had belonged to his great-grandfather.

'Any news of Stapleton?' he asked Howell.

'His plane hasn't landed yet,' Howell answered, riffling the pages in his hand. 'That's all I know.'

'Not very satisfactory,' Orme-Campbell said, rising and stretching himself in what seemed like an endless uncoiling of muscles and limbs till he swelled to the full volume of his great height, towering over the others who shrank as he expanded, the hollow top of the lampshade throwing his imperial jowls into an elaborate chiaroscuro.

'Greg Stapleton? That's a new one. I didn't know we were expecting Stapleton,' said Hamblett, heaving himself into an armchair and adjusting his stomach into a comfortable position. 'What's he got to do with it?'

Orme-Campbell exhaled with a weary satisfaction.

'Don't be impatient, dear boy,' he said. 'You look like the three witches in all this gloom.'

He strode over to the door, and turned on the lights, including the chandelier.

'That's much better,' he said. 'Now listen. This is just a draft that we can muck about with before Greg arrives. I'll have it copied and distributed before the meeting.'

He picked up the quarto sheet and, sitting on the edge of the table, put on his glasses and began to read.

'The board of Orme-Campbell Engineering announces that their holdings of Stapleton (Canada) Engineering Co. ordinary shares, together with the holdings of O.C.E., represent more than 51 per cent of the total voting capital of O.C.E. They are all satisfied that a merger with Levenson's on the terms proposed by Mr. H. Levenson would not be in the interests of O.C.E.'

Orme-Campbell looked over his glasses to see their reaction Howell, blank and haggard, stood with his head drooping, preoccupied with the design of the carpet. Hamblett looked back impassively as if he didn't understand. And Henderson-Kerr was smiling benevolently like a family solicitor listening to an optimistic litigant.

'Yes,' he said. 'Yes.'

It was a mark of attention rather than agreement. Orme-Campbell went on reading.

'The board of O.C.E. will convene an extraordinary general meeting of its shareholders to increase its ordinary share capital for the purpose of acquiring certain important interests of Stapleton (Canada) Engineering upon terms being worked out.'

When he finished, he took off his glasses and waited for the comments of the other three.

'Well?' he asked.

There was another silence before Henderson-Kerr commented with cautious scepticism, 'A very imaginative suggestion. But aren't you jumping the gun a bit? Does the bride —or rather the bridegroom—know about the proposal?'

'Stapleton?' said Orme-Campbell. 'My dear fellow, that's why he's coming tonight.'

'How long have you been cooking this up?' Hamblett asked. 'Don't you think I might have been let in on the—the project?'

'Well,' said Orme-Campbell contentedly, 'you mustn't take it personally. I didn't want it to go off at half-cock. I've been thinking about it and discussing it with Stapleton in Montreal since last Friday. We've had about ten really long talks on the phone. When he heard that Levenson was pressing us, he got in touch with Bryce, Pearson, and they got in touch with our people. He had an idea we might do a deal to hold Levenson off if everything else failed. They started buying voting shares through Bryce, Pearson, and with another ten per cent lying around plus our own holdings, I believe we can block our friend Mr. Levenson for good and all.'

'Ten per cent?'

'About that.'

'Are you sure?'

'Well, I think so,' said Orme-Campbell. 'I think so.'

'You mean,' said Henderson-Kerr, 'it needs confirmation.'

'Yes.'

'What's the Government's view—the Take-over Panel's—Budd's?'

'I don't know. We'll have to see. I think it'll be O.K. Budd's on our side.'

'So what you have in mind,' said Hamblett, 'is to raise our ordinary share capital to acquire what you call "certain important interests" in Stapleton, so that they in turn can buy themselves with our stock into a joint majority in O.C.E. Right?'

'That's it.'

'But who has valued the "important interests" of Stapleton?' said Henderson-Kerr.

'We'll take his word for the time being,' said Orme-Campbell. 'His word, the balance sheets, the Stock Exchange, his banker's readings, the projections. . . . Isn't that good enough?'

'The Treasury mightn't think so,' Howell muttered.

Annoyed at his intervention, Orme-Campbell said sharply, 'If his word's not good enough, the Treasury will take mine. What are you getting at, Howell? We've gone into all this. You've been in this from the start.'

'I've learnt a bit more about it in the last few hours,' said Howell. 'Did you know Stapleton's government contracts are being investigated by a special commission at Ottawa? That there's a Government claim for twenty million dollars going back three years?'

For a few moments Orme-Campbell didn't answer.

'Who told you that?' he said at last. 'Levenson?'

Without returning his glance, Howell said, 'We'd better have this out.'

'Who are you working for, Howell?' Orme-Campbell insisted. 'Levenson or me?'

'Neither,' said Howell. 'The group.'

He became bolder.

'I don't know if Stapleton will be in time for our meeting or not. What I'm now certain about is that this is a piece of self-hypnotism. Stapleton's in trouble. It's a fact. You want him to bail you out, and he wants you to bail him out. And you're planning to do it by papering our stock to take over his "important assets". But they're just not there. You know it, and I know it. You want us all to take in each other's washing, but it's all threadbare. We're in trouble.' He turned to the other two. 'We know we're in trouble. You may hate Levenson's guts, but he's got the assets, the management skills and the energy. . . . Face it, Geoffrey. You're a tired man. You've been a tired man for the last three years.'

He stopped and lit a cigarette, his face white and his hand trembling. Then, putting on a pair of spectacles and taking them off, turning the frames like a bandleader's mace around the long joints of his left hand, he waited. Orme-Campbell glanced from Hamblett to Henderson-Kerr, who sat neutrally, waiting for him to reply, their eyes level with his large, soft hands covered with fair hair and patterned with freckles, the nails spatulate and cared-for, the gold signet ring with a flat bezel an opulent distinction. Their immobile faces said that it wasn't their fight, that they found brawling distasteful and that they didn't intend to interfere. In the arrested moment after Howell's outburst, only Orme-Campbell's fingers moved, slowly and thoughtfully, against the edge of his loose dark jacket.

'I think you're having one of your breakdowns,' he said to Howell.

Then he laughed, and his laugh released the others from their pose of detachment. He walked towards the window and parted the curtains, straining to see the headlights of the car that would bring Stapleton, his broad back and wide rump crouched in a suppliant position between the heavy brocades.

'Any sign of Stapleton?' Henderson-Kerr asked, looking at his watch.

Orme-Campbell turned around and said, 'I can't see any.' He frowned, and added, 'We may have to postpone our meeting. I'd hoped—'

'We'd all hoped,' said Henderson-Kerr, pausing to gulp at the inhaler that he had inserted in his mouth, 'we'd all hoped Levenson would back down. He hasn't and that's point number one.'

'And point number two?' asked Orme-Campbell.

'Point number two is that Budd's not going to be any use at all in stopping him.'

'Rubbish,' Orme-Campbell said. 'He promised—'

'I'm not interested in what Budd promised,' Hamblett intervened. 'I've got nothing against Alf. He means well. But it's no use relying on him, Geoffrey. Have you spoken to the press boys—Parker, Hopkins, Bodley?'

'No,' said Orme-Campbell. 'I've refused to see them—at any rate till we'd come to some decision. I asked them to wait.'

Henderson-Kerr relit his cigar while Orme-Campbell waited for him to continue.

'I shouldn't really smoke these things,' he panted. 'You know what they're saying,' he went on, absorbed in drawing his cigar into a glow. 'They're saying Budd's out.'

'Out?' said Orme-Campbell.

'Out,' said Hamblett. 'Out—fired—sacked.'

'How do they know?' Orme-Campbell asked.

'They always know,' said Hamblett. 'They say the P.M. was trying to track him down the whole evening. He only just got him. It's one of his complaints about Budd. Says he never leaves an address. At any rate, they know what he wanted him for. They always know. They're saying the P.M. has offered him a governorship in the Caribbean or somewhere.'

'It sounds like a joke,' said Orme-Campbell dismissively.

'Yes, it does, doesn't it? The P.M.'s a humorous sort of fellow.'

'It must be a joke,' said Orme-Campbell firmly. 'The Party wouldn't wear it for a minute, if he tried to fire Alf.'

Hamblett chuckled, a rumbling chuckle that ended in an explosive coughing.

'They'll tolerate anything once they get used to it,' he said. 'But they'll tolerate Budd getting the sack better than they'll tolerate most things. They've had to put up with a lot from that little monster. In any case, they're not going to cry about our friend Budd when they remember how he wiped out old Burnaby at the Party meeting ten years ago.'

'That was inevitable,' Henderson-Kerr said judicially. 'He was past it.'

'So he was,' said Hamblett. 'So he was. But Budd was his protégé—his friend. Budd should have backed him. Instead of which, he said—very nobly—"We all owe something to this great Movement of ours. And when the time comes, we must

158

be ready to sacrifice even ourselves." Oh yes, I remember it well! It was in Committee Room 14—he hadn't been long in the House—and all the Shadow Cabinet were peeing themselves with excitement at brash young Alf bringing the spirit of youth to the Party. Then he turned on poor old Burnaby, and said, "It is right that the young should help their seniors, but it is wrong for the old to sit on the young. For the Party's sake, they must give way and not blackmail today's generation with sentimentality over what should be dead and buried." Oh, it was cruel all right. He didn't mention Burnaby—just said that he meant outmoded ideas. There's nothing sentimental about our Alf. At any rate, as I was saying, no one's going to cry over Budd. He got arrogant, you know, and when they get like that, they pass through a phase when their arrogance becomes a cult. Ebullience, bonhomie—those toadying political journalists will always find a word for it. But that doesn't last long either. . . . A politician's cult soon becomes a bore. . . . And that's when people begin to turn.'

No one spoke, and Hamblett, after another puff at his cigar, went on.

'There's a lot of loyalty in the trade unions, but that has its limits too. A chap like Budd can't insult more than a certain number of people without at some time getting his come-uppance. He tried it on young Hughes. Well, young Hughes is now young middle-aged Hughes, and when he called Alf a charlatan at York a month ago, there wasn't a squeak of protest. He just said what everyone was—'

As if his physical presence had been conjured up by the discussion, Budd entered and stood with his hands in his pockets. His face was flushed around the cheekbones, leaving the area from his hair to the bridge of his nose strangely pale.

'You wouldn't be talking about me by any chance?' he began truculently.

'We're always talking about you,' said Hamblett in his

jollying-along voice. 'Everyone's always talking about you. You wouldn't like it if they didn't, Alf.'

Budd looked back at him mournfully, his cheeks sagging like a boxer dog's.

'You can keep that crap for the shareholders at one of your bucket-shop meetings,' he said.

Wrenching his mouth till the teeth appeared, though his eyes were expressionless, Hamblett said,

'That's what we find so lovable in you, Alf. Always *le mot juste.*'

'I said "crap",' Budd repeated. 'Do you find it inappropriate?'

After a moment, Hamblett said, 'No. I think it's a very good word—not a word to use in church but an omnibus word—very good, Alf—very good.'

Orme-Campbell gave him a hostile stare, and then turned back to Budd, with a friendly smile.

'Take a seat, Alf. I thought you might like to hear about our new proposal for reconstructing O.C.E.'

'Not now,' said Budd. 'Another time—yes, another time. I came to say "good-night" to you. I've got to go back to town. I'm sorry, Geoffrey, there's a bit of a flap at No. 10. Perhaps you'd walk me to my car.'

'What's all the rush?' asked Orme-Campbell, hauling himself to his feet. 'Is there—' His sentence trailed away, and Budd's eyes traversed the faces of Howell, Henderson-Kerr and Hamblett, who observed him with the detached curiosity of spectators looking at the accused from the public gallery of a court-room.

'We can leave our friends,' Budd said, 'to get on with the rehearsal.'

The three directors rose to their feet as Budd put his hand on the door knob.

'Rehearsal?' Orme-Campbell asked.

Without bidding the others good-bye, Budd, ushered by

Orme-Campbell, waddled with his short legs into the corridor.

'What sort of rehearsal, Alf?' Orme-Campbell asked him as they walked. Budd took his arm, and said in a loud voice,

'They're rehearsing a murder, old chap—yours. All these comings and goings. They're planning to murder you, Geoffrey. You'll see.'

'What sort of weapons?' Orme-Campbell said, entering into what he called in his own mind, 'Budd's fun-and-games'. 'Old Hamblett couldn't hit a wall at five paces. Howell couldn't light a firework. He tried to when my boys were young. And Henderson-Kerr—'

'It's murder all right,' Budd insisted as he walked carefully down the steps to the main hall, putting his small feet, incongruous beneath his fat calves and thighs, delicately in front of each other. 'It's a night for murder. According to the zodiac. . . . I'm Taurus, you know . . . it's a night for getting people—not with guns, knives—nothing like that.'

His sentences, though emphatic, had a caesura every few syllables.

'You realize Levenson's been at them,' he said.

'Oh, they're all right,' said Orme-Campbell, guiding Budd past the manservant in the hall towards his chauffeur in the cap and blue serge suit who was waiting for him. Budd halted and faced him.

'Like hell they are. Just you watch out, Geoffrey. They're out to get you just like Cranfield's out to get me. But I tell you there's nothing doing. I'm not going. I've still got a lot of friends—a lot of them.'

He had switched the subject from Orme-Campbell to himself, and some of the chauffeurs waiting in the shadows clustered together to hear what he was saying.

'If Trevor wants to get rid of me, he'll bloody well have to say it right out so the Party can judge. . . . I'm not going to be pushed sideways. . . . If he kicks me out, I'm going to tread on every corn he's got.'

'He'd never do it,' said Orme-Campbell. 'Never. . . . If he tried to get rid of you, half the Party at least would be up in arms. He'd have to explain himself to industry as well as the T.U.C. No—don't give it a thought, Alf. . . . But one quick word about our own arrangements. I think we can't come to any definite conclusion tonight. I had hoped we'd get Greg Stapleton out from Montreal tonight.'

'Stapleton?' Budd said, and Orme-Campbell saw that his face was stony. 'Why didn't you tell me he was coming? He's an old chum of mine.'

'So much the better,' said Orme-Campbell. 'I didn't want you to feel in any way involved in the preliminaries. God knows, Alf—you've got enough enemies already to mis-interpret your associations. I'd hoped—anyway, Stapleton can't be here till tomorrow, and you're quite right, I'm having some trouble with Howell and company.'

'They want to murder you,' said Budd, relapsing into his gloomy tone. 'It's a night for murder. What are you going to do about them?'

'We'll have to see,' said Orme-Campbell. 'This isn't the first time—I'll cope all right.'

'That's it,' Budd said wrily. 'Keep calm, keep fit, keep going.'

Orme-Campbell shook hands with Budd, and Budd held his hand firmly, unwilling to lose its friendly assurance.

'Shall we talk tomorrow morning?' Orme-Campbell asked. 'I'm sorry it hasn't been very conclusive.'

'He phoned me, you know,' said Budd, following his own train of thought and shaking his head in time to the continuing handshake. "You can have Bermuda," he said. And I said, "Not on your nelly." And he said, "We'd better have another word together." And I said, "Better make it three or four. I'm coming right back to London".'

'He wanted you to be Governor of Bermuda?' Orme-Campbell asked incredulously.

'That's what the little bastard offered me. I said to him, "Look here, Trevor, you can stick it"—and he said, "It was good enough for my father to be a Colonial Governor, Alf, why not you?" So I said to him, "I'm not your father".'

The two men laughed and Orme-Campbell shut the car door as Budd took his seat at the back of the limousine, but with an afterthought, the Minister wound down the window and said,

'One last thing, Geoffrey.' He lowered his voice. 'If things don't turn out right—'

It was a query rather than a statement.

'Don't worry, Alf,' said Orme-Campbell. 'I gave you my promise.'

They scrutinized each other, locked in their mutual hopes and reassurances.

Budd nodded good-bye and, taking his Despatch Box on his knee, began to study the Departmental papers which were to occupy him on the journey to London.

'Bermuda!' Orme-Campbell repeated to himself as he watched the car draw away. The Prime Minister was undoubtedly a whimsical fellow.

*

Elaine joined Orme-Campbell at the door and, following Budd's car with her glance till its rear lights faded into the darkness, said,

'What's the matter with Alf? He went off like a bat out of hell.'

She didn't expect an answer, but Orme-Campbell replied,

'He made the mistake of being in the wrong place at the wrong time.'

'Would it have made any difference where he might have been?'

'Yes—there's a Law of Organizations—the one who isn't there is always wrong. There's no one in the Government who'd have a row with Alf face to face.'

'The P.M.?'

'Him least of all.'

'Oh, well,' said Elaine, 'I always thought politics a dirty business.'

Orme-Campbell shook his head slowly.

'It isn't just politics that's dirty. When men are fighting for power—it's like sex. There are rules—but how many keep them? And if someone breaks the rules how can you ever trust them again? A woman who betrays her husband will betray her lover too. And that goes for business and politics as well. Isn't that right?'

'You tell me,' said Elaine, drawing her silk stole around her shoulders. 'It's getting chilly. How long are you going on for?'

'I don't know,' said Orme-Campbell. 'You see, Elaine, I'm afraid the agenda isn't working out quite as I planned it.'

'I wouldn't worry about that,' she said crisply. 'Nothing ever works out as one plans it. But I must say I'll be glad when everyone's gone. It's impossible to walk into a room without falling over a lot of strange men drinking—or some rather casual character lying about the kitchens—or Miss Morgan fretting about with her notebook. And on top of that, Levenson and Lattner have been wandering in the corridors like Rosencrantz and Guildenstern. What are they waiting for?'

Orme-Campbell led her by the elbow towards the staircase, and said,

'It can't be long now. I'd hoped to tell Levenson once and for all where he got off, but there are some complications.'

'Like what?'

'Oh,' said Orme-Campbell, and his exclamation came out as a prolonged sigh. 'Like Howell and Hamblett and Henderson-Kerr doing a little fiddle together, and Greg Stapleton not turning up.'

'But he will, of course?'

Her husband had spoken to her of Stapleton as the second long-stop, and for the last two days the name 'Stapleton' first whispered and made mystery of, then transmuted into a magical formula, had become an incantation designed to frustrate Levenson and his associates. During their nightly talks when for Elaine's benefit Orme-Campbell went over the discussions he had had with his financial advisers, bankers and political friends during the day, and analysed the press and radio reports of Levenson's forays and proclaimed strategy, the possibility that Stapleton wouldn't turn up had never crossed their minds.

'He'll turn up all right,' said Orme-Campbell. 'The question is, "will the train or our hero get there first?"'

'Where?'

'It doesn't matter. Have you talked to Levenson?'

'Talked to him? I've been with him most of the evening— billiards, gin rummy—I promise you, there's nothing I don't know about Hackney. Then he disappeared for a time with old Guildenstern, and now he's in the drawing room playing the Schoenberg album Peter gave you several Christmasses ago.'

'Good!' said Orme-Campbell. 'I was afraid it'd never be opened. What a strange character he is!'

'Why?'

'Such an ugly man.'

'Do you think so?'

'Yes,' said Orme-Campbell firmly. 'A very ugly little man.'

'I don't find him so,' said Elaine thoughtfully. 'I think he's very attractive.'

'Good God!'

'No—there's something rather touching about him.'

'Levenson? Touching?'

'Yes—Levenson. He's tough but somehow pathetic.'

'I shouldn't worry about Levenson,' Orme-Campbell said, putting his arm around his wife's shoulders. 'He's doing all right. I think, darling, you'd do better to start praying for us.'

She withdrew from his arm, and said, 'When you finish your meeting, Geoffrey, I want to talk to you.'

'It won't be before three-thirty or so.'

'I don't care,' said Elaine, examining his face that had suddenly become to her an object with contours and scalpel marks but without life. Their eyes met blankly, and he said, 'As you wish. You'll be very tired.'

'I'm never tired at night,' she answered. 'It's only in the day that I feel tired. I have a sort of daylight insomnia. . . . I think I'll go to my room and leave you to it. Who are those?'

She pointed to two men who walked past them in an absorbed conversation. Orme-Campbell kissed her cheek, and said,

'Quite honestly—I don't know. If they're here in the morning, I'll ask them.'

*

After she had gone, Orme-Campbell began to walk slowly up the staircase, resting his hand on the rail above the alternately spiralled and fluted balustrade, and placing his feet carefully on the slippery marble that Elaine had never wanted to cover, even though in the past four years two servants had slipped with overloaded trays and one had broken an ankle. The steps encouraged deliberation, and he welcomed the excuse for his ponderous ascent. The sharp pain that had shuddered through his chest earlier in the evening like a salvo of rockets had disappeared completely, but it had left him shaken and ashen. He should have seen Dr. Kleinwort the first time it happened, but he had put it off. Too much to do. When this was all over, he would definitely arrange to see him. Kleinwort. That was funny. He'd never thought of him as one of them.

But it was nothing. Once it was over, it was over. Orme-Campbell tried to raise himself erect, but it was easier for him to walk with his shoulders hunched. When he had gone about eight steps, he began to feel again a tremor of pain that started at his breast-bone and shot up to his left shoulder and down his arm. He stopped, and waited for the sensation to disappear. And as he stood there, he thought, 'Why the hell am I going on with this?'

The previous year, he had visited the Cayman Islands with Elaine, and he had thought then how pleasant it would have been to sell out his holding in O.C.E. and build a house and live in the Caribbean, less than an hour from Miami, a few hours from New York, and a few more from London. To spend idle days swimming, fishing for barracuda when he felt energetic, drinking at the Tortuga in the evening, exploring the cays, unencumbered by responsibility. Besides, he liked the Caymanians, the grave, handsome seamen who had never seen the inside of a factory. A memory of flame-trees, poinsettia, and the long curve of an empty beach came into Orme-Campbell's mind as he stood on the stairs, and the phrase repeated itself, 'Why the hell am I going on with this?' His sons had no wish to continue in the family firm. Elaine had always hated the factories, the sales directors, the export directors, the financial directors, the Japanese, French, Greek, Italian and Iron Curtain buyers whom she had to entertain. To give it all up—to say to Levenson, 'All right, Levenson. You can have the lot—the works, the strikes, the rows, the meetings in Whitehall, the chagrin of the political decisions that could sweep away in a few minutes the results of a year's planning—it's all yours, Harry. You wanted it, and you've got it. So good-bye, Levenson—Howell, Henderson-Kerr, fat old Hamblett—the whole bloody lot. Next month—next year at the latest—I'll be fishing off Little Cay, and you'll be in Grantham or Coventry or Leicester or in some committee-room in Whitehall, facing an idiot boy calling himself a Minister, flanked by a couple of civil servants with loose collars.'

Twelve more steps to go. Orme-Campbell looked at the portrait of his father staring down from the head of the stairs. It had been painted in the Grantham boardroom; Orme-Campbell knew the mahogany desk well. His father, Sir Henry Orme-Campbell, holding a pen in his hand poised over a blotter without paper—an unexplained omission—was looking directly at those who viewed him, with the searching stare that once made his employees tremble when they invented bogus explanations for negligence or misconduct. Almost till his death at the age of eighty-nine, and long after he had ceased to be active in the firm, he had the ability to terrorise grown men with the gaze that made them feel he knew their imperfections and their guilt.

And so it had been with Orme-Campbell himself. Until late in his adult life, he had been his father's subordinate; even the staff and his fellow-directors had treated him as 'Mr. Geoffrey'. And at his father's dinner parties with Elaine, the favourite, at ease, he himself would sit constrained at the other end of the table, hesitating to speak in case his father overruled his opinion with a dogmatic and crushing judgment. He had been deeply attached to his father, but his death, he had to admit it, had been a liberation.

'You're dead,' he said as he advanced up the stairs towards his father's portrait. And that gave him the advantage, because he himself was alive, and even the Old Man's trusts had been changed by direction of the High Court, and all the post-mortem dispositions, all the orders and all the policies so carefully planned now lay in his own hands. He stood up for a few moments looking at his father's well-brushed hair—he remembered the smell of bay-rum—and his heavy white walrus moustache, the cavalry officer's moustache of the First World War. Framed on the wall behind him was the first catalogue, issued in the mid-nineteenth century, describing the Orme-Campbell lathe. The Orme-Campbell lathe. That was something. Orme-Campbell thrust his hands in his pockets.

The Orme-Campbell lathe had swept the world. The Orme-*Campbell* lathe. Not the Levenson lathe. The Orme-*Campbell* lathe.

He could hear Hamblett and Henderson-Kerr in a loud discussion, occasionally interrupted by laughter. This was a familiar sound, the working music of his life, a sound of friendly men backed by the uproar of machines, the clatter of overhead cranes, the rancid smell of machine-oil and stained overalls in workshops where at least some of the men had known his father and where he was able to call one in ten by their first names. That was the company the Orme-Campbells had built, the company that retained its domestic heart in the name of Orme-Campbell Engineering.

The Caribbean was far away. He could always spend three months in the Caymans if he wanted to. He could well believe that if he spent much longer there—swimming, fishing and drinking with the expatriates—he'd die of boredom. And Elaine too.

So damn Levenson. Damn them all. He wasn't going to sell out. He'd stay and fight.

*

'I'm sorry,' he said to the three men who stood when he came back into the study. 'Do please sit down. Where were we?'

Howell cleared his throat, and said,

'There's a message from Stapleton.'

'Yes?' said Orme-Campbell, stretching his long legs under the table. 'What's he got to say?'

Howell cleared his throat again.

'I'm afraid he won't be here tonight. He's staying the night in London, and he'll get in touch with you tomorrow.'

Orme-Campbell frowned.

'Why didn't someone let me know Stapleton was on the phone? Who took the message?'

'Stapleton sent it through a secretary,' said Howell. 'I spoke to her myself.'

'It's very disappointing,' Orme-Campbell said after a pause. 'With Budd gone—perhaps we'd better postpone our meeting till tomorrow. I'm disappointed in Stapleton.'

'I don't think it will change the overall picture very much,' Henderson-Kerr put in solemnly. 'You see, Geoffrey—we're a deputation—the three of us. There are some underlying matters we wanted to discuss with you on behalf of the Executive Directors. They're not really affected by Stapleton—or even by Budd. They just affect us—O.C.E. We thought it might be worthwhile if we talked about them between ourselves.'

Henderson-Kerr's voice was soothing; the prognosis might be fatal, but at least he wasn't going to let it hurt too quickly. In turn, Orme-Campbell inspected the faces before him— Howell's averted and anxious, Hamblett's suffused but unemotional, an undertaker's face that had looked on many commercial deaths, and Henderson-Kerr's, the face of a man who didn't want tiresome scenes.

'Well,' said Orme-Campbell, 'which of you three assassins is going to begin? Do open the window, Howell.'

Howell, sitting on the nearest chair, resisted the impulse to obey Orme-Campbell's orders.

'Let me do it,' said Henderson-Kerr, tugging at the gilt handle till the long windows parted with a rumble of glass. Outside, the silence was total, and the air blew in coolly, refreshing the atmosphere made stale by cigar smoke. 'Is that enough?' he asked.

'Thank you,' said Orme-Campbell. 'I think that will do. Now, what have you got to tell me?'

Howell changed his position in his chair, and said,

'I've been asked to put a few points to you.'

'Let's hear them,' said Orme-Campbell, and hearing his own voice, he recalled his father addressing a gathering of complaining trade unionists in exactly the same tones.

'I'm afraid,' said Howell, 'I have to say at least one thing that's going to be painful—very painful indeed.'

'Listen, Howell,' said Orme-Campbell, 'I've known you since you were the tea-boy at Campbell's. Diplomatic embellishment isn't really your line of country. Get on with it, man.'

Howell looked up, and for the first time his eyes, at once resentful and apprehensive, met Orme-Campbell's.

'All right, Geoffrey. I'll put it very simply. The directors— and we're speaking for the majority—the directors take the view that the time has come for you to leave the Board.'

Orme-Campbell waited calmly for him to continue, but Howell relapsed into silence. When he went to light his cigar, Orme-Campbell watched his own hand to see if it had a tremor; it was steady, and he approved of himself.

'Well, go on,' he said encouragingly.

'There's not really much more to say,' said Howell. 'You know our articles of association, adopted by special resolution a few years ago.'

'I drafted them,' Orme-Campbell murmured.

'Under article 73(c),' said Howell, 'subject to any contract between any such holders and the company, the directors may from time to time dismiss a director.'

'I shouldn't go on,' said Orme-Campbell. 'I drafted those articles to deal with fellows like you, Howell, who might get a bit above themselves. Yes,' he added ruminatively, 'a bit above themselves.'

He drew on his cigar, and added amusedly, 'Well, what've you been plotting, Mr. Howell—to fire me?'

'I don't think you're being quite fair,' Henderson-Kerr interposed. 'It isn't a simple question of blood and gore. I speak as an old friend. . . . We all want the best for the company.'

'You mean,' said Orme-Campbell, 'if I sell out to Levenson, the situation wouldn't arise.'

'Well, obviously not,' said Hamblett. 'The situation would be different. But I want you to know, Geoffrey, I'm not in on this. I won't pretend Levenson hasn't put up a proposition this very night. But you've given me certain undertakings, and I'm sticking by them. These fellows here have a different view—and I must admit they share it with several of the boys downstairs. You ought to know and face up to it.'

'What are they asking?' Orme-Campbell said, addressing Hamblett as if the others weren't present.

'They want you to resign from the chairmanship of the Board so that they can sell to Levenson and reorganize and restructure the company.'

Orme-Campbell went to pick up his cigar from the tray, but now he noticed that his hand was shaking so that the long ash trembled and fell.

'By what impertinence are they making this—suggestion?'

Hamblett smiled slowly.

'By having looked at the figures. They're bad, Geoffrey. I didn't know till tonight how bad they are.'

'It's a serious situation,' said Henderson-Kerr.

'They say you've ignored the growth areas,' said Hamblett, 'that you haven't been expansionist-minded, that you haven't been flexible enough in the new conditions of the market.'

'It's shown, of course, in the trading figures,' said Henderson-Kerr gravely. 'A steady decline—and the profit forecast—' He left the sentence unfinished, but raised his hands hopelessly.

Orme-Campbell sat without commenting. Then he said to Howell,

'I imagine Levenson's put you up to this, you poor bastard. Do you know how long you'll last with him? I can tell you. Exactly one year. Then he'll start shifting you—first sideways, then downwards, then out. Out, Howell. And serve you bloody well right. . . . But there's quite a long way to go. In the first place, I'm not resigning. My father and his father didn't build up this firm as a bran-tub for you and the Levensons of this world. This is our firm, and by God, I'm going to keep it that way.'

He stood, and said to Henderson-Kerr,

'I'd think it over, old chap—think it over. Don't get mixed up in this. It won't work.'

The pain was rising again above his breast-bone.

Howell stood too.

'As for you, Howell,' said Orme-Campbell, 'I'm going to make arrangements for you to leave O.C.E. I just want you out of the place. And I want you to hand in the keys of your company car tomorrow.'

He dismissed the subject with a flat movement of his right hand.

'That's all,' he said. 'There's nothing more for tonight.'

The three men rose uneasily, and Henderson-Kerr turned the door handle, though without opening the door.

'There is one matter before we go,' said Howell. And now in a symbiosis, the authority of Orme-Campbell seemed to have passed to him. 'If you decide, Geoffrey, that you don't want to resign, the directors have agreed to dismiss you. You can expect a letter by hand tomorrow.'

He looked for a second at Orme-Campbell's white face, his indrawn mouth and his bull-terrier eyes; then he turned with the others and shuffled out.

Chapter Eleven

ISOBEL watched Adrian's face lit by the fragmented moonlight that touched the lake through the fir trees.

'Don't work too hard,' she said. 'If you stop rowing, the current will take us right round to the island.'

'Good,' he said, shipping the oars. 'I was beginning to feel like one of Messalina's galley slaves.'

'I wish you were,' said Isobel. 'You'd be no problem.'

The boat rocked quietly for a few moments before it began to drift slowly in the current, its movement marked by the diminishing sounds from the party, till at last the silence was total except for an almost imperceptible lapping against its sides.

Adrian reached forward and grasped Isobel's wrist, feeling for her fingers in the darkness, then touching their tips, releasing them, touching them again and exploring her palm and enclosing her hand in his own. To change his place, he stood up in the boat, and it wallowed from side to side as if it was being agitated from underneath. Frightened, Isobel clutched at the gunwale and said,

'No, stay there, Adrian. Just sit—let's talk and drift along till we reach the island.'

He laughed into her anxious eyes, and sat down till the boat became becalmed, as still as the temple that they could see through the trees.

'Will we see each other again?' she asked him. And in the darkness, it seemed to her as if she was asking the question of herself.

'I don't know,' he said. 'You have a different life from me. Where are you going to be tomorrow—next week?'

'He'—Harry had become a person outside herself—'he said we might be going to New York next week. It's a possibility. But we'll be back in ten days.'

· It was an eager assurance she didn't want Adrian to think that their separation would be anything more than an accidental interruption.

He was silent, and thinking that she had upset him, she clasped his hand more tightly as if she were holding on to someone on whom she had no claim, who could disappear from the world where she was captive and who with a few words could bereave her.

'I don't want to go,' she said. 'I hate New York. When I walk in the streets, I always feel as if I'm going to be crushed.'

She waited for him to speak and bent over his hand and fondled it with her lips. He accepted her homage.

'Honestly,' she said, 'I don't want to go. What I'd like to do is to come here every single night, and float along in the boat.'

He stroked her hair, then raised a strand and let it fall over her face before laying it behind her ears.

'It would have to be summer every night,' he said. 'I'm sorry you don't like New York. When my father was a special adviser to the UN delegation, we lived on East 64th Street. I was fourteen and very happy there.'

'I wish I'd know you then,' said Isobel.

'I was an earnest and rather disagreeable boy,' said Adrian, 'always sitting at the bottom of the table when my father gave his Saturday luncheon parties. He used to group together what mother called the transient bores passing through New York, just to get rid of them all . . . and I used to love exploring Manhattan—I went everywhere alone—Harlem, Brooklyn, 42nd Street—no one ever mugged me.'

A night bird flew squawking past the boat at water-level, circled it, then faded, phantom-like, in the direction of the island. Isobel shivered, and said,

'I'm terrified of birds at night.'

'What else are you afraid of?' Adrian asked.

'Everything.'

'Me too?'

'A little.'

He put his face against hers, and they sat like that for a few moments while the boat rocked quietly in the current.

'It's peaceful here,' Isobel said. 'It's never like this. . . . There's always some uproar going on—his telephone ringing— someone waiting for something or other.'

He drew away from her, and cupped her face, barely visible, between his hands.

'You know,' he said, 'you're very beautiful.'

She shook her head self-deprecatingly.

'Yes, you are,' he said. 'I don't like to think of you and all those ghastly characters. Business men are like Chinese, they all look alike.'

His expression became sulky.

'I suppose you do—you and Harry.'

She didn't answer.

'It's strange,' he said. 'I can't imagine it. How can you do it with him?'

'Don't imagine it,' she said. Then she added, as if in a soliloquy, 'Before tonight—well, it was all right. Life becomes a habit. You just go on doing what you've become used to.'

'And after tonight?' Adrian asked. 'How will it be then?' His voice was taunting. 'I suppose you'll undress—and he'll come back from the bathroom tightening the cord of his pyjamas around his podgy paunch, and he'll grunt into bed and smoke—yes, he looks the sort of man who'd smoke in bed before going to sleep—and I suppose he'll talk to you about his business deals—and give you all the figures. And afterwards,

176

when you turn on your side, he'll switch off the light and put his arm around your tits—'

'Stop it, Adrian,' she said, putting her hand on his mouth. 'Do stop.'

He took her hand away, and said, scowling,

'Why should I? I've been thinking about it ever since I saw you with him this evening.'

'But we hardly spoke.'

'I was thinking about you and him. And when we were lying on your bed, I still thought about it.'

'You mustn't,' she said comfortingly. 'You mustn't. It's something else—something different—it's just part of my history.'

The boat had drifted towards the middle of the lake, and Adrian peered into the black water.

'How deep is it here?' he asked.

'I don't know. Jonathan says it's the deepest part—I should think about twenty to thirty feet—perhaps more—I don't know. Do you want to take a sounding?'

He didn't smile.

'No,' he said, trailing his hand in the water. 'It's icy cold.'

'Yes,' she said. 'I've water-skied over the lake, but I've never swum.'

'But you do swim?'

'Not very well. Why?'

'Oh, nothing,' said Adrian distantly. 'I can never row on a lake without thinking of that Dreiser novel where the man tips his girl-friend into the water and lets her drown.'

'It was horrid,' she said. 'But then,' she went on, brightly, 'the girl was pregnant.'

'That,' said Adrian, 'was a nuisance—but it was also a symbolic flaw.'

'It involved them both,' she said.

'Yes,' he agreed, 'they were in it together.'

He dried his hand on a cushion, and fondled her throat.

'I like that,' she said.

His fingers became firm on her neck muscles, and squeezed the nape of her neck as his thumb tightened beneath her chin.

'Yes,' he said, 'you like it.'

Her eyes were shut, and she said again, 'Yes.'

He put his left hand on her throat, and slowly pressed till her lips opened to receive his. After a few seconds, she wrestled her head free and gasped,

'I can't breathe.'

The boat had been carried by a slight wind towards the island, and it grounded with a delicate crunch on a bank of reeds. Adrian released her, and went to push the boat away with an oar, but Isobel said, with her hand to her throat,

'Let's just stay put a little. It's so quiet.' She wanted some moments of respite. 'Tell me more about America. Who were your friends? I want to know all about you.'

'What can I tell you?' said Adrian, diverted. 'I knew loads of people, I went for a time to the United Nations school. But it's strange—the person who taught me most—I suppose she was my best friend in a way—was an aunt.'

Isobel waited for him to explain, and he went on,

'She was my mother's sister-in-law—that's it—her sister-in-law—I'm always rather hazy about relations—we have dozens. She took me everywhere—she was the first person who ever tried to explain pictures to me or took me to hear music. I remember we went together to the Museum of Modern Art, and I was just trailing along with her till we came to the Sleeping Indian—you know, that big picture by Le Douanier Rousseau. And we stood there together looking for about fifteen minutes at this strange, green primitive, and all of a sudden, I wanted to go on staring at pictures, and I must have gone to every museum in New York, with her or alone.'

'I'm jealous,' said Isobel. 'I'm very jealous—I don't know a lot about pictures—but I would have liked to have been the first—'

'Well, you see, she was staying with us at the time. Her husband Bruce was in California, where they owned a chain of stores. And as my aunt didn't have any children of her own, she enjoyed educating me.'

'How old was she? What was her name?'

Adrian was thoughtful for a moment, then he said,

'Her name was Margaret. I don't know how old she was. Somewhere near forty, I imagine. She had tiny little wrinkles under her eyes.'

Isobel put her hands to her own eyes.

'Oh, God,' she said, 'you're terribly observant. Have I got them too?'

He leant forward, and kissed her forehead.

'I'm afraid you haven't,' he said. 'I used to like them.'

'It's become cold,' said Isobel. 'Let's go to the island.'

Adrian pushed the boat from the reeds with one of the oars, and rowed without speaking to the stone ramp jutting out from the shore.

Taking Isobel's arm, Adrian felt his way with her over the fern-covered path, shrouded by the overhanging trees.

'It's so beautiful in the day-time,' said Isobel. She lowered her head under a clump of ghostly rhododendrons, and said, 'It's all red with lupins and love-lies-bleeding.'

'That's a sad name,' said Adrian.

A puff of jasmine, carried by the night-wind, reminded her of the scent blowing from the groves at the approaches to Askalon. 'Is it?' she asked, distantly. She remembered the coast road and the violet sea.

'Yes,' he said, sensing her sudden melancholy. 'Would you like me to take you back? We could have a few more drinks. You've gone all sober on me.'

'No,' she said, quickly. 'I'm sorry. I'm very happy. I don't want any more to drink. I just want to be with you.'

With their relationship adjusted, he paused, and said triumphantly,

'I've brought a flask of whisky. Would you like some?'

'I don't think so,' she said. 'Where did you learn to drink out of flasks? In New York?'

'No,' he said. 'In England. At school. Have a drink.'

He held out his flask, and to please him she drank from it.

'Let's have a whisky-kiss,' he said, and drank deeply from the flask, and kissed her. The whisky warmed and excited them, and Isobel clung to Adrian, her mouth enclosing his, while one of his hands waved the flask aimlessly behind her back. When he detached himself from her, he took another quick swig.

'Do you know,' he said as they walked on, 'in New York the flowers never seemed to have any smell. What I remember mostly is the colour—one marvellous morning in the Fall walking through Central Park with Margaret—the kids with their balloons, the baigel-sellers, the chestnuts, the instant art and the people! I don't just mean black and white—I mean all the shades between.'

'Well,' she said, 'you're half-American. What shade are you?'

'Caucasian pink, I'm afraid.'

'With all that black hair and blue eyes?'

'Those come from the Irish bog-trotters. I can't get away from it. Try as I will to identify with my Mit-Europa friends, I always turn out to be a commonplace product of Western migration, descended on my father's side from a line of eighteenth-century time-servers.'

'You're not like that,' she said. 'You said yourself—you're free and independent.'

His arm was around her, and leaning her head against his chest, she listened to his firm heart-beat as they walked on.

'We should have brought a torch,' she said. 'But there is one at the Temple.'

'I like the dark,' Adrian replied. 'Just grab hold of me.'

'It's strange,' Isobel said, 'I don't know you.'

'No,' said Adrian. 'Can you see the way?'

'I can't see a thing,' said Isobel, halting.

Suddenly she felt frightened, and wished that they could have been alone somewhere in the grounds of Marfield, instead of on the island which always made her uneasy at night when she looked out across the lake at its mysterious silhouette.

'You wait here,' Adrian said, 'and I'll go ahead and get the torch. Where is it?'

'In an alcove at the back. We always keep it there. But I don't want you to go.'

'I'll be back in a minute. Just stay here by the tree.'

The scent of jasmine and honeysuckle thickened, and she felt for the tree behind her while Adrian disappeared into the darkness.

Beneath her feet, there was a stir in the thick fern, and her body tightened in fear.

She waited and three minutes passed. Then she began to count. He couldn't possibly be back before, say, another three minutes, so she would count a hundred and eighty. She counted aloud to hear her own voice, and to hold at bay the menacing and invisible environment, creaking, stirring and rustling.

Eighty-three—eighty-four—eighty-five. . . . Each number was a pulse-beat that quickened as she tried to slow down the count. At a hundred and thirty-three, she stopped and listened, waiting yet afraid to hear the silence broken by an approaching foot-step.

She spoke his name aloud in a conversational voice, as if she hoped to conjure him from the void.

Adrian!—she called his name louder, not panicky, she said to herself, just loud, just so that he might make his way back to her in case he couldn't find the torch.

Adrian!—she called his name again, and her voice wailed

181

into a darkness without reply. She must have counted three hundred—more. Releasing her hold on the tree, she took a step into the darkness, then another, and a third on a mound of moss where her leg sank to the calf in a mole's warren. Quivering, she drew her leg away, and fumbled her way back.

For a minute she stood by the tree. Then she called his name again—Adrian!—and this time she cried out with all her fears become substantial, pressing against her in her despair at being abandoned and lost and alone, while the scent of jasmine evoked another sky and Edward, Edward going away said to herself, just loud, just so that he might make his way and never coming back.

In her childhood, returning from dancing lessons, she sometimes had to pass a graveyard on winter evenings, and she used to hurry by, thinking of the ironic dead, rows and rows of them, who lay beneath the dark trees, now knowing everything, and she used to give the glimmering stones a single glance before she hurried on. This was the same terror, but frozen and sustained.

Adrian! She called again, and began to stumble towards where she thought the temple lay. She called his name into the blackness, tripped, clawing at a shrub, her nostrils suddenly filled with the smell of earth mould at its base. In front of her was a dappled white birch, and she held on to it, pressing the callouses of the bark with her palm so that she could stay related to the external world.

'Adrian!' she said again, and this time his name was a whimper. A light turned the foliage an apple-green, and flushed the shrubbery into a pink glow. She screamed, and Adrian lowered the torch.

'What's the matter?' he asked. She put her head against his chest, and began to cry.

'It's absurd,' she said, hiccupping her sobs. 'It's absurd. I thought you'd gone away. I was so terrified. Let's go back, Adrian.'

He kissed the top of her head, and said,

'Good Lord, no. Jonathan's made the temple very comfortable.'

'For snogging,' she said, laughing and crying into his chest.

'Something like that,' he replied. 'I like to think of Jonathan putting out the cushions for us.'

'That's in appalling taste,' said Isobel, wiping her eyes with the back of her hand.

'Yes, isn't it?' said Adrian. 'There's something rather interesting in Jonathan arranging the pouffes for his Mum to be laid on.'

She pushed him away.

'You're disgusting,' she said.

He put out the torch.

'Shall I leave you?' he asked.

'Oh, please don't,' she said quickly. 'I think I'd die.'

He switched the torch on again, and held it under her face so that it was illuminated as if by candlelight.

'You're very beautiful,' he said.

She looked back at him, and said, 'So are you.' Then she said, 'Do you think it ridiculous—you're twenty years younger than I am—do you think it ridiculous for me to fall in love with you?'

'Not tonight,' said Adrian. 'Tonight's rather like reaching a plateau where people are moving about without passports or permits or birth certificates.'

'No,' said Isobel. 'I know what it's like. It's like that picture *L'Embarquement pour Cythère*. No one knows where they're going—all they know is that they're going to an enchanted place—a sort of *là-bas*—no one questions anyone else. They're just accepted.'

'It's a very romantic picture,' said Adrian.

'Is it? Don't you like things to be romantic?'

He didn't answer, and they climbed the terraces in silence till they reached the temple.

Within its curving walls it was warm, and Adrian drew her

183

on to the cushions, taken from the wrought-iron garden furniture and distributed on the floor. She nestled against him happily, and said,

'If it weren't such a waste, I'd go to sleep. . . . Tell me more about New York—about your aunt—the one I'm jealous of.'

'What do you want to know?' he asked, drawing down the zip fastener of her dress. She wriggled herself out of it and they lay for a few moments without speaking, while he twined his thighs in hers and stroked her face.

'Tell me,' she muttered sleepily into his neck, 'what you haven't told me.'

'About her and me?'

'All that.'

'Kiss me first.'

She kissed him, and said, 'Go on.'

'Well,' he said, 'there isn't really much to say. I was fourteen, and I hadn't known many girls.'

'That's not unusual.'

'I'd never seen a naked woman—not even a woman's breasts. And my aunt was the first woman—she'd be around in the mornings in her house-coat, telephoning and talking and taking hours to bathe and get made up, and I'd make some excuse to hang around myself till there was no one else in the apartment, just so that I could look at her. I used to like doing odd jobs for her. She called me her *cavaliere servente*.'

'That was very pretentious,' Isobel murmured.

'Yes, but it made it highly respectable—a family joke that gave me an excuse to be there. She used to like me to brush the back of her hair with a nylon brush.'

He touched the nape of her neck, and laughed in the darkness.

'It was a very voyeurish pleasure. She used to shut her eyes, and as I brushed her hair, I'd look down between her breasts.'

'Were they nice?'

'Yes.'

184

'As nice as mine?'

'Like yours, but bigger. She'd never had children. She was rather tall, and handsome rather than pretty. If you can imagine it, a handsome Daughter of the American Revolution.'

'Yes—I can imagine it. What else?'

'Nothing much.'

'Tell me,' she said.

'There really isn't much to tell,' Adrian said. 'What was strange was that when we were alone, we somehow lost sight of chronology—we were on that plateau I was telling you about. When my father and mother were there with their guests around that bloody long table in the dining room, it was different. I'd sit without talking except when I was tossed a crust. Margaret was a marvellous conversationalist—very much at ease. I used to resent it.'

'But afterwards?'

'Oh—the next day, after I'd sulked a bit, she'd be very attentive and propose some trip or other.'

'I wish I'd known you then.'

She had unbuttoned his shirt and put her hand against his chest.

'I'm glad you didn't. My aunt used to say I was sombre and truculent.'

'So you are. But I like it. . . . Were you ever alone with her—I mean quite alone?'

His hand, which had been stroking her face, paused.

'Only once. . . . It was the night of Latin America Day. I remember the date because we had two Filipino servants, and they had the night off for their ball, and father and mother went to Washington. It was a strange evening.'

'Why?'

'Well, Margaret took me out to dinner to a little French restaurant on West 52nd Street, I think it was La Faronèse or something like that. And, you know, when I was a boy, I was allergic to strawberries.'

185

'That must have been tragic for a little boy.'

'Don't make fun of me. It was terribly uncomfortable. I'd come out in heat-bumps.'

'You poor darling,' said Isobel soothingly. 'So you had strawberries, and it spoiled your evening.'

'No,' said Adrian, 'it wasn't quite like that. When we got home, it was fairly late because the porters were changing their shift, and that must have been about half past eleven—I was feeling miserable with these great welts, and I bathed, and Margaret said she'd put something soothing—calomine or something—on my shoulders. You see, after about twenty-four hours, the allergy goes. But in between, it's hell—'

'Yes.'

'Anyhow, she did that, and dusted my shoulders with powder, and she kissed me on the cheek as she always did, telling me she'd put some more calomine on if I wanted it, and then I went to bed feeling very fed up.'

'And then?'

'Oh, you don't want to hear any more.'

'Yes—I do.'

'Well, I just couldn't sleep because of this thing, and I tossed and turned and went to the bathroom to try and find the calomine, and—it must have been about two in the morning—Margaret came out of her room and asked me what was the matter, and I told her. So she put the stuff on my shoulders in between the blades where I couldn't reach, and she said, "Come and lie on my bed, and if you wake up in the night, I'll do your shoulder again". '

Adrian's fingers moved along Isobel's neck, and around to her hair and back again.

'Go on,' Isobel said.

'It was a stifling night. There was only a sheet on the bed. I could hear my aunt move to the far side and put the light out, and I fell asleep. Then, I don't know, it must have been an hour or so later, and I woke up and the allergy was gone, but I had somehow rolled over and I was lying as I am now—against her naked thigh, and she was asleep with her arm around my head, and I had my left arm on her neck—like this.'

'What happened then?'

'I was terrified and excited. My aunt had always been someone familiar but awesome, a great taboo. I'd as soon have thought of actually touching her as I would of touching a Queen. In my fantasy, I'd always wanted to feel her naked body. But it was secret and private and forbidden. So I lay quietly in the pitch dark, absolutely unmoving, listening to her breathing and feeling her warmth on my arm.'

Isobel didn't speak, and they lay quietly, listening to each other's quickening breath.

'Go on,' she said again.

'I was afraid to move,' Adrian continued, 'but then, very cautiously and slowly, I began to move my left hand over the curve of her breast till I felt the silk of her nightdress that had been rucked up.'

'Did she wake?'

'She was awake, but pretending not to be, I could tell by the change in her breathing, but she didn't move. And very gradually I passed my hand over her body, and all of a sudden she said in a kind of groan, "No—I mustn't", but she held my hand close against her. Like this . . . and she passed her fingers through my hair and pressed my head down—lie back, Isobel.'

'No,' she said, 'no.'

'Yes,' he insisted.

'She pressed my head down,' he said. And Isobel stretched her arms behind her, pillowed in velvet and suspended in darkness.

*

She drew him up into her arms, and all her body felt unhindered, the poignancy, the distortion corrected and dissolved

187

in a smile that lingered into a brief sleep in which she dreamed that she was walking alone in a walled garden when a man whose face she couldn't see appeared and stood threateningly between her and the sunlight. She awoke, frightened, not knowing for a few moments where she was, till she saw Adrian's face against the sky that had now lightened.

'How long was I asleep?' she said. 'What's the time?'

He calmed her.

'Five or six minutes. It's about three, I imagine.'

'We mustn't stay here too long,' she said. 'Harry will be back soon.'

'Not yet,' said Adrian. 'I was looking at that road across the lake. You'd see the headlights of a car turning into the Marfield drive. I could row you back in ten minutes.'

'It's late,' she said. 'I'll put my dress on.'

'Not yet,' said Adrian. She smiled at him, and said, 'I must look a mess. Oh Adrian, I—'

He sat up and took her in his arms.

'Tell me,' she said, 'what happened to your aunt? What happened the next day?'

'The next day? . . . When I woke up, she'd gone. She'd left the apartment, and in the evening when she returned, the staff and my parents were back too. I tried to talk to her alone, but she was never there. And I was never able to get to speak to her alone—she seemed to be very careful that day, talking in a loud voice but never to me. And the next morning, her husband came—he's one of those heavyweights who call you "Young man", and they were both particularly lovey-dovey together.'

'That must have been horrible.'

'Oh, it didn't last long. They went back to California soon after, and that was that.'

'And have you seen her since?'

'No. She died a few years ago. My mother wrote and told me—cancer.'

188

'How very sad.'

He shook his head.

'I can't think of her as being sad. She did what she wanted to.'

'But you loved her, didn't you?'

'Oh, no,' said Adrian with a short laugh. 'I was grateful to her in lots of ways—the ways I told you about. But I hated her too—I hated her when my uncle came from California to collect her, and I've never hated anyone so much before or since.'

'I hope—' she began.

'No,' he interrupted her, and sat up to light a cigarette, holding her hand on his knees. 'It couldn't be the same. Do you want to smoke?'

'I don't think so,' she answered. 'I just want to lie here and talk to you. Tell me—Adrian—what do you want to do now?'

He shrugged his shoulders.

'I'll spend three years at Cambridge—I'll write a few things.'

'What do you want to write?'

'I've begun to write a TV play,' he said. 'It's quite short. It's called "The Hallowe'en Party".'

'Where is it set? In New York?'

'No,' he said. 'In Connecticut.'

'I used to like Hallowe'en,' Isobel said. 'I had a Scottish nanny who used to tell me the most blood-curdling stories of Hallowe'en and ghosts and witches. Is that what your play's about?'

'Nothing like that. It opens in a wealthy sort of house where some children are dressing up in fancy dress and masks—a girl and three boys—pretty American children with their very relaxed and indulgent parents telling them not to get into trouble.'

'Do they?'

'Oh, no—it's all a rather happy smoky October evening—I think it should be in colour. At any rate, these children put

189

their pumpkin masks with the candles on the window-sills and the camera returns several times to establish the comic pumpkins as the Hallowe'en scene.'

'It sounds very interesting,' said Isobel, working out in her mind when Harry would return. She could see the pure line of Adrian's face against the false dawn that touched the horizon, and remembered what he had said of himself . . . 'grown aged in a world of woe', but all that was an attitude disguising his youth, his curiosity about life and his simplicity.

'Well, then,' he went on, 'the children are joined by others as they go to two houses where they rattle their money boxes and collect ransom for something or other.'

'Yes,' she said patiently, and felt tired, and pulled her dress like a shawl around her shoulders.

'And on their way to the third house, they're joined by another child in a happy mask, and everyone falls for this one. The matron—you know, two chins and three rows of pearls—who lives there is absolutely captivated by this little fellow with the squeaky voice who charms everyone, including her guests, with his tricks and somersaults. And when everyone drifts off and they're alone, she takes him on her knee and persuades him to stay, and promises to drive him home.'

'It sounds very cheerful,' said Isobel. 'But, darling, what's the point of it all?'

'Oh,' said Adrian, 'I'm coming to it. You see, Mrs. Henniker—that's her name—keeps trying to persuade him to take his mask off.'

Isobel raised herself, and began to dress. She could see that Adrian was absorbed in his story.

'Does he?' she asked.

'Not at first,' said Adrian.

'But eventually—'

'Yes—she's dandling him on her knee, and he takes off the Hallowe'en mask—and he isn't a child at all—'

Isobel looked at him with horrified eyes.

'—he's a crew-cut dwarf—a circus dwarf with a yellow, wrinkled face—'

'Don't!'

'And he takes Mrs. Henniker—'

'No, don't, Adrian. It's revolting. I don't want to hear any more.'

She dressed, shivering, and Adrian, smiling with a new cigarette between his fingers, watched her.

'Let's go back,' she said. 'Please, Adrian—hold the torch while I make my face up.'

He rose languidly, and shone the torch on her face while she examined herself in her looking-glass.

Then he went behind her and shone the torch with his face next to hers.

'We look strange,' said Isobel, and she was trembling.

'Yes,' said Adrian. 'Don't we!'

Chapter Twelve

OUTSIDE Elaine's door, Orme-Campbell listened. There was no sound but, climbing the stairs, he had seen the sliver of light that told him she was still awake and reading. He hesitated, because if he said nothing about the night's events, she would read the commentaries in the afternoon papers and add still another grievance to her catalogue of reproach; and then again Elaine, though she found commerce and industry such a tiresome and undistinguished occupation, was able instinctively to identify the occult motives of business men. He wanted to study her face as he told her about the transactions, and then at the end listen like an anxious visitor to a fortune-teller as she gave her judgment.

In these matters, she had always been his ally, even after she had moved into the White Room with the draperies of *rose madère* above her bed. What he now needed wasn't technical advice. Bryce Pearson and the other financial advisers had given him more than he required, and besides, Elaine's china-blue eyes became blank when he spoke of asset values, rights issues and market valuations. He just wanted a sympathetic receptacle for his rage against those he had nurtured and been a patron to, the men who had asked for jobs and help and never gone away empty—Hamblett to whom, for example, ten years before, he had given a personal loan of £8,000. It was true Hamblett had repaid the money without any prompting. All the same, it had been a cash loan from his private account. And now Hamblett had backed out of everything they had planned and ganged up with the others.

Tomorrow, he had no doubt, they'd come to him again with a last offer. Henderson-Kerr would produce the formula and the press release to explain that he had left the firm by mutual and amicable agreement, despite their differences of opinion on policy in connection with Levenson's offer and other matters, and that anyhow, he was only retiring two years before the terminal age that had been generally accepted for executive directors.

And then Hamblett—good-natured, hypocritical Lord Hamblett, the interim chairman, would explain to the shareholders his regret that Sir Geoffrey had had to retire.

Well, he wasn't going to resign. If they wanted to sack him, they'd have to do their dirty work openly so that everyone could see what the murderers really looked like.

'Sometimes,' Hamblett had said, 'you've got to change the bowling.' And that was typical too. It was strange that when men like Hamblett wanted to commit a foul, they used sporting metaphors.

Oh yes—Lord Hamblett had to play fair. Where the shareholders were concerned, Lord Hamblett had to stick to the rules. Where business was concerned, there was no room for friendship.

Well, be objective, you fat slob—I'll wait. I'll wait till it's your turn with Levenson—you and Howell and Henderson-Kerr. Henderson-Kerr, the old dodderer, with his trembling fingers, wanted a golden handshake. £100,000. That was a joke! He'd kept Henderson-Kerr on out of pity—because his father had liked him, because on the company reports, with all the bits and pieces of military decoration, he sounded a good man to have. And he was Traitor No. 1.

And Howell. Orme-Campbell's hand tightened around the brass corrugations of the door-knob. Howell was a different cup of tea. He had known Howell over thirty years, but he didn't even know how many children he had. Their communications had always been factual, limited to the job they had to do together. Howell stood up while he, Orme-Campbell, sat. Howell stood and stood, and bought shares—and the Villa from the firm with Orme-Campbell's encouragement. It was as good as a gift, and for himself a convenience, a brief and regretted convenience that came back to him in nightmares.

Orme-Campbell knocked at the door and simultaneously turned the knob. For many years he hadn't entered his wife's room, always meeting her at the end of the day in his study, where they sat comfortably opposite each other exchanging their experiences, discussing matters that concerned them both, and separating finally with a friendly laying-together of their cheeks and the ghost of a kiss.

Though the reading lamp was lit above the bed, Elaine wasn't there. He stood on the dark blue carpet, an intruder, furtively glancing at the Matisse collages above her bed, the Shing Yao porcelain ewer over the fireplace that her father, Lord Hawley, had left her, and from there to the small table where between candlesticks three framed photographs were stacked face downwards. Orme-Campbell approached and cautiously turned them over; there was one photograph of Hawley as an old man in his peer's robes at the Coronation, with his noble expression, chin up, right hand extended and eyes unsmiling, a pose that created a style and a type of English face. Orme-Campbell studied the portrait impersonally. Despite his autocratic stance, Hawley never had any terrors for him; he was only a baron of the first creation who had done well in building. The other two photographs were of their sons, friendly studio portraits which had been taken when Peter joined Lloyd's but before Gerald went into the Church.

For a moment, Orme-Campbell wanted to put the photographs on Elaine's dressing-table, where he assumed they had come from, but he immediately changed his mind. *Mulier*, the scent she used, filled the air and made him uneasy. In the circular looking-glass he could see his face, drooping and ruddy except around his eyes, and his cheeks still smooth and unroughened by a beard which, to his private sorrow, especially when he was a young man, only grew reluctantly.

'Hello, you!' he said aloud to his reflection. 'What are you doing here?'

Since the meeting with the Executive Directors, he had drunk over half a bottle of whisky, but he felt coldly sober. Behind him a cat mewed and he turned abruptly knowing that Elaine never allowed cats in the house. Then he realized that the mewing was the sound of his own constricted breathing, and he walked slowly and heavily from her room.

As the house gradually emptied, there came from below the sound of departing guests, of car doors slamming and of engines revving up. He wondered if he ought to see Levenson and talk to him before he left, but the idea of confronting his triumphant face was repugnant. Eventually he would go downstairs, and if Levenson was still there—well, he'd bid him good-night! And if he wasn't, that was too bad.

Now he felt an anxious need to find Elaine and explain to her what had happened, why it was that so many things had gone wrong since the confident moment when they had greeted Levenson and Isobel that evening. And he wanted to hear her comforting epitaphs on his enemies.

On his way to his room, the anger returned, this time directed not against Howell and Hamblett and Henderson-Kerr but against Levenson—all the Levensons who wanted to take over the structure that the Campbells and the Orme-Campbells had built up, the very buildings that he had inherited or seen rise from ground level.

It wasn't true that he was intolerant. He wasn't a racialist. Together with the engineering unions, he had devised an apprenticeship scheme for coloured workers that had become a model in the industry. O.C.E. had been among the first to employ West Indians as foremen. But they were different from the Levensons. They worked with their hands. In the foundry all faces were black and the eyes all looked alike. He couldn't see the Levenson lot in the hot glare of a furnace. They just sat in boardrooms, surrounded by their bankers, someone else's balance-sheets in front of them, working it all out till the moment when they could move in and kill. If O.C.E. were held up and shaken by them as an inefficient, mismanaged anachronism—and that was Levenson's technique, to paralyse with contempt before the death-blow—then he too would be humbled and destroyed by something that he despised.

But as he thought this, the object of his bitterness changed again. Levenson at least had been an open enemy. He had made a bid in public, stated his reasons, exposed himself to criticism, accepted the insults that met his enterprise not only in the boardroom but in the press as well. No one could say that Levenson had sheltered himself behind front-men, or that he had hidden his personal ambitions, whereas Howell, Henderson-Kerr and Hamblett had toadied to him, lied to him, and finally cheated him. He shouldn't have been surprised. It happened all the time. But it was ugly and squalid. And how ugly and squalid you could only know when it happened to yourself.

On the landing he met Girling.

'Bed, sir?' said the manservant, holding an unemptied ash-tray in his hand. And it was half-enquiry, half-reprimand.

'Where is Lady Orme-Campbell?' he replied stiffly.

'Wandering about,' said Girling, shaking his head. 'Wandering about!'

'Where?' Orme-Campbell asked.

Girling pushed his swollen-jointed left hand upwards to indicate the next floor, and moved off. Orme-Campbell looked at the narrower staircase leading to what they used to call 'the boys' quarters', stood irresolutely, and then continued with his search.

The door of Gerald's disused room was half-open, and the light was on. Orme-Campbell again paused, breathing heavily after the climb up the stairs. How strange it seemed that on this night he should be exploring his own house, visiting places where he had so rarely been, seeking his wife in a room that his sons had abandoned at least ten years earlier. On this floor, the silence had a sea-shell sound, an oceanic murmur.

'Are you there, Elaine?' he called out, and when there was no reply, he pushed the door wide open and entered. Elaine, curved in a wicker armchair with green baize cushions that had belonged to their sons, and incongruously at ease, was reading a school exercise book.

'What are you doing?' he asked.

'Reading,' she answered, without looking up.

On the walls the photographs of rugger and cricket teams, housemaster in the centre, players with their arms folded, stared down unsmiling, while the shelves, emptied of books except for a Wisden, an out-of-date almanac, a Bible, a Book of Common Prayer and an open stamp album from which most of the stamps had been torn, gaped with rows of dis-coloured wallpaper between them. In the corner stood a guitar with two broken strings dangling from its neck.

'Why don't you got to bed?' Orme-Campbell asked. 'It's very late.'

'I was waiting for you,' she said, still without looking up. 'Listen to this, Geoffrey. It's Gerald's essay on "The Difference Between Pleasure and Happiness".' She turned the leaves of the exercise book to its front page and said, 'He was just twelve when he wrote it. Look, Gerald Geoffrey Harrington Orme-Campbell. "Pleasure is what you feel when you are happy. But you do not always feel happy when you have pleasure. Pleasure comes and goes, but happiness is all the time." '

'That sounds about right,' said Orme-Campbell. 'Do you know any happy people, Elaine?'

'No,' she said, closing the book. 'Not by Gerald's definition. You can't be happy all the time. But to be happy none of the time—that's when it's no good.'

'I couldn't say,' said Orme-Campbell, fingering a small silver-plated cup on one of the shelves. 'I've been lucky. I wouldn't know.'

He stood awkwardly in front of her and said,

'Have you heard from him lately?'

'No,' she said, and for the first time since he entered the room the expression on her impassive face changed. Behind her glasses, her eyes reddened with tears. 'No,' she said, standing. 'You know they don't write or phone. Why do you keep asking?'

She walked over to a photograph of Gerald as captain of the school rugby team, and looked at it for a few seconds. Then she turned back to Orme-Campbell and said,

'I must talk to you, Geoffrey.'

He waved his hand wearily, knowing that what she wanted to discuss with him wasn't what he had wanted to discuss with her. 'Not now, Elaine. I've—'

'Not now?' she interrupted him, taking off her glasses. 'It's always not now. It's *got* to be now.'

'I've had a hard evening. I think you ought to know—'

'Every evening's a hard evening. Listen, Geoffrey—I've got to talk to you—not tomorrow—now!'

The room seemed to move in a slow swerve like a ship careening over before righting itself, and Orme-Campbell put his hand on her arm. In his mind he could hear an ill-tuned orchestra of argument, Budd on his enemies, Henderson-Kerr on dividends, Howell on loyalty, Hamblett on shareholders.

'I don't really feel like talking tonight,' he said. 'Not now—not here.'

Questions and answers, propositions and counter-propositions scampered and scurried in his thoughts like rats on treadmills.

With his mouth parched and his legs uncoordinated, he wanted to lie down, drifting far from the debate and his wife's emphasis. The portraits of his sons, their presence haunting the neglected room, their remembered voices mingling with the tinnitus persisting in his ears from the meeting, frightened him. Like someone half-awakening in the middle of the night in a strange room in a foreign city, he felt disorientated, unable to relate himself in time or place to the photographs of his adolescent sons and the memories of a younger Elaine.

She insisted.

'Let's go and talk in your room, Geoffrey,' she said. 'We've got to talk about it.'

He sighed, and said, bracing his body, 'All right, Elaine. But we won't go over all the old stuff—will we?'

He added the last two words hopelessly.

When they reached his bedroom, he switched on all the lights to dispel the unreality that had accumulated around them in their sons' study. Elaine sat in an armchair, and he went to his dressing-table to take off his tie.

'No,' said Elaine. 'I want you to sit there and face me.' She pointed to the bed. 'It's gone on too long, Geoffrey—you must sit there and face me.'

He obeyed her, bleakly seating himself on the counterpane, and waited for her to continue.

'I'm going to leave you,' she said.

'Yes,' he answered. He had heard her say it before.

'I'm going to leave you tomorrow,' she went on. 'I wanted to wait till you'd dealt with the Levenson affair.'

She spoke in a restrained tone lower than her normal speaking voice, and took a cigarette from a box on a side-table. He went to light it for her, and she said, 'Don't bother,' and left it unlit.

'Perhaps before you—' he began, but she interrupted him.

'No, Geoffrey, tonight you've got to let me talk. I've been thinking that next week I'll be fifty-two.' She fumbled with a match and lit her cigarette. 'God knows how long we have to live. Hubert Ensor fell dead last week—Marjorie—you know what happened to her.'

Orme-Campbell nodded his head sympathetically.

'Tomlinson, Collins, Peakes—they're dropping like flies.'

Elaine rose and stood by the curtains, glancing through their gap at the night sky where the stars were already fading.

'I want to live a few years,' she said, 'just a few years the way I want to. Our boys are grown up—Emma too—they're gone—they're all gone.'

She turned as she spoke the last words, and her mouth became tight with anger.

Orme-Campbell stood up, his defensive posture changed into one of resentment.

'No, Elaine,' he said, raising his arm to anticipate her attack. 'Not that again.'

'Yes,' she said savagely. 'That again. You know they couldn't live here—they hated it.' She lowered her voice, and said, 'Put some of those lights out. They're hurting my eyes.'

He switched off all the lights, except for a bedside lamp, and she went on,

'You know why they hated it. And you were to blame.'

'No,' he said. 'No.'

'Yes,' said Elaine. 'They knew what was going on.'

He shook his head.

'It's strange,' said Elaine. 'I loved you. When we were first married, there was nothing in the world I wouldn't have done for you. . . . And even afterwards, there's nothing I wouldn't have done. What happened, Geoffrey? Tell me—it's a serious question.'

He looked up and said, 'Happened? Nothing happened except that we were both what we were.'

'But Galliano,' she said, her eyes following the frieze. 'That was dreadful, Geoffrey—for all of us—you too. How did that happen?'

'It happened,' he said doggedly. 'And that was that. I don't want to talk about it.'

'But you must,' said Elaine, and now she was sad and patient. 'You must. I was very simple—when we were in the West Indies—that young Canadian—Marley—so soon after we were married. And then all the strange, strange things—'

She walked over to the carved wardrobe and tugged at the handle. The door opened and she closed it at once. Then she turned to him unsmilingly.

'The Coachman's Curiosa—'

'Please don't go on,' said Orme-Campbell. 'I can't take much more tonight. I've had a tough time.'

'I'm sorry about that, but you've got to listen. In the eighteen months when Guido Galliano and his friends were around, you paid out in one way or another nearly £93,000.'

'It's not true.'

'Yes, it is—I know it. Bryce told me—you were selling shares.'

'It's old history, Elaine,' said Orme-Campbell. 'Old history.'

'No,' she said. 'Not old history. *I* arranged for his permit not to be renewed.'

'You?'

'Yes—I arranged it. I told Harold Fisher, and he spoke to the Home Office. But it wasn't over. There were Galliano's other friends. There was the Villa Howell. What a charmingly innocent name! Parsons drinking lemonade in the sun. But it wasn't like that—was it?'

She looked at him with hatred.

'It was a rest-home for fags—'

'Stop it, Elaine.'

'—for a gang of fruity spongers. And there in the middle was Sir Geoffrey Orme-Campbell, M.C., with his court, while Mr. Howell looked after the affairs of O.C.E.'

The room filled with silence again, and neither spoke. At last Orme-Campbell said,

'It wasn't quite so simple, Elaine. You know it. We all edit our histories. You, too.'

'Not this one.'

'Yes,' he said in a slurred voice. 'This one too. You've forgotten. You want to forget. . . . The young men on the beaches. After Emma was born—you wanted to catch up. . . . I understood. That was the trouble. Perhaps I understood too well.'

'There was nothing to understand.'

'Yes,' said Orme-Campbell. 'There was a lot. You loved me—I think you did. We weren't just husband and wife. We were accomplices. Perhaps that's part of love. But we loved our children too. Didn't we?'

She passed her hand through her hair in a familiar brooding gesture, and frowned. He waited for her answer.

'I don't know,' she said at last. 'Was it love to dump them in schools, glimpse them at holiday times—and give them a background of Guidos and Giovannis?'

'Oh, no,' Orme-Campbell protested. 'It wasn't like that.'

'It was,' she said simply. 'It was—for them and for me. But it's past. They'll never come back here. Gerald told me. Never. It's the same with Peter and Emma. They don't want anything from us. Neither from you nor from me, Geoffrey. And that's how we must look ahead.'

'Gerald and Peter are a couple of prigs,' Orme-Campbell said with determination. 'If that's how they feel about it, they can go to hell.'

'I don't think so,' said Elaine. 'You don't think that and you don't feel it. But there it is. I've been thinking about this for months. Tomorrow, I'm going to Tipaza.'

Orme-Campbell's face relaxed.

'Tipaza?' he said, as if she had changed the subject. 'I was stationed there for a time during the war, remember? It's got a superb Graeco-Roman museum.'

'Yes,' said Elaine. 'It's one of the reasons I'm going.'

'Who are you going with?'

'Jennifer Roberts, Helen Ruben, Mary Gilmore—'

'Any men?'

'Two or three. Clive Henley, Mark Clifford—'

'Is he still around?'

'Yes,' she said, taking up her handbag. 'He's always around. Have you any objection?'

'No,' he replied. 'Not now.' Then in an afterthought, he said, 'Tell me, Elaine—'

'There's nothing to tell,' she said. 'We're all going with the Friends of Foreign Museums. I'm not coming back to you, Geoffrey.'

'We've had all that before,' he said.

'I'm serious. . . . Please take me seriously.'

'I know. . . . I think you'd better be off to bed, Elaine. You're exhausted.'

She rose hesitantly and he walked with her to the door.

'What happened with your meeting in the end?' she asked him.

'Nothing much,' said Orme-Campbell, looking at her white face with the violet shadows under her eyes. He felt sorry for her and for himself, for everything that had been selfish and callous between them, and above all for the irrecoverable passage of time that had translated them both from their hopeful youth into a wistful and apprehensive middle-age. And looking at her again with resentment, he also felt pity and love. 'Nothing much,' he repeated. 'We just talked and talked—rather inconclusively.'

'Didn't Stapleton turn up after all?' she asked wearily, as if the matter no longer concerned her.

"No—he was delayed at the last moment. But tomorrow, perhaps—'

'There's one I wouldn't rely on ever again,' she said.

'No,' he replied.

'Well,' she said, 'I'm glad things aren't worse.'

'Oh yes,' said Orme-Campbell. 'Everything went off as well as could be expected.'

He patted her on the cheek, and opened the door.

'Good-night,' he said.

She stood irresolutely.

'I want to talk to you about a few practical matters,' she said.

'Tomorrow morning.'

'Very well, Geoffrey. . . . Don't drink any more tonight.'

She turned to go, and he said, remembering,

'Strange—Mark Clifford—I haven't seen him for ages. What's he like now?'

'He hasn't changed much—getting rather grey.'

'I imagine he's a bit pompous, now he's gone to the Lords.'

'Yes—just a little.'

'How long have we known him?'

'Thirty-one years.'

'That's a good snap answer.'

'Well, I remember,' she said calmly. 'We met almost a year before Gerald was born.'

Orme-Campbell gave her a quick glance, closed the door, and sat on his bed. The pain in his chest had returned, and he thought that if he died before morning, he wouldn't have to meet Levenson again or preside over the shareholders' meeting or cope with Howell and Henderson-Kerr and all the others, and that *The Times* would give him a column and a photograph for his obituary and that Hamblett would write a short tribute and that Elaine and his two sons and daughter would be described as the chief mourners and that the service would be attended by the whole Orme-Campbell family— Mr. Henry Orme-Campbell, brother, Mrs. Henry Orme-Campbell, sister-in-law, Sir Roger and Lady Blackstone, cousins, Mr. and Mrs. Neil Orme-Campbell, Mrs. Henrietta Cuspar, Mr. John Hurford, Lady Bettina James and all the other collaterals. And leaving the church, Mark Clifford would comfort the widow, and afterwards they'd all get out of their black clothes and scatter off to some party or other. And Levenson would say, 'Poor chap, he looked very well the other day,' before talking down his own bid so that he could get O.C.E. cheaper.

Orme-Campbell bent to untie his shoe-laces, but the effort left him panting, and he straightened himself again.

There was a hesitant knock at the door.

'Yes,' he said, and the sound came out in a thin gasp.

The knock became louder.

'Yes,' he said again, and Girling appeared.

'There's someone outside who wants to say good-night.'

'Tell him I'm in bed—fast asleep.'

'Hello, Orme-Campbell,' said Levenson, appearing behind Girling's shoulder. 'There's just something I want to put to you before I go.'

'Hello, Levenson,' said Orme-Campbell without rising. 'I'll join you in the drawing-room in a few moments. Shut the door, Girling.'

He continued to sit on the bed, wondering what Levenson might add to all their long discussions about his bid. He was feeling better now, and feeling better he put his earlier anxieties aside. Levenson's call had given him an unexpected hope, and he rose, thinking of Elaine's visit and of Galliano— the tall, slender Galliano.

'No,' he said to himself. 'No.'

Then he thought of the Coachman's Curiosa, and what his executors might make of his collection if he died.

'I'll put it up at Christie's,' he said aloud. 'Some of it, anyhow.'

He liked the idea, and he savoured the future description in the catalogue:

Carrosserie et Cuirs: 18th and 19th century: Sundry Items of Equipment.

Then he added to himself,

'The Property of a Gentleman.'

Chapter Thirteen

LEVENSON was in a hurry to get back to Marfield, but in business he had learned that it was a mistake to leave too soon. There was always someone who might turn up at the last moment to frustrate the most elaborate plans, some possible information to falsify everything that had gone before. He wanted to make sure that there was nothing—no phone call and no visitor, that before morning could reverse a victory that now only needed formal confirmation. Besides to have left without saying good-bye to Orme-Campbell would have been discourteous as well as imprudent, and that was why he had followed the butler to Orme-Campbell's room.

The directors of O.C.E. had left in a straggling procession and Levenson, sitting alone in the drawing-room and waiting for Orme-Campbell to descend, smiled contentedly at the change in the demeanour of Henderson-Kerr and Howell since they had first greeted him, their hostility now turned to obsequiousness, their unfriendly detachment into an urgency to impress on him their merits.

With his ability to visualize systems and programmes even without seeing them on paper, Levenson planned in his mind the new structure of the merged companies. He had already decided to edge Howell towards some peripheral job where in due course he could be pensioned off. Henderson-Kerr would get a terminal payment. Not what he expected, perhaps a quarter, perhaps £25,000 and he'd be lucky to get it. As for Hamblett, he'd find some title for him in one of the company's new divisions, and give him a salary appropriate for a part-time job. The man, after all, was no fool. And besides, he'd been very useful in the last couple of hours. Cleaning out the old management was going to be tougher than bringing in the new one. There'd have to be a lot of phasing-out as well as phasing-in. It might take as much as a year to make all the changes. Still, that could keep for tomorrow.

'Well,' said Orme-Campbell, entering the room and surprising Levenson so that his cigar ash crumbled and fell, 'I was afraid you might have gone.'

Levenson brushed his jacket and said,

'No, I'm still here. I felt I'd like to say good-bye to you before I left.'

'Very civil of you—very,' said Orme-Campbell. 'Let me get you a drink. Do be seated.'

'I won't drink,' said Levenson, sitting opposite Orme-Campbell. 'I've got to get back to a party.'

'A party?' said Orme-Campbell. 'At this hour?'

'It's my son's,' Levenson said apologetically. 'You know, he's down from Cambridge.'

'Yes,' said Orme-Campbell, pouring himself a whisky. 'I remember now. Isobel told me. You're very fortunate, Levenson.'

Levenson watched Orme-Campbell's blonde face with suspicion. The large, relaxed figure, at ease and apparently friendly, didn't have an air of defeat. On the contrary, Orme-Campbell wore the auspicious look of one who could see an outcome shrouded from others, and didn't seem displeased at what he saw.

'I *am* fortunate,' said Levenson. 'But what makes you think so?'

Orme-Campbell sipped his whisky and said,

'I like it undiluted. . . . What makes me think so?'

'Yes.'

'Well, it's not the obvious things. You may get O.C.E.—we'll all know more tomorrow. But that isn't why I think

207

you're lucky. You're going to have a lot of headaches if you get it—a lot more than you think.'

Levenson grinned, and his dark face brightened as if the very challenge stimulated him.

'I'm an old hand at headaches,' he said. 'Ever since I was fourteen.'

Orme-Campbell said ruminatively,

'I think you're lucky to be going home to your son's party. . . . I suppose you're about ten years younger than I am. You look fairly fit—perhaps too much weight for your height—but then I myself—well, never mind that. There you are: Levenson—tomorrow's hero of all the Business News—going home to your son and your beautiful wife. That's very lucky.'

Uncertain as to whether Orme-Campbell was mocking him, Levenson said,

'You're home already.'

'That's true,' said Orme-Campbell. 'Very true.'

He poured himself a second large measure of whisky, and Levenson could see that he was getting drunk.

'Home,' he went on, 'means more than a bed, board and four walls. You're going home to a party, Levenson—you're going home to your son and your wife. Have a brandy.'

'No, thanks,' said Levenson. In counterpart to Orme-Campbell with his flushed face and watering eyes, he felt cool and clairvoyant.

'I have two sons and a daughter,' Orme-Campbell went on. 'My daughter Emma lives in Chicago.'

'That's a long way away. How often do you see her?'

'Hardly ever,' said Orme-Campbell. 'Don't get on with her husband—he makes such hair as I have stand on end.'

'Why didn't your sons go into O.C.E.?'

Frowning, Orme-Campbell took a gulp of his whisky and said,

'That's a rather unpleasant question, Levenson.'

'Unpleasant—why?'

'It's unpleasant,' said Orme-Campbell, looking down at his glass. 'I'd like to know exactly what are your motives in putting it.'

Levenson said, 'No motives. Just curiosity. In a family business, sons follow their fathers—that's all.'

'It's a bloody unpleasant question,' said Orme-Campbell. Then he added, as if to himself, 'But I might have expected it.'

His voice was truculent, and Levenson could see that he was seeking to be provoked and unwilling to be appeased.

'My dear fellow,' said Levenson, 'you're entitled to expect what you like. If you want to treat a friendly question as an insult, I'm sorry. Forget it.'

Orme-Campbell brushed the apology aside.

'I'm not interested in your explanations, Levenson. You ask me a bloody unpleasant question, and then you think you can get away with it by saying you're sorry. It reminds me of my daughter Emma.'

He took another swallow of whisky.

'Tell me about your daughter Emma,' said Levenson, watching him carefully.

'Well,' said Orme-Campbell, and suddenly he became benign, 'when she was a little girl she'd do the most extraordinary things—the most outrageous—'

He sat holding his glass, and his thoughts drifted away in a fugue that left him looking marble-eyed into the middle distance.

'What sort of things?' Levenson asked.

'What's that?' said Orme-Campbell. 'Oh—like climbing out of windows on ropes—the usual little girl tricks—she always wanted to get away. And then, when Elaine complained, she'd come to me and say "I'm sorry, daddy. I'm sorry." Ridiculous words, Levenson—a kind of sponge to wipe away every blemish and make it good again. .... And yet there's a lot to be said for confession. Confession's a statute of oblivion. That must be very nice. It's what I want myself. A statute of oblivion. . . . You know, I've often wished I was a Roman Catholic so that I could do a *mea culpa* for everything I've done wrong—everything that went wrong. That must be pretty good, Levenson. Imagine, old chap. . . . Here we are—two middle-aged men, both of us loaded with all the guilty baggage we've collected over the years. And then, tomorrow —what do you say?'—he had a bright idea—'Let's stay up all night—let's just go along to St. Elizabeth's—tomorrow morning—just you and me, Levenson.'

He finished his glass of whisky, and went on with his urgent apostrophe.

'You, Levenson! Imagine it! We'll go to St. Elizabeth's tomorrow morning at eight o'clock, and we'll ask for a priest and he'll say, "What do you want?"—something like that—and we'll say, "Father, we've come to confess." I'll do the talking if you like. I'll say, "This is Mr. Harry Levenson, a Jew, and I'm Sir Geoffrey"—no, there aren't any titles in Heaven—I'll just say, "I'm Geoffrey Orme-Campbell, an Anglican, a poor bastard who got his sums wrong. All of them.' He'll take us into his little box, one by one, and after we've said our piece, he'll say, "In the name of the Father and of the Son and of the Holy Ghost, I give you absolution," or whatever they say. And we'll both go out in the sunlight, Harry, cleansed, purified, absolved!'

His voice faded away and he lay back, brooding. Then, after a pause, he added dejectedly,

'No, I don't think it would work. I don't think they take Jews . . . or Anglicans for that matter. It's an interesting subject, though—very interesting. What do your lot do? . . . I know. You do it all in advance, once a year. You do it wholesale. Confess now—sin later.'

He relished his summing-up, and began to laugh in an accumulating roar till his face reddened and he felt the pain, inexorable and menacing, compressing his chest, and he stopped. The sweat on his forehead was glacial, and with a sudden sobriety he became aware of Levenson's scrutinizing eyes.

'Are you all right?' Levenson asked.

'Of course I'm all right,' Orme-Campbell replied, his hand to his chest. 'Just get a rheumaticky twinge every now and again. . . . It's going now. I'm sorry, Levenson. I've been pulling your leg a bit. At one time, I wanted my sons to go into the firm. But they didn't like engineering—must have skipped a generation. Or perhaps they take after Elaine. . . . How about your son?'

The pain had ebbed as the pallor was replaced by a flush and the small red veins on his face were reabsorbed into the robust appearance of his complexion.

'My son,' said Levenson, 'hasn't made up his mind, except —like yours—he doesn't want to go into the family firm.'

'Strange,' said Orme-Campbell, 'to hear you talk of family firms. . . . You sound like a sentimental hangman. . . . They're going—the family firms. They're being killed off in clusters, and one day we'll all wake up—you too, Levenson—and you'll see what's been lost.'

'What?'

'Personality. We live in an age where everyone prattles about the rights of personality, and where most people spend their time trying to blot it out. A firm that's been built up by individuals who've worked in it—that's an organic entity. It's got a personality where brains and limbs and nerves have some relationship. What you're doing, Levenson, is to de-personalize—dehumanize. Oh yes—it'll be all right for a few years. You'll grab a hundred other firms—you'll build new conglomerations—as the Yanks say. You'll computerize your management. You'll deal with a hundred thousand workers, and you won't know more than a dozen, and in the end they won't even know who they're working for. . . . Then, one day, it'll all start going to pot. The man in the engineering works will find that he's lost his job because there's been a falling-off of the demand for beer or washing powders or TV rentals.'

'Oh, no.'

'Oh, yes. You'll make these conglomerations, not because you want to manufacture this or that or even to match up the selling of organizations. You'll marry beer and washing powders and lathes and TV rentals, just so that you can diversify, and hedge your bets.'

Levenson wanted to interrupt, but Orme-Campbell went on.

'No, old man. Don't interrupt. I'm not blaming you personally. You're not an engineer, Levenson. I'd doubt if you can read a drawing. You're a financier. Your raw material isn't metal; it's money. All I wanted to say to you is that in the long run, you and the fellows like you—you'll destroy every-thing that made Britain great.'

He stopped, and sank his head between his shoulders, gratified that he had told Levenson what he thought and wanting their interview, the long night of argument, the dialogue with Elaine which still intruded into a jumble of voices somewhere inside his skull, to come to an end. The ticking of the clock was an accompaniment to their silence. For a few moments, Levenson sat watching Orme-Campbell, still entangled in his own thoughts.

'Well, come on, Levenson,' Orme-Campbell said at last. 'Say something offensive.'

'I don't think so,' said Levenson. He leaned forward from his chair towards Orme-Campbell, who was lying back with his long legs extended. 'You'd like me to say something offensive so that you can go to bed with a nice easy conscience. Tomorrow, you'd like to say, "He was a sod to the last." Right?'

'Quite right,' said Orme-Campbell.

'Well,' said Levenson, 'I'm not giving you that satisfaction. You see, Orme-Campbell, a few minutes ago when you were drunker than you are now, you said something that was quite true.'

'What was that?'

'You said you'd like a statute of oblivion—you said you'd like to make a confession that would wipe out your debts—purge you—something like that—of all the guilt that's grown on you over the years.'

'That's it,' said Orme-Campbell in a melancholy voice, pouring himself another drink from the whisky decanter now three-quarters empty. 'I'm an old hulk covered with barnacles.' He drained the glass and added, 'Past repair—past repair! A scuttled old hulk, covered with barnacles and seaweed.'

Levenson smiled.

'Well, in a way, we're all like that.' Then he stopped smiling and went on grimly, 'But not entirely. . . . Tonight, Orme-Campbell, you've been giving me a few sermons.'

'Oh God, no,' said Orme-Campbell.

Levenson stood up, and said, 'Oh yes, you have. Let's begin with the Jews.'

'Oh no,' said Orme-Campbell. 'We've had enough of them.'

'Not quite. You see, Orme-Campbell, you've been arguing tonight—and no one's contradicted you—that if our bid goes through, your firm will be taken over by the Jews.'

'It's academic,' said Orme-Campbell.

'It wasn't academic just two or three hours ago,' said Levenson. 'Because you know, Orme-Campbell, that apart from me with my personal eight per cent, there isn't a single Jew among our directors or major shareholders. It's neither good nor bad. It just happens to be a fact.'

'I didn't count them,' Orme-Campbell said calmly. 'I'm not anti-semitic, you know.' Then, like a boxer setting up his opponent against the ropes and measuring the distance for the knock-out, he added, 'It's just that where Jews are concerned, I find two's company and one's a crowd.'

Levenson stood stock-still, and Orme-Campbell looked up

at him questioningly, waiting for his reaction. Then he slowly heaved himself to his feet, and said,

'I'm sorry, Levenson, I'm very sorry.'

Levenson stared in front of him without moving.

'I'm sorry, Levenson,' Orme-Campbell repeated. He was feeling sick. 'That was unforgivable. Please sit down. . . . You know how it is. Sometimes you intend to be smart—and it comes out as a balls-up. I'm sorry, Levenson. Please sit down. I'm sorry.'

Levenson continued to stand without answering him. His attention was fixed on the tall portrait of a woman in a blue dress behind Orme-Campbell's head.

'That's a very fine picture,' he said. 'Is it a Reynolds?'

'No,' Orme-Campbell muttered. 'It's a portrait of Lady Axton, attributed to Gainsborough. My grandfather bought it—he thought the blue dress would look well against the grey wallpaper.'

'Yes,' said Levenson. 'It does.'

Orme-Campbell waited uneasily for him to continue. Then he said,

'I've apologized to you, Levenson. I hope you accept it.'

'That's unimportant,' said Levenson dismissively. 'What does it matter one way or another if I accept your apology? You'll still go on thinking that I'm a bloody Jew—'

Orme-Campbell tried to interrupt, but Levenson continued,

'You and your friends in the City will still go on spreading nasty little stories about "Levenson's first £100,000"—no, don't bother to deny it. It's already part of the myth. I can chase it as long as I like—issue writs galore. You're still ahead of me in the muck stakes. . . . I understand the reasoning. If that man's an outsider, we'll keep him there. And if he's outside and not inside, there's something wrong with the man. We'll have him to lunch at the Savoy Grill if we have to; but we won't have him home. Except when we're fighting for our lives. . . .'

Levenson walked across the room to examine a secrétaire, decorated with Sèvres plaques.

'You are fighting for your life,' he said. 'I don't mean your financial life'—he waved his hand towards the furniture and pictures—'you won't be on the dole. It's got nothing to do with that. Do you know what you're up against, Orme-Campbell?'

'I don't think you can teach me how to face a challenge,' said Orme-Campbell stiffly. Now that Levenson had brushed aside his insult, he no longer felt at a disadvantage and was ready for another clash.

'I think I can,' Levenson said harshly. 'What you're afraid of, Orme-Campbell, is being on your own—of losing authority. You wanted to be someone, because you were just the son of your father—"young Mr. Geoffrey" if you lived to be ninety. You wanted to go into politics, but you wanted it the easy way. . . . You asked the Prime Minister for a peerage—'

'That's a lie,' said Orme-Campbell.

'No,' said Levenson patiently, 'I know exactly what happened. You sounded Budd out to see what chance there was. Budd said he'd put it up to the Prime Minister, and the answer was "No". So that when Budd told you there was nothing doing, you put out the story that you'd turned down his offer. But that isn't the point. . . . You wanted to make a splash in politics. You hitched up with Lord Mayland and his Renewal Movement. . . . For God's sake, man, how on earth did you think you'd win public respect in the long run by identifying yourself with Mayland?'

'I don't expect you to understand,' said Orme-Campbell. 'Mayland's Renewal Movement was concerned—is concerned —with restoring the quality of our society—giving morality some place in our public life—creating a Government of dedicated men—patriots—'

'I know,' said Levenson. 'I know. You're all a splendid lot of public-spirited men, independent and sprouting morality all over. I'm glad you roped in Hamblett for "Renewal". He fitted.'

'Hamblett?' Orme-Campbell said wistfully. 'He was a disappointment.'

'It won't do,' said Levenson, slowly shaking his head. 'Mayland with his mistresses, Hamblett who walked over corpses to get his job—Percy who double-crossed everyone in the City—you with the Villa Howell—'

'What do you mean by that?' asked Orme-Campbell, standing face to face with Levenson.

'I mean,' said Levenson, unflinchingly, 'that I've got nothing to hide from the public. But you have.'

'I think you'd better go,' said Orme-Campbell, and his voice had begun to tremble. 'If you have any other communications with me—'

'Yes,' said Levenson. 'Lattner will see to that.'

He turned his back on Orme-Campbell, and hurried out of the room to the hall, where his chauffeur Wardle was already waiting.

*

There was scarcely any traffic on the road between Orme House and Marfield, and the headlamps conjured up strange walls of light on the hedges as the car rushed along. Levenson shut his eyes, impatient now to be home again, to see Isobel, and to sleep away the hours till the new day when he could tidy up the night's arrangements.

He had won, and he wanted to enjoy the exultation of victory. But instead, he felt an amorphous anxiety, heightened by the plunging of the car through lonely and unidentifiable roads. A rabbit froze in the car's headlights, and Wardle pressed the brakes sharply so that the car skidded and screamed. Levenson's hand tightened on the strap, and when he relaxed it, it was moist. He resisted the inclination to tell the chauffeur to slow down. That would have been a weakness.

And he lay back, trying to savour what had been successful in the evening.

He had won. That was certain. There was nothing that Orme-Campbell could do in the face of the Articles of Association which gave Howell and his friends the power to dismiss him. Nor was there any chance that the shareholders would reverse the decision. Orme-Campbell had asked for it, and he'd got it. Tomorrow, the new Board would accept Levenson's offer and everyone would be happy—Levenson, the shareholders of O.C.E., and Edgar Waltham, who, according to Parker, was going to take over Industrial Reconstruction from Budd. Everyone, that is to say, but Orme-Campbell and a few of his hangers-on.

Tomorrow, he was sure, the afternoon papers would be full of the sacking of Budd. That was, perhaps, the most satisfactory part of the evening. Budd—hectoring, bullying, rollicking, insulting—Budd who had thought himself a fixture—was going. And even if his own relationship with some people in the City had contributed to his downfall, he deserved what he'd got. And Levenson was glad that he had signed the private letter of complaint which ten chairmen of leading companies had sent to the Prime Minister about Budd's handling of affairs at the Ministry of Industrial Reconstruction. Edgar Waltham was a different matter. They were old friends. He had discussed the matter sympathetically, and besides, Edgar couldn't stand Orme-Campbell.

'Two's company, one's a crowd.' Levenson tensed at the recollection, and the surge of sympathy that he had felt earlier in the evening for Orme-Campbell disappeared. At one time, he had thought of offering him some honorary title in the merged companies, something like life chairman or life president. It was one of the reasons why he had dawdled to bid Orme-Campbell good-night. And for his pains, Orme-Campbell had turned the knife in him yet again. Perhaps it was as well. It relieved him of the need to feel sorry.

And yet, Levenson thought, the night had brought a devastating blow to Orme-Campbell. To be kicked out of one's own firm by a gaggle of yes-men, converted by panic into what was, after all, a betrayal. A justified betrayal. But a betrayal, whichever way you looked at it.

And this was his second big betrayal. The poor devil had been blackmailed and betrayed for years. That was why he had put so many of his shares on the market at a time when every commercial consideration would have encouraged him to hold them. It was common talk in the City, and it was a pity. There was a lot about Orme-Campbell that, in a curious way, Levenson respected. Like his unhappy face after the insult. Not that Orme-Campbell had regretted the insult. He was only unhappy that he had offered it to a guest.

But to be blackmailed—that was hell. Once, Levenson recalled, an accountant had tried to blackmail him, alleging that he had ordered him to make an insertion in the books. It was a lie, and he had dealt with the matter by informing the police. The blackmailer turned out to be a paranoiac who had been in several hospitals before working for Levenson. But he remembered with nausea the weeks after the first long letter of accusation.

How could Orme-Campbell have kept it up, year after year—even after the Act had made things easier—coping with the anxieties of his daily affairs and the squalid pressures of his coterie? It wasn't surprising that O.C.E. had lost its dynamism. The flabby centre. That was it. The flabby centre.

It would be a deed of kindness to turn the car around, even now, and go back to Orme House. Levenson would ring the bell, and Orme-Campbell would come down, probably in his dressing-gown, as grumpy as hell, and Levenson would say to him, 'Look here, you've been damn silly and offensive.' Then, Levenson ruminated, he'd be magnanimous. He'd go on to say,

'I accept your apology, Geoffrey. It would, I think, be in

218

the interest of all of us and it would maintain the family connection and all the goodwill that goes with it, if you'd agree to become life chairman of the new firm.'

Orme-Campbell would hesitate, but after a moment, he'd shake hands and see Levenson to his car. And that would be that. The venom would have been sucked out of the wound. And everyone could start tomorrow happily.

The Mercedes lurched around a corner, and Levenson put out his hand to steady himself.

No. It wouldn't be like that. 'Two's company, one's a crowd.' Orme-Campbell would send a message. Everyone's gone to bed. Sir Geoffrey has nothing to say. Nothing at all.

Well, to hell with you too, Sir Geoffrey.

'How far are we from Marfield?' he asked the chauffeur. Wardle switched on the lights of the dashboard, and said,

'About another four miles, I reckon. Everything looks different in the dark.'

'Yes,' said Levenson. He glanced through the rear window at the blackness behind him, and added, 'It'll all look different tomorrow.'

Chapter Fourteen

THE driveway at Marfield was encumbered with cars, spikily parked, abandoned wherever their owners had found space, a chaos that made it impossible for the Mercedes to advance beyond the gate.

Wardle pulled up and Levenson said to the chauffeur, sallow-faced in the light of the entrance-lamps,

'You'd better take it on through the meadow-gate, Wardle. Sorry to have kept you so late.'

The chauffeur muttered politely,

'What time tomorrow, sir?'

'Eight,' Levenson said, opening the door.

'Eight?' the chauffeur queried, glancing at the car clock. 'It's going on for four already.' He touched his face grey with his morning beard. 'I won't be in bed till half past four.'

'Neither will I!' said Levenson curtly. 'All right, Wardle. Make it a quarter past. I've got to be in London without fail by ten. Good-night.'

There were no lights in the house, and no sign yet of the dawn. The enveloping heat of the early night had yielded to a fragrant coolness, and he stood for a few seconds inhaling the washed scent of privet, stock and honeysuckle in a darkness broken only by the glint of windscreens and chromium, before he began to feel his way towards the house. He had hoped that the party would have been over by now, that the litter of the cars would have disappeared with Jonathan's friends to wherever they had come from and that he could have regained the solitude that the remote thump of the pop group still troubled. Though the arithmetic of the bid continued of its own volition to reproduce problems and sums in his wakeful mind, he felt exhausted, on the edge of sleep, drained of blood as he had once felt long ago when he had had a duodenal haemorrhage. A roundabout of faces, Budd, Howell, Henderson-Kerr, Orme-Campbell, aggressive, hostile, flushed, defensive, arrogant, humble, hectoring and broken, recurred to him in time to the music that reminded him of the panatrope in the fairgrounds of his youth.

He wanted an interval between his arrival and the moment when he would again feel Isobel's warm presence, her sleep-filled voice, her familiar arm across his chest and the security of being home again. And tomorrow, he would suggest to her that after he had dealt with the practical consequences of the merger, the board meetings, the Press, the confrontations with the Trade Unions, the Ministries, the reorganization of the main Board and the subsidiary companies—Copeland and Fisher would certainly have to go—they could leave for a holiday, perhaps to the Caribbean via New York.

To be her escort was a fulfilment in itself. To enter a restaurant with her, to travel with her at his side, to leave a reception with her at the moment of his command, enhanced and completed something in his own personality which he was reluctant to acknowledge. Often in their married life, he would force her into tears by disparaging the clothes that she wore or an idea that she proposed. It was an act of redress for the humility that he felt in front of her beauty, her knowledge of worlds beyond his own. He punished her for having the qualities that he most admired.

And it always seemed to him that his possession of her was a fragile one that had constantly to be protected. The admiration of other men for Isobel was something that he accepted as a familiar and inevitable experience, though it never failed to excite in him a mingling of eviscerating jealousy and tumescent pride. Not that she ever consciously gave him cause for jealousy. At parties, she always stayed as close to him as she could, so that frequently their hostess had to separate them with coy remarks about how long they had been married. She never coquetted nor accepted gallantries with anything but a friendly courtesy in which she involved her husband. Levenson had once overheard an Amazonian peeress say of Isobel after a dinner party in London: 'She's so lovely. And he's really a rough piece of quartz—so incongruous!' But it hadn't worried him. On the contrary, it had pleased him, and he hadn't held it against the peeress' husband when he sought a directorship in one of his companies.

So when everything was tidy, Levenson thought, they would go away and he would have Isobel to himself without the disturbing presence of Jonathan. It was a demeaning admission, even to himself, even in the lonely darkness. To be jealous of a boy—his wife's son! He pushed his hands in the pockets of his jacket, and walked around the house so that he could look down towards the party. Yes. He had to admit it. He was jealous and it was shameful, and he would be glad when Jonathan no longer intervened in their lives.

Above the trees, there was a faint glow from the braziers, an aureole which the house had earlier shrouded. The Chinese lanterns were pin-points through the foliage, and the house was inert and closed.

Levenson took a few steps towards the swimming pool and stopped. His cigar was still alight and before throwing it into the bushes he drew on it twice, breathing in its scent and visualizing its blue drift through the roses while he disentangled the door-key on his chain and made for the house.

She would be warm and heavy with sleep. On her brow, there'd be a faint moisture, and she'd stir and say 'What time is it?' and she'd fall asleep again before he could answer. And then she would turn her back, coiled up with her knees raised till morning and her cat-like stretch and the words of waking.

Levenson's hand hesitated on the switch, but he didn't

press it. Contrary to her usual practice, she had left the curtains drawn, and except for a fringe of light filtering around their edges, the room was in total darkness. He smiled. She must have been very tired, and he felt guilty about his last telephone call that had awakened her. He walked cautiously to the edge of the bed, and put out his hand to touch her. The pillow was cool and he felt the buttons of his pyjamas under his hand.

Suddenly alert, he pressed the bed-lamp switch and in the blaze of light he saw that the bed had not been slept in though the pillows were crushed and his pyjamas usually neatly disposed by Carmella next to Isobel's nightdress, were crumpled and disordered. He frowned. Isobel must have been lying on the bed when he telephoned her. But she had said that she was already *in* bed. Or had she said that? Perhaps she had meant she had dozed off. 'Isobel!' he called her name, and opened the dressing-room door. He sniffed. There was a faint stale smell of cigarette smoke in the air, and in the ash-tray a cigarette butt without a filter-tip. And that was strange because Isobel only smoked cigarettes with filter tips.

His chest felt constricted, and he sat on the bed trying to think things out. Complex memories of old anxieties flowed into his mind. 'One day I'll just get up and walk out'—a long time ago. 'You make me feel as if nothing's worth while. I'd like to be blotted out—' The sleeping pill time, two years ago. 'Yes,' laughing. 'I could float and drown in the lake like Ophelia—by the reeds.' There was the time of the burglary. He got up with a new thought and walked over to the wall safe, hidden behind the dressing-table. It was intact. He went to the cabinet and took out a decanter of whisky. His hand was shaking as he poured it, and then he tried to raise the glass to his mouth, but had to put it quickly down, sloshing the surface with its overspill. Then he took it in both hands, drank the whisky in two gulps, and began to feel better.

'She probably couldn't sleep because of the noise,' he said

223

to himself. 'If you can't beat 'em, join 'em. She must have gone to the party.' He wanted to smile, but the tremor had reached his face and he stood waiting for it to pass. Then he resolutely switched on all the lights in the room and on the staircase, and hurried out in search of his wife.

Approaching the dance floor was for Levenson like entering a rowdy and unknown city at night through suburbs of laughter and chatter, shrieks of delight and singing. He stumbled over a couple sitting enlaced on the stone steps and said 'Sorry.' Another couple stood in his path, their mouths adhering like rubber suckers that have created a vacuum and can't be detached. He skirted them. Although he had only offered a hesitant doubt to Isobel, the whole idea of the party had been disagreeable to him, and now he saw his forecasts realized. The noise had become an uproar, a din of the amplified guitar, drums and hysteria and loud talk. Between the braying mouth at the microphone and the quivering, convulsed dancers and onlookers around the Group there was a conspiracy that he didn't belong to. This was his house; these were his gardens; the trees, the shrubs, the lawns, the pool, the lake—they all were his. But the self-absorbed young men and women with easy manners masquerading as Regency elegants with their ladies talking, strolling, embracing, dancing, lying about and laughing at jokes that excluded everyone but themselves had taken possession of them all in a way that he couldn't understand.

Four men and three girls were standing by the bar, hunched as if in a rugger scrum, with the tallest man encircling a girl with each arm.

'Excuse me!' said Levenson.

They ignored him.

'Excuse me,' he said again.

The tall man turned languidly and looked at Levenson without speaking.

'Any of you seen Jonathan?' he asked.

'Who's Jonathan?' asked the tall man.

'Who's Jonathan?' echoed the two girls and that was the signal for a rattle of giggles that ran from side to side as they turned their backs on Levenson and resumed their mysterious plot before he could formulate the anger that stuttered to his lips. Who's Jonathan? Where's Jonathan? His dinner jacket made him conspicuous among the guests but he felt that he walked like a ghost in daylight, invisible to the others. What the hell was he doing there? What the hell were they doing, these strange figures turned to ice blue by the illuminated fountain? 'Jonathan!'

He called the name sharply to his step-son on the dance-floor in the marquee. In the hubbub, Jonathan, dancing closely with Henrietta, didn't hear, and Levenson started to thrust himself through the dancers.

'Jonathan!'

Indifferent to the looks of surprise and outrage as he elbowed his way, breaking conversations, interrupting laughter and spoiling rhythms, Levenson called out the name in a loud command. Jonathan stopped dancing, though still holding Henrietta, and said,

'Hello, you're too early!'

Levenson didn't smile. Instead, he put his face close to Jonathan's and shouted,

'Where's your mother? She's not in her bedroom.'

'She's probably having fun,' said Jonathan, wiping the spray of his step-father's anxiety from his cheek.

'What are you getting at?' Levenson asked, menaced by the happy look in his step-son's face.

'Oh, nothing,' he replied defensively. 'I just mean she's been having a good time at the party.'

'Where is she now?'

'I do wish people wouldn't shout,' said a passing girl dancer. 'It makes them look so ugly.'

'Let's get off the floor, darling,' Jonathan said to Henrietta.

225

With his arm around her waist he led her off followed by Levenson.

'Where's your mother?' Levenson repeated, pleading, no longer bullying.

'I honestly don't know,' said Jonathan. 'She must be about somewhere. She was dancing about half an hour ago.'

'Dancing?' Levenson asked. He himself had given up dancing several years earlier. From time to time, he attended Charity Balls in London, but always sat at his table with Isobel at his side waiting for the earliest moment when they could leave.

'Dancing?' he repeated. The idea seemed to him as far fetched as if he had been told that his wife had sung an aria on one of the lawns.

'Yes—dancing,' Jonathan said. 'She's a very good dancer. I danced with her myself'

And when he said that, his step-father's face creased into a smile, a grateful smile that his assumptions hadn't been disturbed and that his wife had danced once with her son in a manner befitting a hostess He didn't want to know anything more about Isobel's presence among Jonathan's noisy friends on the dance floor. All he wanted to do was to find her and restore her to the stable mood of yesterday before the party had intruded into their systematic life together.

'How did the deal go?' Jonathan asked. He had never seen Levenson with the crumpled, apologetic expression, and he imagined that it was the result of a defeat. Henrietta was resting with her eyes closed, her face against his shoulder, and he wanted to get rid of his step-father so that they could start again where he had interrupted them.

Levenson grunted.

'Oh—all fixed.'

He had taken a step to leave them when Henrietta, waking from her doze, said,

'Why don't you try the island, Mr. Levenson?' but her last

words were overlaid by a sudden blare in the microphone, a wail about love, that took Jonathan and Henrietta away, hugged together, while Levenson stood uncertainly, trying to reconstruct the distorted vowels and consonants. He thought she said 'the library'—she couldn't have said the island—there was nothing on the island—and that was reasonable enough. Isobel used to read for hours into the night when she had her bouts of insomnia. And that was where she would be. The possibility now became a certainty, and he returned to the house, preparing his words of greeting as he might have prepared the opening of a speech.

The door of the library was shut. He turned the knob, and it was locked. For a second or two, he stood incomprehending, while in the corridor the old Labrador, somnolent but curious, pulled himself to his feet, a tawny figure in the dim light, and came up, wagging his tail in a slow pendulum movement.

'Go to sleep, Trott,' Levenson ordered. He rattled the door-knob, and the dog, excited, began to bark angrily in time with the clatter and drumming of the door.

'Go away,' said a male voice from inside. 'You'll wake the neighbours.'

Levenson hammered at the door with his fist.

'Open the door at once,' he shouted.

There was a sound of urgent talk inside the room, and Levenson waited in silence while the dog's barking fell into a low growl.

A key clicked on the other side of the door, and Levenson pushed his way in, brushing aside a young man with his hair falling over his face who stood in his way. The room was in darkness, and Levenson switched on the light.

'For God's sake—' said the girl on the sofa pulling her blouse together.

A couple, acrobatically entangled on Levenson's red armchair, looked up, and the man mumbled:

'Put that bloody light out!' before returning to his previous posture.

The desk that Levenson had always prided himself on keeping free of anything not connected with his immediate work was a slum of beer bottles, remnants of sausages, coleslaw, half eaten sandwiches and glasses with dregs.

'This room is private,' Levenson said.

He stood looking at the defiant and insolent face of the one who had opened the door, and from him to the disorder in the room; and it seemed to him an expression of the battle that he had always had to fight against the presumptuous and the casual.

He moved into the room without speaking, halting at the centre of the carpet where a girl was coiled up, asleep and faintly snoring. After the fresh night air, the room smelt stale, an amalgamated smell of breath and scent. As he stood there, the room itself appeared to disentangle. The first to leave was the man who had opened the door, trailing with him, hand in hand, the girl who had been clutching at her blouse. Blinking and grumbling, the two from the red chair followed. Like some brooding policeman watching a Black Maria being loaded, Levenson waited until the room was emptied except for himself and the girl on the floor. She was drunk, and as he bent to look at her, she breathed over him a mixture of regurgitated whisky and cheese.

For a few moments he contemplated her in distaste. Her long dress had rucked itself up so that her thighs were exposed with a plump gap between her stockings and suspender belt. She looked about nineteen, but her eye shadow, smudged over her lids, and her smeared lipstick gave her the air of a Hogarthian drab. Levenson wanted to find a covering for her, but there was nothing suitable in the room.

He hesitated, then pulled her dress down, before starting to lift her on to the sofa. She opened her eyes, the cornea reddened, and said in a clipped voice,

228

'What are you doing, you filthy old man? Leave me alone.'

In a mingling of rage and panic, Levenson let her slide to the ground where she lay muttering, sniffed at by the dog. Leaving the light on, Levenson returned to the gardens to continue his search.

'Don't look now,' he heard a voice say as he hurried past. 'There's Orpheus looking for Eurydice.' And then the giggles and guffaws.

Williams, the gardener in charge of the fireworks, stopped him near the river, and said,

'Pardon me, sir, but what time do I let them off?'

'Have you seen Mrs. Levenson?' he asked.

'Not lately, sir. What time do I let them off? It'll start getting light in half an hour.'

Levenson looked around him impatiently.

'When did you last see her?'

Williams pondered, shuffling his tweed jacket into a better position on his narrow shoulders.

'About half an hour ago. . . . No. I'm a liar. About three quarters. I heard it striking.'

'Where was she?'

'All over the place—looking very pleased. She said to me, "Hello, Williams, don't go and blow yourself up." '

'Was she alone?'

And as he asked the question, he saw Williams' eyes looking at him enquiringly, pityingly and knowingly while the mouth moved with the beginning of a smile.

'Not when I saw her, sir,' said Williams. 'There was always one or two with her.'

'Who?' and asking the question, Levenson felt that he was handing himself and Isobel to Williams as a hostage for his understanding, and he averted his glance from Williams to the shrubbery. 'And, incidentally,' he added assertively, 'this shrubbery is a disgrace—you can see that, even in the dark.'

'Yes, sir,' said Williams evenly. 'You were asking me about

229

Mrs. Levenson. I've just remembered. I saw her being rowed out.'

'Rowed out?'

'On the lake—with that young fellow—the friend of Mr. Jonathan—good-looking lad. What time shall I let off the fireworks, Mr. Levenson?'

But Levenson had already moved off.

Levenson started the engine in the motor boat, and it moved away in a mutter towards the island. Within seconds, the shore receded and the party became a small bonfire in the black landscape. The island itself should have been marked by the lamp in the temple, but now it too lay in a darkness, only broken by the fringe of light where, as his eyes became accustomed to the night, he could see the contours of the trees meeting the sky. Long ago it had been like this in Italy, when Isobel had gone swimming on a lonely beach, and he had read a book, and when he had looked up after half an hour, the vast sea was empty and Isobel was no longer there; and he had rushed up and down the shore, desperate and praying until she had appeared from the pinewood where she had walked after her bathe, to meet his rage and desperate relief.

A red star rose with a whoop from the mound, and he followed it to its apogee over the lake where it burst in a saffron spray. Briefly illuminated the island looked like a heavenly vista in a painting by Mantegna, a fire of roses and azaleas. But before the image disappeared, another rocket exploded in the air, festooning the lake with pendants and girandoles that burst a second time, crackling in the sky like gunfire, garlands of light dropped by raiders over a city in pain.

This was a dream. The slow chugging towards the lake in search of Isobel. The artillery in the sky. The absurdity of the dinner jacket. He pulled at his tie and threw it in the water and undid the button at his neck. And then he took off his jacket and tossed it into the stern. And the act of doing so made him feel that he had shaken himself awake from his dream, that he had abandoned a masquerade and recovered his identity.

At the landing stage, the rowing boat was swinging lightly against the bank, tugged and rejected by the currents. He cut out his engine, and let the motor boat drift quietly inshore. Then he tied it up, and taking with him his heavy torch, began to climb through the tangle of fern towards the temple. There was an interval in the fireworks, and he switched on his torch so that he could pick his way across the undergrowth. As he left the boat he had twisted his ankle and the pain made him pause against a tree about thirty yards from the tessellated precinct. He was sure that he could hear voices and he listened. But the only sounds were the rustle of a rodent, the scream of a night bird, and the sudden lunge and clatter of three rockets in succession.

In their light, he could see Isobel standing by a column, and he wanted to shout her name but the sound was swallowed in his tightened throat. She switched on the lamp above the arch and said calmly as he stood staring at her, his thought dominated by her loosely hanging hair,

'Hello, darling. Come to see the fireworks? It's quite the best view from here. This is Adrian—you've met. He did all the hard work, rowing.'

His expression did not change and she went on talking.

'Do you think we should have the torch off? It's like being on the bridge at sea. You can see very much better without it.'

He didn't move till Adrian who was standing behind her said,

'Perhaps I ought to be getting back. I'm due in London.'

Then Levenson said to Isobel, his face unsmiling, his lips scarcely stirring, his eyes on the shirt that Adrian was wearing,

'Get in the boat.'

She tried to preserve her authority.

'Come on, Adrian, we're going back to the mainland.'

'No,' Levenson ordered. 'Just you, Isobel. Get in the boat.'

She turned to Adrian and said, 'Perhaps we'd better say good-night.'

Without looking at her, Adrian replied, 'Yes, indeed. Thank you very much for a very pleasant evening.'

'Yes,' she said and took his hand. 'It was a very pleasant evening. I hope we'll meet when I come to see Jonathan at Cambridge.'

Levenson struck her across the face with a slap that sent her reeling against the column. She stroked her cheek with the back of her hand, and said to Adrian who, seeing Levenson's white face in the half light, now put up his fists:

'No, Adrian, it's only a game we play. We call it Happy Families. Good-night. It was a lovely evening, despite everything.'

She hurried down the path in front of her husband, half-running to avoid his contact, and climbed into the motor boat. Levenson started the engine, revving it up into a roar. The rockets were now bursting overhead like Very lights and they could observe each other in bow and stern as the boat gathered speed and the lanterns on the lawns drew nearer.

Neither spoke, but each of them knew that soon they would have to explain to each other. The explanations would be lies and half-truths; those who asked questions would get questions in return; and in the end, before sleeping, they would both withdraw into the pillow of their own truths where they were private, no longer inquisitors without real hope of answers.

Chapter Fifteen

In the first morning light, the party was breaking up, and a disordered cortège was moving from the marquee and the gardens towards the house. Some of those who had held each other most closely during the night were walking a few paces away from each other, already absorbed with their thoughts for the new day. Almost everyone, especially those who the evening before had looked radiantly tanned, seemed jaundiced. In the chilly air, a few of the men were wearing pullovers, the girls silk coats. The chatter had become subdued, overlaid by the sounds of the cars manoeuvring in the drive, the confused shouts of 'Left lock down,' 'Hard on the right hand,' and the cries of thanks and farewell.

Isobel shivered as she walked in silence at Levenson's side. His mouth was grim, and he stared ahead fixedly like a gaoler —or perhaps a prisoner. She wasn't sure which. She folded her arms around herself, cocooned in the consciousness of her own personality, raising a palisade against her husband. Her face was throbbing where he had struck her, and in her ear was a thin pain that sang inside her head, confusing the voices outside. Trott followed happily, swinging his pendulum tail.

Jonathan was standing by the swimming pool with Henrietta who was due to stay at her aunt's house in Abingdon, and as Isobel saw him exchanging friendly waves with his departing guests, she recognized the unhappiness in her son's face that she knew so well.

'For God's sake, do you have to make a terrible fool of yourself?'

The words he had used to her when she danced with Adrian tore at her dignity, mangling and lacerating her pride. As if a coin had been reversed, her love for Jonathan had turned and briefly uncovered a resentful hatred. But it was fading, leaving only a regret that the party he had looked forward to had been marred because of her, that she had trespassed on his joy, and that she had blundered into an alien world of youth where she had no bearings.

'A fool of yourself.' That was a kind of death sentence. 'Good-night, Mrs. Levenson. We simply loved it. I know *you* enjoyed the party.' 'Good-night, Annabel.' 'Good-night, Mr. Levenson.' 'Venetia Cohen had to leave early. She wasn't feeling awfully well. She asked me to say "good-bye".' 'Good-night, Peter. Good-night, George.' 'Good-night, Elizabeth. Yes, bacon and eggs at the Mill House is a very good idea—but I'm much too old for that.' 'Kippers and strawberries and cream—you're joking.' So good-night again. Good-night, good-morning and good-bye. Isobel Levenson, shutting her mind with three sleeping pills, is going to bed at last.

*

When they reached the bedroom, Levenson sat on a chair, watching her as she went to the dressing table to remove her make-up and brush her hair. She tried to behave indifferently, casually throwing the paper tissues into the basket and examining her skin in the circular looking-glass with an absorbed scrutiny. But her husband's face, reflected next to her, insisted. The argument went on in silence, each waiting for the other to give it the first words. The yellow birthday roses had faded, the petals curling, the water in the vast bowl stale. I must throw them away, she thought. Tomorrow. That seemed to her the most important intention that she could form before she gave herself up to darkness and sleep.

'I want to talk to you,' he said.

'There's nothing I want to say,' she answered.

234

'That's too easy,' said Levenson, still sitting and watching her as she walked across the room to pick up her nightdress. She stopped, holding it in her hand.

'Well, what do you want?' she asked in a resolute voice. She felt awake, and turned to face him.

'I'm not sure,' he answered slowly.

'Well, what do you want to ask?' she said in a harsh tone.

'Why,' he said in the same slow voice, 'why did you pretend to go to bed, and then go back to the party?'

She looked at him coolly.

'Sometimes I think you're mad. Who would believe that a man who had spent the whole night working on the biggest merger in—oh, for heaven's sake! To the *party*—my own son's party! What crime is there in that?'

Levenson stood up.

'Don't give me that,' he said. 'I'm not Edward. That was the formula you used for him. When you had that American. You told me.'

She looked at him in loathing, aghast at his bitter eyes, the scarcely-moving mouth from which the accusations seemed to go on and on, resurrecting and deforming the confidence given in trust between sleeping and waking.

'It's not true,' she said, and her hands were shaking as she confronted him.

'Oh, yes, it is true,' he said, and now he moved towards her. 'You've forgotten. You told me so.'

'I didn't,' she said. 'It isn't true.'

She could feel the panic rising, the water in the lock, and she wanted to clench her eyes till it had overwhelmed her so that she could re-emerge.

'Yes, it's true,' he said, gripping her arms. 'You told me so. I've got a good memory, Isobel. I know every machine in every one of the works. Do you think I could have forgotten that?'

'It's not true,' she said, begging for charity, her head

235

swinging from side to side with her eyes tightly shut. 'I was never unfaithful to Edward—never, never, never.'

'Not at the conference in Rome—that American—the one you told me about?'

'It's a lie,' she said. 'You didn't understand. You misunderstood what I said.'

He pushed her away from him.

'I understood all right,' he said.

Yes, that was true—partly true. There had been a session of the International Endocrinological Conference at the Villa Lubin in the Viale David Lubin, and she had spent the evening in the Borghese Gardens, dining with the attaché from the American Embassy who was an observer. There had been nothing—almost nothing—so it had seemed—nothing that counted, nothing that she wanted to remember except her relief late that night to find herself enclosed in Edward's presence again, the unreachable sanctuary. What had she told Harry? What he remembered was only what he couldn't understand.

'Don't listen to him, Edward.'

It was the injunction inside her mind, the fear that in articulating his accusations Harry could destroy the past. 'Don't listen. No, don't listen.'

She put her hands over her ears to blot out the voice. She wanted to apologize to Edward for the infidelity of having married Levenson. The man who wanted everything he could reach. Not only her present but her past. Not only what he could touch but her thoughts as well. His voice went on and on about the party, about the island, about Adrian.

'Stop it!' she suddenly screamed. 'Stop it! Stop it! Stop it!'

Levenson looked at her in amazement as she flung herself on the bed, weeping uncontrollably. He put his hand on her shoulder, and she said, 'Leave me alone. Oh, I hate you. I hate you.'

Beyond logic and reason and argument, she lay on the bed,

no longer obliged to face either her husband or the past, indifferent to the future, exhausting herself like a child in the tears that relieved her of the need for self-justification. He tried to speak to her, but she clapped her hands over her face and ears, rolling herself in a sheet as if it were a shroud, and screaming,

'I hate you. Go away.'

'Isobel,' he said. 'They'll hear you outside.'

'I don't care,' she said. Her voice was a wail. 'I don't care about anything. I don't care if I live or die.'

He pulled the sheet away from her, and took her two hands and drew them away from her eyes. Her cheeks were blotched and mottled with tears and her hair, trailing over her forehead, was wet. Levenson touched her swollen eyes, and she said,

'No, keep your hands off me. Go away.'

Through the open window they heard a woman call, 'Good-night, Adrian,' and Levenson stood without moving, contemplating Isobel on her bed. One of her shoes had fallen off, and her knees were drawn up towards her chin.

'Why were you on the island with that boy?' he repeated in monotone.

She didn't answer, and in a new access of rage he seized her shoulders in his hands, turning her face upwards and shaking her till a vein at the side of her forehead stood out.

'Why were you on the island with that man?' he shouted.

Her eyes were wide open, staring past him towards the ceiling. She didn't answer, and his fingers unclenched.

'Why don't you kill me?' she asked. 'Why *don't* you? Whatever you can't get, you destroy.'

'If it's useless—you bitch!'

'Yes, if it's useless. When you don't need it any more.'

'What were you doing on the island with that—that—'

'Nothing. Nothing at all. You've got everything in the world—but you're afraid. Afraid of a boy.'

She slowly raised herself, and said, 'You're afraid I'll

discover one day that there's something better, someone more capable than you.'

His fingers with their fuzzy backs that once had made her feel tender towards him, moved as if beating time to her goading. She went towards him, and said, 'Yes—that's the truth of the matter. Harry Levenson, the great take-over bidder, the Merger King, has been frightened.'

He raised his hand to shut her up, and she said,

'Go on. Hit me again. Prove how brave you are.'

Abruptly, he turned his back on her and went into his dressing room, taking off his jacket as he went. A habit of orderliness made him remove his keys, his wallet, his loose change, his wrist-watch and his gold cuff-links, and put them in a leather tray lined with red plush that Isobel had bought for him at Aspreys. They had just returned from a holiday near San Stefano, relaxed and happy, and had been walking down Bond Street when they saw it in the window. Levenson sat on the sofa, facing the open door and the four-poster bed where Isobel lay unmoving, and took the tray in his hands.

A quarrel was a death. The savage words were intended to kill. Why shouldn't she have gone back to the party? After all, Jonathan hadn't had a party for years. But she had said she was going to sleep. Perhaps she couldn't. Sometimes she would get up quietly in order not to disturb him, and read in the library till early morning. Adrian's face—handsome, mocking, with the hair falling over his forehead angered him again. They were all insolent; and because they were young, without responsibility and indifferent, they had the advantage.

And Isobel, by her deference to their youth, had formed an alliance with them—with the boy in his shirt against him.

It was a commonplace design. A blue check. A shirt he might have got anywhere. But that was impossible. She'd said so. Again the doubt, rising in his stomach, eviscerating, annihilating his certainties, ending his pride in his triumph over Orme-Campbell, Budd, and the whole lot of them. Levenson put the tray on the table and went to the window.

There were a few cars in the drive—dark shapes left over from the party by Jonathan's friends lost in the gardens. They were the relics of an untidy, distasteful evening that he wanted to wish away and forget. He looked through the open door again, and saw that Isobel had her hand clasped to her ear, and all he wanted to do was to beg her forgiveness, to expunge the night, and to start again.

*

The whine inside her ear had become sharper like the high pitched tone of a circular saw, and the sounds outside were dulled as if by a layer of cotton wool. Her ear-drum hurt, not intolerably but naggingly. She welcomed the pain that evened out her feeling of guilt towards her husband. Now she might sleep, in a kind of innocence, the rage, the mania, all ended. She couldn't remember Adrian's face, not even its expression. And lying on the bed, she couldn't imagine how a few hours earlier she had run from her bedroom to the lake, to the marquee, to the house in a desperate search for a boy twenty years younger than herself, a friend of her son who now seemed little different from any of the others. 'Do stop. You're making a terrible fool of yourself.' No one would know. Not everything. No one, not even Jonathan. And Adrian? He might boast as he had boasted about his successes in the Sorbonne. But that didn't matter either. It was nothing—not even like the American. It hadn't happened. Nothing had happened. The Villa Borghese. The Carozza. Carozza. Carezza. That was all a long, long time ago.

But she hadn't wanted to hurt Edward. Nor Harry. She turned on her bed and looked with open eyes at the canopy. Harry was kind and generous. He had saved her when she was in despair, and had helped her to bring up Jonathan, sent him to school and university, ministered to her comfort and luxury,

239

supported her father and, though he brushed aside the fears that he couldn't understand, gave her security and sanctuary. He loved her, and she had wounded him, and she felt sorry.

Levenson was standing by her bedside in his dressing gown. His dark, heavy-lidded eyes were tormented and humble. He looked at her a few moments, and she smiled to him slowly.

'You're very silly,' she said. He sat on her bed and stroked her cheek where her tears had dried.

'I'm sorry I hit you,' he answered, and bent over her and kissed her cheek, and she was glad that he was there.

'What time is it?' she asked.

'Twenty past four. We must get some sleep. I've got to leave at 8.15 for London.'

'Poor Harry! she said. 'Yes—let's go to bed.'

*

So in the familiar comfort of her bed, feeling his weight above her and the repertoire of his movements, the hand passing from knee through the inside of her thigh to her breasts, and her neck, returning over her back and hips and flanks—the sword, the wound and at last, the sad pleasure—she felt the night end in its last throes, the kicking death followed by a white dawn. Above her, the familiar stranger panting, diminuendo, the heart-beat, the weight slowly sliding from her body, the seal sliding from a rock. The heart-beat diminishing, diminishing. Then a silence in which there was nothing for either to say.

'Cigarette?'

'No, just sleep.'

Just sleep.

'They thought they had us over a barrel. They—'

Just sleep.

Budd—Orme-Campbell—Lattner. The Tivoli Gardens and the water-organ. Inconsequential thoughts. The cascades and the Villa Borghese. The candles in the gardens. A quick dream

240

of Jonathan and a tall fountain. A silence. The habitual post-orgasmic dream of the squalid, bearded old man. She woke trembling. Harry was fast asleep, snoring lightly.

In the light that filtered through the curtains, she saw that it was 5.20—she had slept for about an hour. By the bedside, the three pills were untouched.

But that was wrong. She wanted to sleep. She looked again at her husband's grey and exhausted face, the half-open mouth, the slight frown as if he still carried the night's burden. And then, he seemed to recede and dwindle, to become a stone, inanimate, unrelated to her isolation. Everything around her was remote. The canopy, the curtains, the bed-covers, the pictures, all surrounding and observing her, present and hostile. She got out of bed, holding the three sleeping pills in her hand, and stood by the bedside, not knowing what she wanted to do, still trembling, scarcely able to breathe. She glanced at her face, reproduced in two facing mirrors, and the multiplied image added to her terror. She was sweating, and she passed her left hand over her face to wipe the sweat away.

The curtain was stirring in the early morning breeze, and she stood by the window feeling its movement so that she could be aware of a contact with the physical world. She struggled with her dread, wanting to escape from her daylight nightmare into the extinction of darkness.

The drawer where she kept her sleeping pills was open. The carpet prickled against her bare feet as she walked towards it, and the draught was now chilling her body. 'Mrs. Levenson—two to be taken as prescribed.' Twenty-eight. He wouldn't give her more.

*

Levenson groaned in his sleep and mumbled. Hearing his voice, she hesitated, and guiltily closed the drawer. Then taking care not to disturb him, she dressed quickly in a white polo-necked sweater and black slacks and made her way to the stairs, where on the landing outside Trott muttered in his sleep but didn't stir. The birds too, after waking at daybreak in a chattering turmoil, seemed to have fallen asleep again. The only sound over the gardens was a girring of doves that deepened the silence of the woodlands.

'*And what is the purpose of your protest, Adrian?*'

'*To protest.*'

'*And what is your purpose, Mrs. Levenson?*'

'*To have no purpose.*'

Jonathan? To have no purpose to protest.

And Harry? To have purpose.

That was perhaps right. Not to be a victim but to be a dominator. Not to allow things to happen, but to make them happen. Or perhaps for her, as a compromise, to create the conditions in which such things would have to happen. In September, after the arrangements for the merger, Harry had said they would go away, perhaps to New York, perhaps to Turkey, perhaps to Australia. Perhaps just away. To a fictitious place without problems.

The sun hadn't risen yet above the trees, and the sky looked washed in a white water-colour. When she reached the swimming pool, she saw that the curtains both in the house and the annexe were drawn, giving the buildings a secretive and yet vulnerable air, asleep. But she was awake. Inhaling the morning scent of the roses, the privet and the wet grass in the silence around her, she felt liberated from the night that had passed, from all that had made her rush in a frantic urgency to the lake and the island, from the fear of the quickening years. On the lawns were the remnants of fireworks, burnt cardboard and sticks. The braziers by the yew trees were silvered with ashes. Candlesticks, the dead barbecue, a scarf hung on a tree branch, a garden chair on its side, a string of fairy lights still lit—she walked slowly as if over a battlefield, making an inventory.

The miniature cascades on the way to the lake were gurgling

over the moss, and she followed them, thinking again of Adrian, whose face returned more precisely to her mind. The sullen expression, the dark hair, his mocking blue eyes, his hands, thin and eager, clutching at strangers and systems as a substitute for the ever-absent parents. Adrian recalling Jonathan. Jonathan recalling Edward.

*

Her son was standing by the stone column at the lakeside and she said, 'Hello, Jonathan,' as if they had arranged the meeting.

'Hello, mother,' he answered casually. 'I imagined I'd find you here.'

'Why?'

'I just did.'

They stood looking towards the island at the rushes and the water-lilies that were opening in a pink flush. The trees were as quiet as the temple, the water untroubled.

'It's very peaceful after all that noise,' said Isobel.

'Yes,' said Jonathan. 'I'm glad it's all over.'

'Are you warm enough in your pullover?' she asked.

'Yes,' he said. 'I'd better fasten that rope.'

He climbed down to the rowing boat that was loosely moored to the landing stage and, tying a new knot, said,

'Adrian asked me to say good-night to you. He had to get back to London.'

'Did he? That was very formal of him.'

'He *is* formal,' said Jonathan. 'His problem is to force himself not to be.'

'Oh, well,' she said, 'all that was last night.'

'Yes. I'm sorry I was so rude to you.'

'Rude? I didn't notice.'

She took his arm, and they began to walk along the path skirting the lake.

'I mean,' said Jonathan, 'when you were dancing with Adrian.'

243

'You weren't rude. You were quite right.'

Jonathan puckered his forehead. 'No,' he said, 'I've been thinking about it. That's one of the reasons I couldn't sleep. You see, it wasn't just that I was afraid you might be sneered at.'

She waited for him to continue.

'What I didn't like about you—with Adrian—was—I suppose that he was taking you away from me. I was jealous.'

He spoke the last words defiantly, and she said,

'Yes, I can understand that.'

'I mean—it was like a substitution.'

'Yes,' said Isobel. 'In a way.'

'And I felt somehow that I was on Harry's side—I'd never felt it before—against you.'

The sun had risen over the trees, diamonding the grass and turning the long windows of the house into looking-glasses. She didn't answer, and he went on,

'Then, I thought, perhaps she's unhappy. And that's why she's behaving like this.'

Isobel stopped walking and looked at Jonathan's puzzled face.

'That was very understanding of you, Jonathan. Very. . . . I was unhappy last night, and that's why I behaved like that. But it's all over now. It's a new day.'

'We've decided to go to Avdat on Monday instead of waiting.'

'You and Henrietta? . . . She's a very nice girl.'

'Yes,' said Jonathan. 'And next term'—it was intended as a consolation—'you'll come and see us at Cambridge.'

Luigi and Carmella were opening the curtains, and the sleeping house had wakened to the distant sound of early traffic.

'Not too soon, darling,' said Isobel, kissing her son on the cheek. 'Let's wait till we've all settled down.'